A CALLING OF THE BLOOD

"He was born a [obscured by barcode] ed a
warrior, as I wa[obscured] battle."

"Four hun[obscured]

"Yesterda[obscured] giant said softly.
"Yesterday, my bonnie lass. To a Highlander,
all the battles are yesterday, and the blood
as red and wet. I want him to recall what he
is. And who." His eyes were humorless, set
aflame by lantern light.

"How?"

He turned away a moment, and onto
the table he set them one by one. A clump of
dried heather. A single scarlet feather. A
scrap of bloodied tartan fabric, darkened by
age. A clan badge, and the short, small knife
called *sgain dhu*.

"Do you believe that is enough? And if
not, then surely this . . . " She looked upon it
in his large, powerful hand: a crudely made,
withy cross. "He'll answer," the man told her.
"No Highlander, no Jacobite sworn to the
Stuart kings of Scotland, can turn his back
on such."

"The cross of war," she murmured.

"I need only set it afire and put it
before him, to summon Duncan MacLeod of
the Clan MacLeod to Scotland's aid again . . . "

HIGHLANDER™

SCOTLAND THE BRAVE

JENNIFER ROBERSON

ASPECT®

WARNER BOOKS

A Time Warner Company

WARNER BOOKS EDITION

Warner Books, Inc.
1271 Avenue of the Americas
New York, NY 10020

Visit our web site at
http://pathfinder.com/twep

Ⓦ A Time Warner Company

Printed in the United States of America

First Printing: September, 1996

10 9 8 7 6 5 4 3 2 1

Acknowledgments

To Ashley McConnell, for information and impetus;
Betsy Mitchell and Wayne Chang,
for opportunity and amusement;
Bill Panzer and Gillian Horvath, for saying yes;
Michael A. Stackpole, for the joke;
And the cast and crew
of <u>HIGHLANDER: The Series</u>, for inspiration.

Author's Notes and Acknowledgments

Annie Devlin was first introduced in the second-season episode titled "An Eye For An Eye," written by Elizabeth Baxter and Martin Brossolet, featuring singer/actress Sheena Easton in the role. I am indebted to all three individuals for providing me with such a complex, complicated, and fascinating character with which to play. Such is a writer's dream.

I am grateful also to Donna Lettow of the HIGHLANDER staff, whose brief inquiry regarding Annie Devlin's Watcher inspired me to create Mattie O'Connell, and to adapt the actual documented historical incident that gave birth to Annie's fanaticism.

History buffs will recognize the references to the documented theft of the Stone of Scone and such prominent historical battles as Killiecrankie and Culloden; to the Scottish supporters of the exiled Stuart monarchs, called Jacobites; and to such individuals as Prince Charles Edward Stuart, aka "Bonnie Prince Charlie"; John Graham of Claverhouse, Viscount Dundee; and William, Duke of Cumberland, third-born son of King George II, later known as "Butcher" for his ruthless management of the English Army at Culloden.

Because of this near-annihilation of Jacobite troops, the Highland culture was all but destroyed. Some members of the Parliament suggested all Jacobite women be sterilized. The Gaelic language, the kilt, and bagpipes were outlawed under pain of immediate execution in an attempt to destroy any continued loyalty to Jacobite monarchs and Scottish causes.

Duncan MacLeod is infinitely Scottish, bred of its peoples and culture. I refer anyone who wishes to learn more about the actual Scottish history that had the shaping of the fictional Duncan MacLeod, particularly in this novel, to a sampling of selected reference materials: *Scottish Lore and Folklore*, compiled by Ronald MacDonald Douglas; J.D. Mackie's *A History of Scotland*; Charles MacKinnon's *Scottish Highlanders*; *Glencoe*, by John Prebble; *Scotland's Story*, by Tom Steel. For information on Macbeth, the High King, I refer readers to Peter Beresford Ellis' Macbeth, and of course William Shakespeare's historically inaccurate but nonetheless brilliant play.

—Jennifer Roberson

Prologue

Scotland, 16 April 1746

Carnage. And no consolation at all in it, save that a man would go to God.

Save that a man died for his country.

Save that a man died for his king.

Oaths sworn, held, died for. Oaths to clan and man and monarch, the prince who would be king when his father was dead; but that father lived in Italy, not in Scotland, not in England. And the son of that man, firstborn, royal-born, bred up to be a king, came home at last from Rome to a place he had never been. He spoke next to no Gaelic at all save what he had been schooled in prior to landing at Eriskay, then later at Glenfinnan where Scots met him, men of the Highland clans, Jacobites bound to his grandfather, his father, to him, in the name of a holy alliance, a political mission: of oaths made and held, and died for already at Prestonpans.

Now at Culloden.

But it was rout, not victory. The Duke of Cumberland, as much the son of a king as Prince Charles Edward Louis

Philip Casimir Stuart, had schooled himself well in such things as battle. And in the bravery of the Scots, whose courage was unquestioned and whose dedication now was turned against them.

Carnage. In less than an hour an army broken by artillery, shredded by grapeshot, trampled by cavalry. Blood turned Drummossie Moor into bog.

He spilled his own share, did Duncan MacLeod. He would not die of it—unlike others, he could not—but the loss was debilitating, the pain real. Nothing of it was felt or known in battle, merely the cold and calculating analysis of how best to kill a man, to cripple the enemy's offense; and yet in retreat, in the awareness of defeat, every wound hurt, every bruise ached, every breath set his lungs afire. So much powder inhaled, the acrid taste of war. So much breath and strength expelled, and knowing it now for naught.

But not alone, in this. Men he knew, of every clan, lay dead around him, lay dying; fell as failing bodies acknowledged defeat. Others yet lived, cursing, crying; bloodstained, powder-stained, gritty masks of faces were channeled by tears of extremity, of sweat, of frantic haste to find something of honor in that which now seemed without. Swords, dirks, sgian dhus, Spanish pistols, muskets, even Lochaber axes: undone against cannon.

Undone, all of it. Scotland was defeated.

But there was more a man might do for his kin, his clan, his country, and for the Italian-born prince who would be King of Scotland, of England, were he given time to claim them.

No time at all, now . . . and then a man beside him, who had fought there as desperately, as coldly, with the same fierce dedication, the same passion, the same oaths sworn and held, here before the Sassenachs and their cannon, their royal prince known as the Duke of Cumberland.

MacLeod was not alone. The Scot with him was tall, as so many of the Highlanders, though now shrunken by adversity: hunched, bent over, collapsed in upon himself. Duncan believed him a stranger, though he could not be certain; it was difficult to recognize even a kinsman when so many wore masks of blood, brain matter, mud, and sweat, even Mac-Leod himself, and this man was badly wounded. Flesh was torn, bone shattered, blood poured from badly broken nose and shattered jaw; from the gaping hole in his chest. Amidst the mass of shredded shirt and sodden plaid: abused flesh, sundered ribs, violated viscera. That he lived at all was testimony to his great strength and determination; in a moment more he would be dead, surely, as a mortal died, with the spirit fled from the house.

But he lived. He and MacLeod clung to one another in the wreckage, in the carnage, bonded as brothers by battle as they stumbled over dead men, dying men; slipped in blood-soaked turf; shuddered and gasped and swore and went on, staggering, falling, up again amidst worse curses, throats raw from the sting of powder, shredded by their warcries, their shouting, the extremity of battle.

The young and powerful fighter was dying now even as he ran, staggered, stumbled; going down into death so he might be reborn again out of mortality into something else, something more. And yet MacLeod could say nothing of it, that death, that rebirth. Could only be there to ease the passing, to make certain the Scot understood he had survived, and would. More truths could come later, more knowledge; for now they must get away, go to a place apart, where a dead man might come again into life, suddenly and painfully, when a mortal man would remain dead—and by that rebirth would know himself Immortal.

Miracle, Duncan MacLeod had named it in Glenfinnan one hundred and twenty-five years before, rousing from death into life. Demon, his father had called him, then and in exile.

Not for this Scot, such things. He would die apart but in the company of a man who knew what it was, what he was; would know, would be told he was no demon, but a man who would live as long as his wits and sword skill permitted.

It was, MacLeod supposed, the best way for a Highlander to die: in battle for his king. And the best way for an Immortal to be born: in the aftermath of carnage, in confusion, where those who survived must go into hiding; where reports of deaths were not to be trusted, framed on such uncertainties as Culloden.

Uncertainties. When the most obvious certainty was they had lost the battle. Perhaps even lost Scotland.

Beside him, the clansman sagged. MacLeod caught him, dug fingers into cloth, into flesh; saw the slackened jaw obscuring the shape of his face, the pouring blood.

There were easier ways, surely. But this was the way of it for this dying Highlander: the threshold of Immortality.

"I am here," MacLeod managed, who recalled his own threshold and its manifold shocks. "I am here wi' ye, aye? You willna be alone in this, I promise—" Not as he had been, and given no welcome save damnation and curses from those who had been kin and clan. "On my honor as a Scot, a Highlander, as Duncan MacLeod of the Clan MacLeod."

Thunder boomed again: a final comment from the English who won the day, held the ground, sent the Highlanders to hell. A volley from the cannon, when none was necessary.

"I am wi' ye," MacLeod gasped. "You willna die alone—"

He went down. Not the other. He did. At first there was nothing, and then pain blossomed in his side. He cursed it weakly, thrust himself upright, caught and clung to his companion before the man could fall, to steady him, because no one would bring him up again from the ground.

So many Highlanders, dead. So many bodies sprawled upon the ground.

"Come," he said, "we'll go apart, aye?" Where a man could die, and live again with impunity. "I'll see ye through this. My oath on it." The dying man could say nothing, could form no words. Blood bubbled in his throat.

There was no "apart." There was only here. Smoke rolled across the field, took them all. Blinded, eyes streaming, throat clogged with powder grit, MacLeod felt his companion waver.

He meant to say no, to urge him up and through it; but there was no voice in him left save a wracking cough, the black and bitter phlegm that rose out of his lungs and fouled his throat, was spat onto the ground. And the young Scot was down at last, the strong body failing, the heart giving out.

Breath wheezed in his throat, hissed through torn lungs. On his back now, eyes staring: and he was frightened now, all the fine courage stripped of him, all the passion, the determination. He was a dead man, and knew it.

He gave into nothing, but fought it still. One hand clasped MacLeod's, closed; bruised flesh, threatened bone. The broken jaw shifted, but shaped nothing. In the mask of blood and powder, the whites of his bulging eyes were stark as a dirk in the belly.

He drew breath, noisily, painfully. Drew breath, held it, hoarded it, then shaped a word of it, plea and command. No jaw formed it, but sheer determination, the efforts of tongue against teeth. The sibilant hissed, abraded into thickness, into warped word by the travesty of the shaping, the requirements of the remains of his mouth and jaw. "S-Stay—"

"I will. I will. I promise you."

Barely a word. An exhalation. "S-Stay—"

MacLeod tried to settle the head, to arrange the limbs more comfortably. But there was no comfort in it; it was himself, survivor, who required the semblance of life, of humanity, in a dying man, instead of the slack surrender into death.

He wanted so badly to say it, to give the young man the truth: that for all he died now, he would live again. The memory of pain would abide forever—not even an Immortal escaped the pain of the dying—but he would rouse again into life, into wholeness, into strength. Into awareness tempered by knowledge, because a man would be with him who could tell him, could instruct him, could ease him into comprehension, with answers for all the questions.

"S-stay—"

"I swear it. I am here. I will be wi' ye." His own pain was manifest, but he would not die of it. Already his body worked to repair itself, to heal the holes in his flesh, to knit broken bone. Even as a mortal he wasn't wounded unto death. But his clothes were bloodied, his movements slowed. Anyone looking at him might believe he died even as the other died, in the thunder of English cannon, in the pall of powder-smoke.

Carnage. Defeat. The ending of Scottish freedom, and the quest for a throne.

Was it the last? Would they never more rise up for Scotland against the Sassenachs? Or would he, Immortal, live to see Highlanders join again in the efforts, the oaths, to put a Scotsman on the throne?

"You there! Highlander! To me!"

It startled him, that shout. Not English. Gaelic. A Scot, then, and not the enemy.

"To me!" the voice shouted.

MacLeod twisted, looked across his shoulder. Powder drifted, obscured his vision; but he saw a cluster of clansmen holding a horse, and a man upon it.

MacLeod drew breath, expelled it. "I canna," he said. "The man is dying, and deserves my comfort."

"MacLeod? Of Glenfinnan?"

Duncan recognized him now. "Fergus MacDonald?"

Fergus was startled by recognition, but dismissed it instantly. "You will come, MacLeod. Now, aye?"

"I canna . . . This man here, this Highlander—"

"And this one," declared Fergus MacDonald. "Dinna ye ken your own prince, man?"

And Duncan looked then, harder; looked through drifting smoke, through gritty eyes, and saw the horseman. Knew him.

"You will come, MacLeod," Fergus said. "For this man, so we may get him from the field." His face spasmed. "Or we'll have died for naught, aye? All of us!"

Oath warred with oath. "I made a promise—"

"And swore to this man, to his father, to the Cause of Scotland!" Fergus MacDonald cried. "In the name of Sweet Jesus, man, you'll come to his aid or I'll kill ye myself!"

A man was measured by his oaths, and the quality of their keeping. MacLeod had sworn to both men, but that man upon the horse, white-faced and dazed by defeat, was a realm.

He glanced down at the dying man beside his knee. He saw no lucidity in the slitted eyes, no recognition. Breath bubbled out of lungs, rattled in bruised throat. The young

Scot was as good as dead, as near it as a man might be, who had not yet crossed over.

"This is your prince, MacLeod!" called Fergus MacDonald. "'Tis treason to turn from him!"

So it was. Torn, MacLeod bent closely to the shattered face. "God be wi' ye, Highlander—"

One hand groped, caught muddied sleeve, dug split nails into MacLeod's flesh. "You swore. . . . S-swore—"

"I must go. In the name of our rightful king and his son, I must. If Scotland is to rise again." Called to a greater oath, it was all he could offer. The Scot would die, but would rise again, even as Scotland. And he would find and make his way as every Immortal did.

Chapter One

The Present

Rain now was mist as the sun came down. He had left unlocked a side door to the theatre in the city's plush new Cultural Center; she slipped inside and shook back the hood of
her raincoat from auburn hair, marking potential escape
routes as she always did. She was accustomed to secrecy, to
subterfuge; it was dangerous, too dangerous, for a woman of
her notoriety to go where she wanted, and when, without
care, without preparation.

Inside, in muted light, she deftly untied the belt of her
raincoat and let the navy-blue fabric fall open. Beneath it she
wore a black silk sweater, black jeans, boots—and the accoutrements of her kind: a deadly steel blade honed for taking
heads.

He had given her directions through the maze of new-built
corridors, far removed from the stage where even now stage-
hands labored to put scrims and backdrops into place. It was
a new theater, glorious with glass, part of a massive complex
designed to restore some semblance of civilized life to an

urban area gone to crime and grime; the papers said it could revitalize the city, that the bond money was well-spent. Such things did not matter to her; she had witnessed the new and old brought down by time, by man, by catastrophe. Had herself labored to bring them down, where it served her Cause and her country.

She heard pounding, shouting, hissed invectives; only hours now until the curtain rose, and the play began.

She smiled. *On the stage, and off.*

Up catwalk stairs, metal grid beneath her boots—a woman afraid of heights would not look down as she ascended, but she feared little beyond a blade against her neck—and then another narrow corridor hedgerowed by doors. Photos, posters, notices, and fliers plastered walls and bulletin boards: detritus of coming productions.

He had not told her which room, but there was no need. The air was alive with it, unmuted by wooden door, by lock; by the wardings of the mortals. There for the knowing, the taking: the presence of power, terrible power, raw, unfettered power—and the promise of a coupling others named bizarre, who couldn't understand; a passionate union of body, of soul, of spirit, of *essence*, entire and inseparable, and an immense satisfaction no one wholly human, so ineffably mortal, could ever comprehend. Even in dreams, in nightmares.

She lingered there and smiled. *I could take his head.*

Oh, indeed, she could; and the Quickening would fill her, would assuage, would content, would gift her with more power, more experience. For he was older than she, stronger, larger, more physically powerful, and a woman, albeit Immortal herself, could use all the power it was possible to claim in the way of her kind. Because if she did not find it, did not take it, did not protect herself against those who sought her own life and power, she would not be the one left standing at the ending of the world such as only they knew of: one, left alive, with all the others dead.

Her mouth stretched again into a brief, ironic smile. *Heads will roll* . . . And she slid her hand beneath the raincoat to close slim fingers around the hilt of deliverance.

* * *

Duncan MacLeod felt it as he kicked shut the door of the dojo, arms full of groceries. Indefinable, indescribable, simply *there*, sudden and stark as a warning light, piercing as an alarm.

Immortal.

But he was home again, and he knew very well who the visitor was, though there was never anything so specific as tangible recognition in the moment of awareness.

Logic, not magic: Richie Ryan had been there earlier in the day, and now apparently was there again. It was his habit to work out in the dojo, then hunt up Mac for conversation, company, a meal when he could get it.

Well, the meal had only just arrived in MacLeod's arms, but he supposed Richie might have scrounged enough out of leftovers in the refrigerator to tide him over for something more substantial. Richie was no longer a kid—hadn't been for some time—but old habits . . .

MacLeod grinned reflectively. His own particular habits were older than most.

So, cooking for two . . . he hitched the rain-dampened sacks into one arm long enough to trip the latch on the door, then shifted them back again as he crossed the wooden floor. Boot heels thumped as he walked through, oblivious to the mats set against the walls, the speed-bags and heavy bags depending from beams, the hand weights neatly racked, the barbell plates carefully stacked beside the benches.

Without conscious thought he mentally catalogued reactions should he require them, were it not Richie above after all: bags dropped, open coat jerked aside as the katana was grasped, and introductions.

Duncan MacLeod, of the Clan MacLeod.

The ritual performed, as always, prior to engagement, to center himself in his heritage, not so clear-cut as a mortal man's: as foundling, fosterling, taken in and then cast out.

Duncan MacLeod, of the Clan MacLeod.

And one of them would die.

But it was Richie, and none of it necessary.

He rode the refurbished freight elevator to the loft, saw through the wooden slats shoes he recognized hanging over the end of his leather couch—and eased the subtle preparedness that lived always in his shadow, servant as much as master.

Joe Dawson had once described it as preternatural, an uncanny awareness at his core, wound like wire, that allowed Duncan MacLeod to intimidate any moment simply by being *in* it; MacLeod himself rather cynically felt it was merely a matter of age. Four hundred years should teach a man something, when others hunted his head.

As he stepped off the elevator into the loft the shoes at the end of the couch moved, and proved themselves attached to feet. Familiar feet attached to jean-encased legs. "Mac!"

Richie Ryan scrambled up. He was a clean-featured young man, grown over the past few years out of the indeterminate softness of adolescence into a harder adulthood. He was more mature, and now more at ease with his body than when MacLeod had taken him off the streets and given him a job, prior to his first "death." Mac had known what Richie was and what he *would* be, and guided him over the threshold into Immortality even as Connor MacLeod had his kinsman, Duncan.

Sandy hair was damp, drying into curls brush and comb never tamed for long; now untamed altogether as Richie shoved a splay-fingered hand through his hair. "Listen, hey, I showered, came by—figured you'd be here, so I'd just hang out."

MacLeod nodded mutely, depositing grocery bags on the countertop. The loft was spare, rustic, inherently wide open, spacious with little beyond a scattering of furniture clusters—haphazardly assembled in style and period, yet oddly complementary—to divide one space from another. The pieces were eclectic, unpretentious—and priceless in today's market.

"I found this note slipped under the dojo door," Richie said, retrieving an envelope from a table. "I guess it's for you."

"I think it's logical to assume a note slipped under my door might be for me, yes." MacLeod did not at once reach for the note but began fishing items out of the sacks.

"Well, I can't really tell," Richie said. "I can't read the writing. It's Greek to me, but I *think* the first letter is a 'D.'"

Curiosity piqued, Mac took the envelope, read the writing easily, and laughed. "No, not Greek. Gaelic." His tongue slipped easily into familiar cadences and throaty enunciation, though it had been long since he had spoken the language that was his first. *"Dhonnchaidh."*

Richie blinked, then shrugged. *"Sounds* Greek, too."

"Gaelic. It's my name: Duncan. Yours would be Risteard."

"Really?"

"Really." MacLeod opened the envelope flap, pulled out a printed card resembling a wedding invitation. Something fluttered to the ground, slid across hardwood to Richie's feet.

"I got 'em." Richie bent, picked up the fallen enclosures. "Tickets . . ."

MacLeod read the card. An invitation indeed: he and a guest were requested to attend the opening night performance of "the Scottish play" at the newly opened and reportedly elegant Cultural Center downtown.

"Macbeth," Richie said, reading the tickets.

MacLeod's hand shot up in an eloquently silencing gesture. "Careful," he said, "Don't say the name."

"Don't say the *name*? Of a play?" Richie laughed incredulously. "That doesn't make any sense. Kind of hard to advertise, isn't it?"

MacLeod shrugged. "You're not supposed to say the name in the theater. Bad luck."

"We're not in the theater," Richie pointed out.

"Humor me."

" 'The Scottish play,' " Richie dutifully echoed, then grinned. "Well, okay. Still doesn't make a lot of sense, but if you say so . . ."

Mac nodded, smiling, and reread the invitation. An infinitely *Scottish* play, "the Scottish play." "Tonight," he said consideringly.

"Short notice, wouldn't you say?"

Precisely because of that MacLeod was not moved to accept; and then he looked again at the envelope with his name scrawled in Gaelic. Someone had gone to a great amount of trouble to personalize the invitation. The play was part of his heritage, his ancestry. Macbeth—Shakespeare had altered the spelling from MacBeth even while anglicizing it—had been the *Ard-Righ*, High King of Scotland, and he . . . well, *he* was indisputably not. He was something less than a normal man with regard to knowing his lineage, the circumstances of his birth, but far more than merely mortal.

Mac Bheatha Mac Findlaech, who had fought for Scotland as valiantly—and violently—as Dhonnchaidh MacLeoid.

Gaelic, after so many years. And to hear those words again, those lines; the music of the language an Englishman had shaped out of the mists and high-grown heather of Scotland's past . . . MacLeod tapped the creamy, gold-printed card against one hand. "So—do you want to go? It might teach you a little Scottish history."

"Ah, no, I've got *you* for that, Highlander." Richie grinned. "Besides, I've got a date."

"A date?" MacLeod feigned surprise. "Fast work, Richie —you've only just gotten back into town."

"Hey, listen—I may not be *you*, Mac, who can lay a woman out with the merest glance from those brooding Scottish eyes, but, well . . . I have my ways, too." Richie grinned, slapped him on the arm. "Speaking of, I'd better get going. I'm taking Teresa—you remember Teresa?—out for a nice dinner at a fancy restaurant, my treat, and afterward . . . well, who can say? I might get lucky." He headed toward the elevator. "I'm not much in the mood for a play tonight—and anyway, didn't you live through it?"

"Eleventh century," MacLeod said dryly. "As you very well know."

Richie laughed. "Okay, okay. Maybe I'll read the book."

"It's Shakespeare," MacLeod reproved pointedly as Richie slid closed the slatted doors. "Better heard than read." Even as Gaelic was.

"But you knew *him*, right?" He grinned, waggled fingers. "Later, Mac. Tonight it's—Risteard?—and Teresa."

MacLeod stared after the descending elevator. "I guess you could say I knew Shakespeare . . . . met him in a book."

And Macbeth as well, in that book, the year Timon taught

an illiterate Scot to read English in the monastery, safe with Paul on holy ground, before Kalas was banished.

Three hundred years before. And Macbeth older than that, the long-dead King of Scotland, slain on the field of battle with his head chopped off.

MacLeod looked again at the invitation, the hand-written name on the envelope.

Macbeth, with his head chopped off. Dead to all but history, and the literature of a Sassenach.

Scotland had birthed and bred many Immortals, after all. Duncan knew several of them himself, including his kinsman, Connor MacLeod, who had found and taught him.

It would, MacLeod decided, cast an entirely different light on the Scottish play, to watch while wondering if perhaps that Scottish king, so vilified by the greatest of English playwrights, had been an Immortal.

Softly Duncan quoted, " *'My strange and self-abuse is the initiate of fear, that wants hard use . . . We are but young yet in deed.' "*

She waited in the corridor, listening. Footsteps, from the other side of the door. The latch rattled, was undone. And the door fell away, swung open into darkness. Into invitation.

More tightly yet her hand shut around the hilt of her sword. *Ah, but I could take his head—*

If he let her.

He moved away from her: a tall man, very tall, wearing dark clothing as she did, indistinct in the shadows, but the fabric was cut loosely so as not to bind the massive frame, nor the arm from drawing sword. She was auburn-haired, but his was red, a thick, vigorous red mane springing from his scalp to curl against wide shoulders, and the shadow of a ruddy beard upon his averted profile.

A match was struck, flared. She smelled the sharp tang of chemical, heard the muted hiss of ignition, saw the brief small strobe of illumination across freckled hands—skilled, strong, powerful hands—before those hands cupped and warded the match, transformed transitory light into permanence. He set flame to wick, let it catch, then dropped the match onto the tabletop. It died, smoking, was spent, but left behind it flame enough upon the lantern wick to illuminate the table, and the man beside it.

Light born of lantern, of fire and wick, not incandescent, fluorescent, or halogen. Old vector, not new. *As we ourselves are old.*

"Come in," he said: a soft, deep rumble as much from chest as from throat. "There is trust in this."

Trust. Oh, there were some she trusted. Perhaps even this man.

"Come in," he repeated. "Come in out of the rain." He smiled in the silent interplay of lantern-bred shadows, and the hard, high angle of harsh cheekbones softened. "Come in out of the darkness into the light."

The accent was there, though slight and soft as her own, and bred of a different country. She took her hand from the hilt, let fall the flap of damp-dappled coat. She moved beyond the hallway into the room, into the light as invited, though his light was not of flame but of soul, and swung shut the door behind her. "I've said that myself to many a man."

He arched a single expressive brow in devastating eloquence. "No women?"

It amused, if briefly, with excess irony. "Women give me little chance to speak of light, and truth."

"Oh, aye. I can see that." He grinned. Widely. Warmly. Wickedly. With such charm as to strike her down, if she were the woman who could be struck. And if she were, undoubtedly she would be dead. It was dangerous for a woman such as she to allow anything but immense self-control to dictate her responses.

And yet there were those who said she was *out* of control, had lost it too many years before. And perhaps she had, though none of them knew precisely how many years before, nor how many she had survived.

None who lived knew, save those who were like her.

"So," she said. "Light to banish the darkness." She tossed back mist-curled hair, then raked it from her face. "How poetic."

"And truth," he answered. "Truth, light—poetry. There is

power in such things. We are Gaels, are we not?" His eyes, smoky-amber, warmed as he studied her. "There must be that between us. Truth, and poetry."

"And?"

He turned away briefly, turned back. Set down upon the table a bottle, two glasses. "Whisky," he said. Then the grin bloomed again, framed by a brilliant beard, and the Gaelic they both spoke though born of different lands. "*Usquabae.*" Water of Life.

She laughed. Oh, a bonnie lad indeed, this Scot, this red-haired, red-bearded giant, broad as a barn and equally hard and strong as the stone of its begetting. A lesser woman would succumb, surely, to so much power and charm. *And I?*

She thought not. Too much at stake, for now. And there was another between them. Another man, another Gael. Another Highlander.

They knew him both, that man, that Highlander. One as a warrior, in war; another as a woman, equally a warrior but on a different, less rocky battlefield, and in a wholly different battle.

Amusement was banished by recollection of the man who was not present except in their thoughts. Once. Only once had they shared that ground, danced that dance, the Irish woman and the other Highlander. When both of them had been lost in abject grief and anger, in confusion, in the black, incomparable pain of unconscionable loneliness, the kind of deep, bleak anguish no one else might comprehend, not even of their own kind, because each of them had done what was warned against: lost a part of their Immortal souls to fragile, human mortals whose deaths were permanent. Seeking that one night to remember what had been lost, seeking to renew, to reaffirm in their own souls that they yet survived. Solace, and survival. Something more than sex. Something significantly less than love.

So much love for each of them lost in the spray of bullets miles and months apart. She, a man she loved; he, a woman.

And now: this man. Who looked straight at her and said a single thing. "I want Duncan MacLeod."

Chapter Two

She drew a quiet breath, let it go silently between parted lips. Here it was, as expected, springing up between them, but also to bind them. It was as much a challenge the man offered as simple comment.

"He will not come," she said. "It isn't as simple a thing as you might wish it to be."

"He will come. He is a man of honor, of commitment—"

"And he has committed to *peace*," she interjected sharply, dismissing the odd note of precise irony in his dark-timbred tone as she framed her own reply out of a personal frustration. "No more the warrior is Duncan MacLeod; he has given it up. As for Lent."

Once again the quick, engulfing grin amidst trimmed beard, and the thick, intentional dialect: "Och, lassie, I dinna think so, aye?" He shook his head, dropping the burr that once had been as breathing to a Scot; yet now was merely for roles and readings other men wrote for drama. "Not Duncan MacLeod."

"I know him—" she began.

"As do I."

"Younger," she said, persisting. "Both of you were younger then, in the way of our kind. He is older now, in spirit if in nothing else—"

"He'll come."

"Into the light?" She shook her head. "I've tried. More than once."

"In Ireland, I heard . . . and that incident here, with the boy newly made one of us?" He shrugged, smiling faintly. "Oh, I know, you've told me he refused to join you—but 'twas different, that. Now is—now."

Mention of him as 'the boy' annoyed her, set her on edge with remembered humiliation; that 'boy' could have taken her head for his very first Quickening, had he not given up the chance. But she set that memory aside in lieu of present business and personal conviction. "MacLeod hunts no one—"

He overrode her. "Nor do I, at the moment. What I hunt now, the tangible and *in*tangible, those 'things' others can't understand save for the worth of the jewels and the gold"— his expression made plain his contempt —"is done for the land of my birth, not for the Gathering. As *you* well understand. We were patriots first, before ever we were Immortal." He smiled faintly, at ease again, assessing her expression. "But he is no less willing to take a head than you."

She conceded that. "For survival, when pressed to it."

"Not for revenge?"

"He has," she answered. "But—he isn't like me. Not now. Not then. Not ever." She recalled it so clearly, his urging of her to turn away from the violence seventy years before, in an Irish cottage moments before the volley of shots exploded the window. And Kerry had died in it—

"Och, aye, I can see he's nothing like you." The man eyed her more openly, not as a man a woman, but in judgment of her dedications, her intentions. "You take heads . . . but also mortal lives of no consequence to our kind."

On edge already, she bristled. "No *consequence?* Sweet Jesus, can you not see what it is we do, mortal and Immortal, to fight the Sassenach? You are a Gael yourself, man, and—"

"—*and* I'll fight my battle with less mortal blood shed, English or otherwise, for now. No blood need be shed at all, in such unsubtle activities as the recovery of stolen property. Though if later they insist—well, that will be later, aye?" He tapped one long, thick finger against the table. "We'll have him with us, lass. You'll see."

"He will not come. As a thief?" She shook her head. "He will not." They spoke English, as they had for decades, but now, before one another, they fell back too easily into the constraints of Gaelic: there was no such answer as simple as the English "*No.*"

"Because he's a man of peace, now?" Broad shoulders hitched briefly. "One cannot change what is ultimately one's nature, lass. Not even as we take in the natures of others like us, as we take their heads. He was born a Scot, a Highlander, reared a warrior as I was to feuds and blood and battle—"

"Four hundred years ago!"

"Yesterday," he said softly. "Yesterday, my bonnie lass. To a Scot, to a Highlander, all the battles are yesterday, and the blood as red and wet."

She bared her teeth at him briefly. "Do you think I don't know it? That blood runs in me, as well—"

"*Irish* blood." He smiled disarmingly. "Did they not say, the bloody Sassenachs—and the historians, after—that if the Irish and the Scots had stopped fighting *one another* long enough to unite, we could have defeated the world?"

It stung, as he intended. And yet she suspected it was true. Scots and Irishmen fought themselves, like mirror images, rather than the enemy as a united force.

"So," she said, "you'll have him with us."

"I will, aye. I want him."

"How?"

"By making him recall what he is. And who." His eyes now were humorless, set aflame by lantern light. "Duncan MacLeod, of the Clan MacLeod. Highlander."

"How?" she repeated.

"He was born of violence, born *into* violence, as every Gael, my lass. He cannot deny it, any more than you can. He may walk away for a bit, but he'll come back to it. He will always come back to it. A man such as he needs only to find that single element, the one abiding truth, that is far more important to him than personal peace. For him, once, it was oaths and honor, and brotherhood sworn in blood, in battle—" But he broke it off sharply, his generous, friendly mouth in the wide bearded jaw now compressed to a seam within the granite of his skull.

"I know what it is for me," she said sharply. "Separation from England. The flight of the English from Ireland, as the 'Flight of the Earls' of our history." She thought of them briefly, the brave Irish earls, men of her ancestry fleeing their own land from the depredations of a Sassenach queen. "But for a man who isn't political?" She paused, clarified. "*Now*." He had been, once, had MacLeod. They had fought side by side for something far greater than personal survival.

"He's a Scot," the man said. "There are—inducements."

She folded her arms. "Oh?"

He turned away a moment, gathered something, swung back. Onto the table, into lantern-light—a prop, surely, in this theater where even mortals wielded swords—he set them one by one.

A clump of dried heather. A single scarlet feather. A scrap of bloodied tartan fabric, darkened by age. A clan badge, and the short, small knife called *sgian dhu*, worn, she knew, strapped around a man's calf.

Around MacLeod's calf, once, and another around this man's. She met amber-colored eyes. "Do you believe that is enough?"

"Perhaps. If not, then surely this . . ."

She looked upon it in his hand, his large, powerful hand: a crude-made withy cross.

"He'll answer," the man told her. "No Scot alive, no Highlander, no Jacobite sworn to the Stuart kings of Scotland can turn his back on such."

"The cross of war," she murmured.

"I need only set it afire and put it before him to summon up Duncan MacLeod to Scotland's aid again."

In her heart, at last, hope burgeoned. And the pipes beat in her blood.

Deftly she took up bottle, poured whisky—*usquabae*—

into the glasses, set it down again. He lifted one, she the other.

"*Slàinte*," she said—*Gaelic "cheers"*—raising smoky-hued liquor into smudgy lantern light. A prop, that lantern; but sufficient unto the moment.

"*Alba gu brath*," he answered: Scotland forever.

Well, she was not Scottish. But it would do, this. Gaels, Celts, united, to take back from the enemy what had been stolen from them, from Irish and Scot alike, for time out of mind.

And Duncan MacLeod among them.

Holy ground. A place of quietude, of refuge, for any man, but also for an Immortal, be he in need of such respite. And so even Duncan MacLeod had gone there to the monastery where Paul saw to it no man broke the peace, mortal or Immortal; where fools lived so long as they had a mind to, and those of more wit found the chance to rest, to renew a spirit weary from the Game.

MacLeod, that most unlikely monk, had too much choice in partners to be moved to celibacy, yet nonetheless found peace there, and respite, and education: at the behest of Timon, he learned to read English. He had, he claimed, a bit of Latin, some Italian, but not enough of either, and nothing at all of English. But Timon had given him a book and bade him learn; that he would find comfort and entertainment, and such things as he knew.

And so with instruction he learned the English, read the book, and found Timon's words true. Shakespeare's Macbeth, *the story of a Scotsman who was also a king, and weary of a game nearly as exhausting and deadly as the one MacLeod played, and other Immortals like him.*

In the tiny cell he read the play again, sprawled belly-down across the narrow mattress in inelegant abandon, one leg hanging off the edge, torso levered up on elbows. He was not yet fluent, for that took time, but he could read, now, could comprehend, could make sense of the words that sang, and yet told him tales of such things as he knew, as Timon had promised.

Scots, and war, and battle; the fight for a kingdom; murder and machinations, tragedies and griefs, stirring triumphs.

An attentive forefinger found his place, marked it, underscored the printed words so he might keep track of them, knitted them together into sentences he understood, and emotions that rang true and real and right. It passed beyond his awareness that the fingernail was cracked, with a thin line of grime beneath it; that the bruises of his own life, the aches of his battles had only just begun to fade. Immortality did not preclude him from injury, from pain, from stiffness and sore bones. It merely meant he healed faster.

Of all the characters, MacLeod had a liking for Macbeth. He admired the whole play, but it was to Macbeth he returned time and again, to sort out the language, the disputations, the declamations. To comprehend the ambitions and emotions, the helplessness and the ruthlessness, all in one man. A most human man, and mortal man, Macbeth. And the playwright, this William Shakespeare, grasped an Immortal's spirit if not the concept of his existence.

MacLeod mouthed the words, then set them together, found the rhythm, the cadence that made it sing. That made it and the man come alive.

> "Tomorrow, and tomorrow, and tomorrow,
> Creeps in this petty pace from day to day,
> To the last syllable of recorded time;
> And all our yesterdays have lighted fools
> The way to dusty death. Out, out, brief candle!
> Life's but a walking shadow; a poor player,
> That struts and frets his hour upon the stage,
> And then is heard no more: it is a tale
> Told by an idiot, full of sound and fury,
> Signifying nothing."

MacLeod thought it over. Read again the first three lines, felt those three lines, as if Shakespeare spoke of Immortals and the slow unwinding of their lives.

Aloud, so that the words echoed back from the stone walls, he read: " 'Tomorrow, and tomorrow, and tomorrow, creeps in this petty pace from day to day/ To the last syllable of recorded time—' "

He considered that. How true it was. The petty pace of mortals, lived by men and women who had no need of clocks, of days to measure the years, of years to measure the centuries.

" 'And all our yesterdays have lighted fools/ The way to dusty death.' "

Fools such as mortals, with no choice but to live and die a fixed moment in time, so short a moment upon the earth. He scratched idly at his cheek. " 'That struts and frets his hour upon the stage, and/ Then is heard no more . . .' "

MacLeod frowned. But what of Immortals? They perhaps had more time, but left less by which to remember them. They outlived mortals, or left them, and were thus forgotten. They played the Game and lived or died; if they lived, it was to step closer yet to the Gathering, when only one would survive the final battle.

" 'Life's but a walking shadow . . .' "

He looked up from the book, stared hard into distance despite the confines of the tiny cell, scowled fiercely. Such truth, and such eloquence. What was his life at all but a shadow upon the stage, despite its longevity? There was nothing known of Immortals, nothing written down to transcend the years. Macbeth lived still because of Shakespeare's talent, but what of Immortals? What of men and women who transcended the years of mortals, and yet were unknown? What of Duncan MacLeod?

His mouth twisted into irony. Softly he quoted: " ' . . . a poor player/ That struts and frets his hour upon the stage, and then is heard no more.' "

James Douglas leaned toward the mirror, deftly adding shadow along a cheekbone, darkening it into a pronounced shelf of bone. Theatrical makeup changed a man into a ghoul, but it was necessary if the audience was to distinguish features from a distance-muted blob of flesh shallowed by lighting effects. On the stage features were overemphasized, as were gestures, enunciation . . . Shakespeare caused a man to spit, were he not meticulous in his diction.

He examined his reflection, studying his face as if another wore it. Smoky amber eyes fringed ordinarily by pale, ginger-hued lashes, now darkened. Trimmed red beard framing a wide, mobile mouth, underscoring the hard line of jaw beneath from ear to ear; heavy eyebrows, penciled for effect; strong, straight nose; freckles banished beneath makeup. Women claimed he was not a handsome man, that his appeal went far beyond the superficiality of his features, born instead of immense size and power and an equally towering spirit.

He bared his teeth in a predatory grin. " *'O horror, horror, horror! Tongue nor heart . . . Cannot conceive nor name thee!'* "

Someone rapped briefly at the door. He knew who it was, and that he need not fear.

The door opened and a light voice said, "Half hour to curtain, Jamie."

"So it is." He continued applying shadow, looking now into the mirror to see the man who had entered his dressing room. Colin Cameron, Banquo to his Macduff. "Tonight will be a very special night, Coll."

"Will it?" Cameron was dark in place of red, though pale of face beneath the theatrical makeup. He was young, perhaps eighteen, though the makeup aged him. Beneath it the bones were good, though softer, more delicate than Jamie's. His eyes were bright with anticipation. "Will he come, then?"

"Och, aye, he will." Jamie grinned. "Dhonnchaidh MacLeoid."

"But—you're not after his head."

The doubt in the young man's tone amused him. Douglas arched a hedge of brows. "MacLeod's vaunted head, seated so long upon his shoulders? It would be something, aye, to be the man who took that head. So many of us have tried."

"But—"

Cameron was worried now, and Jamie took pity; the boy learned quickly, but his feelings were transparent. Duncan

MacLeod was something of a legend, and Cameron was fascinated. "No more after his head than after yours, Coll. There's more to this than the Game. I've sworn that to you on my soul, on the blood of a Scot."

"They say MacLeod has given up war."

"This isn't war, Coll—at least, not that kind."

"Nor Annie's kind?"

Jamie capped the pot of makeup. "Annie Devlin has agreed there are to be no deaths in this."

"Annie Devlin couldn't swear any such thing," Cameron answered flatly, youth banished by the pragmatism required for survival. "She's a stone killer."

"Of Sassenachs, and Irish traitors." He hitched one massive shoulder as he cleaned his hands on a cloth. "This is for Scotland. We are not the IRA, and we're not known for killing folk, are we?"

Colin's gaze was steady. "Nor for stealing, Jamie."

"Oh, aye—not *yet.*" In the mirror, he met blue eyes. "Have you changed your mind about our own Cause?"

After a brief moment, Cameron averted his gaze from the intensity of the giant's. "I have not."

"It's the right thing to do, lad."

"I know that. You've taught me enough of our history, of what was taken from us—"

"Freedom. Culture. Our living. Even our language, our kilts, and the music of the pipes . . . after Culloden." Tension knotted heavy shoulders, set tendons into iron. With effort he banished it. "We'll have all of it back, our treasure. And our pride."

Cameron nodded, but he had not entirely learned to ward his expression. As yet it divulged his concern.

The huge Scot smiled. "We'll leave his head on his shoulders, Coll. He's a clever man, my Duncan . . . I'd sooner have his wits *with* us than his blood on my sword."

Quietly Cameron challenged, "Or his Quickening?"

Jamie laughed softly, a quiet rumble deep in his thick chest. "Now, that would be something, aye? He's older than us both." He pushed his stool away, stood up. "We'd best go out, before we're late. This is important, for the first night in such grand surroundings as well as our own plans. . . but 'the play's the thing.' " And he grinned, amused that Shakespeare, as ever, provided in the sixteenth century that which was as timely four centuries later.

Colin Cameron grinned back, affecting an accent. "Och, aye, 'tis that . . . and other things, tonight."

"Invitation," the man said, "for a Scot, a Highlander, to come back to his own."

Colin's eyes were steady. " *'A heavy summons lies like lead upon me, And yet I would not sleep'* . . ."

"Oh, he'll not sleep tonight. I promise you that." Jamie gestured sweepingly toward the door. " *'Out, damned spot!'* "

Laughing, Colin went out. " *'May flights of angels'* . . ." And his voice trailed off into the corridor.

"Wrong play," the giant said quietly, taking up his sword, the lengthy trefoil-quillioned claymore. Its weight was comforting, made for the massive hands of a Highland warrior. "Better, I think, to say: *'Confusion now hath made his masterpiece!'* "

Chapter Three

The rain had stopped, though fresh asphalt betrayed the pewter-hued sheen of moisture. MacLeod didn't bother with the valet stand at the Cultural Center and parked the Thunderbird himself. He'd just as soon look after it than risk it to someone else.

Joe Dawson had arrived already and stood waiting in front of the entrance. MacLeod, coming up the stairs from the underground garage, checked his watch, quickened his step, glanced at the huge building's glowing facade. A cliff of glass met his examination, hundreds of transparent panes set into a massive framework. In front of the windows stretched an expanse of granite-and-marble plaza and the cascading cataracts of a series of fountains; beyond that a greensward of clipped, perfect grass. The wall of glass was alive with illumination and reflected images. It painted the waiting man into a chiaroscuro of light and darkness, silhouetted against a webwork of silvered spray.

Joe Dawson was younger in body and spirit than his hair and beard suggested, currently in the process of transforming to pale silver out of pepper and salt. Clearly a fit, vital man,

solid in torso and shoulders and lacking the paunch and softness of many men in their forties, he stood nonetheless without the natural balance of a gifted athlete, though once he
had been such: a mine in Vietnam had robbed him of his
legs, though not of his life, or his warmth and humanity.
Prosthetics permitted him mobility, a cane aided it; but there
was nothing in Joe Dawson that hinted at disability, including wit, decency, kindness. Of all the men Duncan MacLeod
had known over four centuries, Immortal and mortal alike,
Dawson was one of the best.

"Some joint, huh?" he asked as MacLeod joined him.

"Expensive," Mac observed.

Dawson grinned. "And you're part owner, MacLeod. We
all are. Taxes, after all . . . even Immortals pay them." His
pale eyes were alight. "Nice to see them going for something
that will last, something about arts and beauty and talent, instead of everyday things."

"Everyday things feed a lot of people." MacLeod straightened the fit of one sleeve, a black velvet evening jacket over
black silk collarless shirt; he wore simple clothes, as ever,
but elegant in their simplicity, in cut and fabric. He was not a
man who paid much attention to clothing, though women
had told him he could wear anything at all in any company
and put every man to shame.

Or wear *nothing*, some of them said, tending to it deftly—
though the discussions that followed had nothing at all to do
with clothing. Or with taxes, for that matter.

"So," Dawson said, "have you seen 'the Scottish play'?"

MacLeod arched eloquent eyebrows. "You know about
that?"

"The superstition? Of course. I did some plays when I was
a kid." Dawson laughed then, chagrined. "I suppose that was
a silly question. What Scot hasn't seen this play?"

Mac considered that. "Probably the ones who don't like
having history rewritten."

"How would you know? The real Macbeth was about five
hundred years before your time."

"We weren't exactly neighbors," MacLeod agreed dryly.
"But Shakespeare—well, let's just say he took liberties."

"That old argument about Richard the Third maybe murdering the princes in the Tower?"

"Among other things." MacLeod glanced toward the entrance, where stragglers in costly opening-night finery hurried inside. "We'd better go in, or we'll miss the curtain."

Dawson set his cane for balance and swung toward the massive glass facade. He pitched his voice into theatrical rhythm and precise enunciation. " *'When shall we three meet again/In thunder, lightning, or in rain?' "*

"You make a lousy witch," MacLeod declared, laughing. "Wrong gender."

Unperturbed and in high good spirits, Dawson quoted one of the Weird Sisters cheerfully, " *'Fair is foul, and foul is fair/Hover through the fog and filthy air.' "*

"Eleventh-century smog," MacLeod said crisply as they made their way to the doors.

Backstage, as the curtain rose, James Douglas sat upon a rock. It wasn't a real rock, being handmade by the prop department, but it was a worthy seat nonetheless for a Scot born of the Highlands. He sat with head bowed, hands clasped loosely across the pommel of the claymore balanced vertically against the floor. Separated by scrims, backdrop, curtain, the sounds of battle were muffled. Men shouting, dying, the clangor of swords, the sounds of life extinguished in the name of a play.

He had time. His entrance was not until Act I, Scene VI, a good hour or more away, and this was but the prologue before the witches' entrance. Always time, when he was Macduff. Macbeth was never his role, and certainly not this night; there was another actor needed for that infamous role, though he did not yet know his part.

Swords clashed, shouts rose. To this tour they brought more realism, this particular company, because the swords were real, the swordsmen expert, the unscripted language during the fight born neither of Shakespeare's pen nor of ambitious but foolish directors. James Douglas himself was director.

The red-haired Scot shut his eyes. For that moment, with

effort, he could cast himself back, let the staged battle become real, with blood running wet on the ground . . . and then his eyes snapped open. *He is here—*

A man stepped into his vision: Colin Cameron, as Banquo. " *'Good sir, why do you start; and seem to fear'*—" And then Cameron saw his expression, his stillness, and a light came into his eyes.

It was not Jamie's line to answer, but he replied nonetheless, albeit not of Shakespeare. "I told you he would come."

Cameron released a breath. "Duncan MacLeod . . ."

He expelled a low laugh. "Christ, Coll, one would think you *worshiped* him!"

Cameron colored splotchily beneath his makeup. "You've taught me a lot, Jamie. But—"

"—he's older, reputedly better, and you don't worship me." He laughed softly. "Well, I didn't expect it, did I? My goal is merely to teach you to live out the centuries you're due."

"*If* no one takes my head."

Jamie grinned. "When I am done with you, you'll know enough to see you through. On the day you die and become Immortal, you'll know what you are. And what it means." *Not like me,* the thought finished in his head, unvoiced. He jerked his head toward the curtain. "There's the drum, lad. You'd best go make your entrance."

Cursing silently, Colin Cameron hastened around the curtain. Jamie, still clasping the pommel of his claymore, looked into the wings and saw the table holding various props: flagons, goblets, rolled parchments tied with ribbon, even a severed head.

Macbeth's severed head, that would be stuck upon a pike and carried out into the stage in triumph for Macduff's final lines, some of the most stirring of the play.

Yet those were not the lines Jamie spoke now, beneath his breath so softly. From earlier in the play, the final confrontation before Macbeth is slain by Macduff: " *'Then yield thee, coward . . . We'll have thee, as our rarer monsters are, painted upon a pole'* . . ."

*   *   *

In the wings, in deep shadow, away from actors and stage-hands, the woman watched the play taking place both on-stage and off. Colin Cameron skidded around the curtain, paused to catch his breath, then went out onto the stage. Behind him, behind the curtain, perched upon tumbled "rocks" as if they constituted a throne—perhaps the Stone of Scone?—sat James Douglas, teeth set as he murmured something she could not hear. But she *could* hear Cameron stumble over his first line, catching himself and continuing as best he could. He was a well-meaning boy, ripe for manipulation. But he was Jamie's tool, and she would not interfere.

She looked again at Douglas, at the wicked steel of his claymore, the legendary broadsword of the Highlanders. Friends, he had said: he and Duncan MacLeod, sworn companions before battle and during. And he was certain of his friend, that he would answer the call in the name of the land of his birth. That was their goal, to bring MacLeod to their number, to the fold, to their Cause, not to his beheading.

She was Irish, not Scottish. But their peoples were bound nevertheless by blood and birth and language, even similar customs; even the pipes, by God, the wailing of the pipes calling Celts to war.

This is war, too. No matter what Jamie called it. This was as much a war as the one she conducted, and for that reason she would aid them.

For them, and for MacLeod.

They had lost so much, the two of them, and people they had loved. Was it not time now that they found one another and put the past away?

Dawson felt the man next to him tense, stilled into immobility. There was no sound, no sign, but Joe knew Duncan MacLeod too well now. A glance at the striking profile, cut clean as king's coin; the tautness of perfect features; the sudden startling sharpness in brown eyes beneath the deep arch of heavy brows as he searched the audience, the actors on the stage. An unheard, unseen indication, felt by none but those who were of his kind; MacLeod had said he simply *knew* when an Immortal was near. Not who or exactly where—it was not so precise, and even the distance varied—but that one was present.

Banquo hesitated, then stumbled over his first line. He caught himself quickly enough and went on smoothly, but Dawson thought it a pity the actor's entrance was ruined. Opening night nerves.

He glanced down at his program. *Highland Shakespeare Company*, presenting Shakespeare's *Macbeth*. The young man playing Banquo was listed as Colin Cameron, with an italicized name in parentheses: *Cailean Camshron.*

It was the only visible mistake of the evening, though Dawson was certain there were other missed cues or missteps. It had been twenty years since he'd seen *Macbeth*, and he had never memorized it save for a few lines that appealed. He felt most of the actors acquitted themselves well—Lady Macbeth was particularly effective, though her "husband" was less so despite his leading role—but it was the giant red-haired Macduff who stole the show. From the moment he walked onto the stage, though he had no line in that scene, no one in the theater could look at anyone else.

And it was Macduff who killed Macbeth in a superb display of swordsmanship, good enough that Dawson, who had witnessed MacLeod in action, held his breath. It was hard-fought, violent, filled with the clangor of steel as well as the grunts and shouts of extremity, as two strong men fought for crown and country, for revenge and redemption. The choreography carried them offstage, and a hideous cry rang out.

Dawson barely heard the rest of the dialogue recited by supporting characters. He was transfixed, as was everyone, by the entrance moments later of Macduff, a severed head carried aloft upon a pike. Upon the tumbled stones he stood, red hair bristling, and declaimed his final lines in a clear Scots-laced English far purer than Duncan MacLeod's centuries-softened accent.

> *"Hail, king! for so thou art: behold, where stands*
> *The usurper's cursed head: the time is free:*
> *I see thee compass'd with thy kingdom's pearl*

That speak my salutation in their minds;
Whose voices I desire aloud with mine,—"

And thundering through the theater: " *'Hail, King of Scotland!'* "

As the others onstage roared the refrain, Dawson glanced at MacLeod. What he saw in that face stunned him by its tension, its palpable rigidity. "MacLeod?"

But Duncan did not hear him, or chose not to answer. He merely stared, transfixed, at the head upon the pike, the dark-haired, brown-eyed head—supposedly Macbeth's—that looked exactly like his own.

Chapter Four

Scotland, 1632

This time, he knew. At once.

The enemy was English. A Sassenach soldier in crimson coat—an outlander, to use the Gaelic. But he was an enemy far more than because of the land of his birth, the language he spoke. He was also Immortal, and he was hunting heads.

MacLeod felt the enemy even as the enemy felt him. Connor had taken pains to make certain he knew that sensation, that alarm, lest he lose his head out of sheer ignorance. But he had not expected this, this sudden burgeoning knowledge that the man wished to kill him not for anything he'd done, or might do, but because of what he was.

Immortal. Not because he was a Scot, a Highlander, a warrior—which was enough in this time and place to make an English soldier his enemy—but because he was part of the Game.

So quickly the enemy came, without preliminaries beyond the warning of his closeness, the violence of his charge, the single shout of challenge.

A horse, bearing down, with the sunset at its back: mouth agape, eyes bulging, shod hooves striking sparks against the granite of a stony Scottish hillside where Duncan MacLeod tended dinner: a single lean hare, spitted.

A hard-used horse, as much a weapon as any blade could be. The animal couldn't kill him, but most assuredly it could cripple him long enough for the enemy's sword to do its work.

Silhouette, and sparks; the bellows-bark of breath expelled through massive equine lungs. But MacLeod was up and away, thrusting out of his squat as the horse came down, came down from the sunset; scrambling for the sword set aside, though in reach; ducking the whistling slice of Sassenach steel.

"I'll have your head!" cried the soldier. "I'll have it off your shoulders and set upon a pike on London Bridge, you bloody Highland savage!"

Two purposes, then, this enemy claimed: to behead an Immortal within the rules of the Game, but also to kill a Scot, whom the English detested as much as Highlanders hated the English.

Duncan threw himself aside against the earth, rolled, came up instantly, kilt a-tumble, bare feet planted against turf-clad earth, automatically kicking aside small stones that might interfere. He drew breath and shouted it: "I am Duncan MacLeod of the Clan MacLeod!"

The other offered nothing now, no more shouting, only an eerie, contained silence. The first rush had failed; now the man came off his horse and engaged on foot, battering at MacLeod's broadsword to cut away his defense.

There was no more speech between them, no sound at all save the screech and clangor of steel, the grunts of mutual exertion, the noisy inhalations and exhalations. Time slowed even as the day died, lending MacLeod the ability to see each move before it was made, to decipher the maneuvers, to stop and turn the blade. He had not known so much prior to Connor, prior to the training, prior to understanding what Immortality meant.

The first test, this. This was not Connor, who played with

his kinsman even as he taught him, proving with ease how a man might fall to another's sword. Duncan had been a warrior prior to his first death, but the war between Immortals, Connor explained, was different. So were the rules of engagement, and so was the enemy's goal.

If the blade got through, if the blade pierced his heart and took his life for so brief a time as an Immortal could die a mortal death, decapitation would follow, and also the true and binding death, the final and permanent death.

He was Duncan MacLeod of the Clan MacLeod. He had only begun to live in the way of his kind, and he would not die yet.

The soldier grinned at him, goading him. "I'll have your head, Highlander—I'll carry it with me all the way to London, and put it upon a pike!"

Back, back and back . . . now it was MacLeod who advanced, MacLeod who held ground and advantage, MacLeod who drove the other into extremity and fear. There was no sense in telling the Sassenach the truth: that Duncan MacLeod of the Clan MacLeod had taken no heads, no Quickenings. All that mattered was he had to do both now, or surrender his life before it was properly begun.

Block, block and block . . . and the opening, unexpected; the flutter of anticipation deep in his belly, his groin; the understanding that the question was answered, the ultimate question for which Connor had told him there was only one answer.

Yes, he could kill. In the way of his kind.

The other stumbled, went to one knee. Tried to bring up the sword even as he wavered, balance undone; lost the weapon as MacLeod struck it away with a clean, sharp blow of his own blade, steel against steel, sending the English weapon spinning to the ground.

Unweaponed. Unmanned. Soon to be beheaded.

The soldier knew. He knelt there on one knee, empty hands outstretched, chest heaving as he tried to catch his breath. Fear was in his face, fear and acknowledgment, a hybrid MacLeod had seen before in other men at the doorway, yet this was different. This knowledge was bittersweet, this fear of a loss no man might comprehend save he was Immortal, faced now with the transformation into pure mortality.

Death lived in his eyes.

The Englishman moved then, yet did not flinch as Mac-Leod's blade nicked the flesh of his throat. The other knee was set against the ground. He was neither supplicant nor servant; was merely prepared.

MacLeod had died once, that first terrifying death that was to mortals final. He recalled it so well, that pure and clean comprehension that he would end, would be no more, erased from the present as a fire was doused beneath a drenching rain. There had been pain in his death, physical pain from the spear thrust into his chest, shattering bone, sundering viscera. No peace in that death, merely pain and a sick, consuming fear that he had failed his clan, had dishonored his father.

This man had died, too, and was resurrected. Perhaps many times. But this was the final death.

"My head goes on no pike in London," MacLeod told him. "It stays here, aye? On my shoulders and in Scotland, ye bloody Sassenach!"

"Do it," the soldier said. Then, in clear derision, "Do you believe I wish to pray?"

What god could they pray to, those who were Immortal?

"Do it!" the Englishman cried.

MacLeod drew breath and asked what he had never been able to ask Connor. "How many deaths? How many Quickenings?"

The Englishman's expression underwent a startling transformation from taut preparedness to incredulity. "How many?" he echoed. "Do you say I am your first?*"*

"First," MacLeod said. "But no' my last, aye, if they all come for me as you have."

"Oh, they'll come. One after another, they'll come. They must. We must." The other's mouth twisted briefly. "There can be only one."

"Aye, well," MacLeod said, "here, and now, 'tis me."

The Englishman laughed at him. "You've not got the stones, Highlander. You've waited too long. And I am not one of your savage clansmen who will give you a reason ... if you want me dead, you'll have to do it while the blood is running cold." He smiled thinly. *"Can you do that, Highlander?"*

Without waiting, without permitting himself one fleeting instant to think of what he did, to consider repercussions, to question the savagery, Duncan MacLeod carried through the motion that severed flesh, vessels, bone.

He had not killed, had never killed, as he killed now.

The body fell as the head tumbled away. Blood gouted as the heart continued to pump, ignorant of the truth; but then truth was known, acknowledged, and the body collapsed.

MacLeod's breath ran harsh in his throat, expelled in a noisy gust. He stood over the body tensely, hands gripping hilt, lungs gulping air. The enemy, killed; his life, preserved. "Not my head," he said. "Not upon a pike."

Satisfaction. Relief. And then acknowledgment: because of this man he had begun the road Connor traveled, that other Immortals traveled, that was required.

Because there could be only one.

And then the maelstrom took him.

Shook him.

Remade him.

And it began again in the theater, in the head upon the pike—meant to be Macbeth's—that looked so much like his own. Taking him back to that very first time.

Applause, shouted approbations. More than three hundred years later he sat in a brand new theater. He was not back in Scotland; not on his knees, gasping, with blood running over splayed and shaking hands pressed rigidly against sodden earth; not twisted and wracked by that first terrible Quickening, the firestorm of raw power and an alien, unexpectedly interior *presence* he feared might destroy him thrumming throughout his blood, his bones, his brain—except he could not die after all, after all, and the Quickening was proof of that when he took another's head. Unless that other took his.

Shock, and hunger. A wild, sweet hunger, an abrupt satiation—and an awareness of *differentness*. He was not the same. Would never, *could* never be the same. Whatever he was.

Curtain calls. Whistles. Continuing applause.

Demon, they had called him.

Duncan MacLeod of the Clan MacLeod, banished by the man he believed to be his father. Forgiven later by the woman who had not birthed him, but reared him, when he had avenged the murder of her husband, Ian MacLeod, whom he had called "father"—and still did.

Iain MacLeoid.

So much Gaelic, warring with his English. He closed his eyes briefly, banishing images and overlays, then opened them upon the present, upon reality, and saw the curtain calls, the actors onstage: maligned Macbeth, his mad and driven Lady; Malcolm Canmore, new-hailed king; murdered Banquo—and, of course, Macduff. The huge and massive man, red-haired head bowed in quiet acknowledgment of the audience's overwhelming approval.

"Not bad," Dawson commented. "Although it was a bit unsettling to see Macbeth get his head lopped off. It looks a lot like yours."

So, Joe had marked the resemblance also. MacLeod shrugged, ignoring the opening. "Not a bad performance, on the whole."

"Pretty fair Scottish accents, wouldn't you say?"

He smiled. "As real as mine ever was."

"Thicker than yours."

"Well, after four hundred years a man loses something of himself." Duncan smiled again, but it faded too quickly. He had lost too much of himself, the Dhonnchaidh MacLeoid who was, and "the Scottish play" had just proved it.

Lost—but also gained. Surely he had gained. Somehow. Some*when*.

But losses were easier to remember, especially when one least wished to.

The curtain dropped a final time, hiding the cast, and applause died out. People began leaving, discussing aspects of the play itself, historical implications, Shakespearean elocution, performances. Mostly commenting on the swordplay, presented in the flesh for everyone to see instead of offstage as it so often was, relying on manufactured sound effects. These sounds had been real, not manufactured, any more than the footwork was rote.

"The guy playing Macduff was pretty impressive, don't you think?" Dawson asked as they waited for the worst of the crowd to leave.

"Hard to miss," Mac agreed, seeing again in his mind's eye the red-haired giant holding aloft the severed head. Abruptly he opened the program, sought and found the appropriate name: *James Douglas.* Next to it, in parentheses and italicized, *Seumas Dubhghlas.* "Gaelic," he murmured.

"What?"

"Gaelic spellings, for all of them." MacLeod closed the program. So much in so short a time: the invitation, his name scrawled on the envelope, the very real swordplay, the head upon the pike . . .

"Well, it *is* the Highland Shakespeare Company," Dawson said lightly.

"Highland names, Highland spellings . . ." MacLeod felt renewed tension, eased it with effort. "It means nothing, Joe. How many Americans claim they have Celtic blood and 're-create' something they know nothing about?"

Dawson looked at him more attentively. "Bitterness, Mac-Leod? That's not like you. I'd suspect you have an axe to grind with such things as the Highland Games."

MacLeod smiled crookedly, hitching a shoulder. "Let them have their fun."

"*Weren't* there Highland Games?"

"Now and again," Duncan agreed. "But—they weren't always games." Most of the audience had departed. He pushed to his feet. "Let's go—" And stopped, for in the aisle blocking his way was a lovely strawberry-blond young woman in Scottish dress: saffron-dyed blouse, long tartan skirt, a matching tartan sash drawn slantwise across her bodice. Green eyes were bright with alertness.

"Welcome," she said. Then, with a wider smile: "*Se do bheatha.*" And waited.

He could not help himself: "*Tapadh leibh.*"

She nodded once, though he couldn't tell if she understood it or had been told to respond to any answer. "I'm to give you this." She put a card into his hand, cream-colored, printed in gold ink. "We hope you will come." She curtsied briefly, then went back up the aisle to the open doors letting out into the lobby.

"What was that all about?" Dawson asked. "What did she say? What did *you* say?"

"She welcomed us. I thanked her. Formally, as we've never met."

"Yeah?" Dawson was clearly fascinated; MacLeod realized he'd never said much about—or *in*—his birth language before. "And what would you say to someone you knew?"

"Someone like you?" MacLeod smiled. *"Tapadh leat."* He held up the card. "It's an invitation. Opening Night Reception, with refreshments." He offered the card to Dawson. "I think I'll head home, but if you'd like to go—" And then something caught his eye on the other side of the invitation. "Wait—" Frowning, he turned it over, saw the same scrawled handwriting that had scribed his name in Gaelic on the envelope containing tickets to the play.

Alba gu brath.

Dawson looked over his shoulder. "Alba—what? More Gaelic?"

"Alba gu brath," MacLeod answered.

"And?"

"It means 'Scotland forever.' " Duncan slipped the card inside his breast pocket. "I think I'll have a drink after all."

"Scotch whisky?" Dawson asked, grinning.

MacLeod smiled back. *"Usquabae."*

From an adjoining room off the reception area, James Douglas and Colin Cameron watched the wealthy Cultural Center patrons and angels glitter their way from darkness into light, laughing and talking, shaking hands, kissing cheeks, beginning to gossip already: dissecting the play, the presentation, the performances. Among their number, less inclined to boast of anything beyond a predeliction for nonconformity—and thus conforming—came the wannabes: the students, the hangers-on, the has-beens. Black-clad, most of them, the girls and women artistically wan and ethereal in net-mesh, beads, and draperies, the young men equally pale but less ethereal, favoring raw silk and leather, moving with studied grace, most of them, and a consciousness that they must be *noticed*, for surely they counted for more than the others beside them.

"There!" Cameron said breathily. "My God—he's dark as a Spaniard!"

Jamie smiled. "He's a Black Scot, Coll . . . not a red Celt, like me."

Cameron inspected his own fine-boned hand, pale as Jamie's but lacking altogether in Douglas' freckles, the wiry ruddy hair springing out of older flesh. "Well, I'm not a red Celt, either . . ." Then he grinned, shrugging. "Who's to say where *any* of us come from? Red, black, blond, anything in between." His hand dropped again to his side. "I thought he'd be taller."

"You're used to me, laddie. He's taller than you. And you know better than that: judge our kind by the length of our blades, never the weight of our bones."

Cameron grimaced wryly. He was five inches under six feet, but did indeed judge himself small next to James Douglas, who was very nearly seven feet tall. But then any man was small beside Jamie.

"Who's that with him?" Cameron asked.

"Does it matter? He's not our kind."

The young man watched avidly. "Jamie—?"

He waited.

Cameron looked at him. "Could you take him?"

"D'ye want me to, then?"

"*No!*" The young man laughed, embarrassed by the explosiveness of his answer. "I only meant—*could* you?"

James Douglas smiled. "We're evenly matched, Coll. I'm stronger, he's quicker. I'm younger—as a mortal would reckon it, that is—but he's wiser, or was. Had we met in the field games"—Jamie grinned—"Well, I imagine I threw the stone harder, tossed the caber farther. But no one, I've heard, outran Duncan MacLeod. Nor outwitted him. Nor stopped him at *camanachd.*" He saw Cameron's incomprehension. "Shinty, lad—field hockey, in a way. Have you forgotten already?"

The young Scot sighed. "Eighteen months ago I was a shoe clerk in Edinburgh, Jamie, a 'wee mortal' dreaming of the stage—"

"And now you're on it." He clasped a shoulder briefly. "You'll do. When you've had your first death and awakening, your first head and the taste of the Quickening, you'll know all you need to know. All that is important." He pressed him forward. "Now, go out and greet your public. I'll be along."

After a momentary hesitation, Cameron went. As he made his way through the crowd to the cash bar, moving self-consciously, a smattering of applause rang out for "Banquo."

"Good lad," Jamie murmured. But he did not look at Colin Cameron. He looked only at MacLeod, Duncan MacLeod, whom he had not seen for two hundred and fifty years.

So much changed. So much *un*changed. The Spaniard-dark skin and eyes, near-black hair—shorter now, tamed, pulled back into a ponytail instead of the loose curling mane—and the startling, uncanny grace of a man born to move in the swift brilliant economy of a body honed and hardened to fitness, to agility, to power.

"To battle," Jamie murmured. "Och, my Duncan, you wear the clothes of a gentleman now, but you're no more at ease in them than I am in mine. 'Twas always the belted plaid for us, aye? The great kilt, and our swords—and a curse for the enemy."

He bared his teeth in silent laughter. *And so we will curse them again, taking back what was ours.*

Chapter Five

———

MacLeod was slightly taken aback as the actor who'd played Banquo swept up, but the young man's expression was open and friendly. "It's you," he said on a rush; and Duncan recalled his name from the program: Colin Cameron.

MacLeod arched brows. "Maybe," he said mildly. "I think it depends on which 'me' you mean?"

"Which—? Oh." Color betrayed embarrassment; he was very young. "Not, not like that. I mean . . . I knew you were here—Jamie said—but that's all I meant. Acknowledgment. Not—not anything else. Anything *more*." The young actor glanced quickly at Joe Dawson who, wearing a carefully neutral expression, turned away as if oblivious to the conversation.

MacLeod tried not to laugh; the boy was awkward but well-meaning. "You did well tonight."

"Thank you. *Thank* you. I'm new to the company . . . but the man who was to play Banquo died unexpectedly before we left London, and so they needed me after all." He shrugged, clearly self-conscious. "Some of them felt I'd do better to play Macduff's *son*—"

"Rather than his friend?" MacLeod considered it; the actor *was* very young. "Jealousy puts hard words in too many mouths."

"Yes, yes, it does." The actor thrust out his hand. "Colin Cameron. Of Edinburgh."

MacLeod grasped it, gripped briefly. "Duncan—"

"—MacLeod; I know." Cameron lowered his voice, but seemed certain Joe Dawson's attention was elsewhere. "I understand, you see—about Immortals. Jamie's explained. Everything. And he says you're famous." The young man colored again. "I'm sorry—we're expected to circulate . . . but thank you, thank you for coming." He nodded, grinning, then took his leave hastily.

Mac heard Joe cough to hide laughter. He knew what was coming as he turned a baleful glance on his friend. "Don't start."

"Famous," Dawson said only, innocently, eyes alight with laughter.

Duncan sighed. Smiled in self-mockery. "Famous." He raised the glass to toss back his whisky, but stopped short. *Immortal*— He turned swiftly, hands moving away from his body.

"Duncan MacLeod of the Clan MacLeod," said the red-haired Macduff.

MacLeod barely felt Dawson reach out quietly and take the glass from his right hand, freeing him of encumbrance. It took but a moment to assess the height, the weight, the bulk, the strength of the man. It would be lengthy, brutal, excessively painful to engage this man. Possibly even deadly.

With exquisite precision, MacLeod inquired, "Have we met?"

The man froze. Something akin to shock flickered briefly in smoky amber eyes. Then he boomed out a laugh. "What, have I taken you by surprise? Duncan MacLeod?" Despite the laughter, the glint in his eyes now was hard and assessive as he slipped into dialect, the elegant singsong rhythm of broad Scots. "Och, bonnie Duncan, what's become of you? D'ye no' recollect me?"

Duncan did not. Not in the least.

One large, freckled hand flattened against the massive chest. "A blow to the heart, that." The tone was friendly, but the eyes were not. "And here I'm told no man forgets Jamie Douglas!"

The man was taller than all present, but MacLeod, in four hundred years, had met many tall men, especially tall Scots. He caught Dawson's eye and arched an eyebrow; Joe immediately swung away purposefully and moved two steps to signal a passing waiter for another drink.

MacLeod turned back to the actor. "How many of you are there?"

"Of me?—only the one. Scots? The company—and you. Of *us*?" He grinned, flicking a glance at Dawson's back. "One is as good as an army."

"In your case, one *is* an army," MacLeod commented. "As for the other . . . " He glanced at those nearest people; no one was close enough to overhear. "Have you come for me?"

Jamie Douglas laughed. "I've taken my head for the night, MacLeod, and put it upon a pike." He paused with the exquisite timing of a trained actor. "Of course, that one I bought from a catalogue, then modified it to match the actor playing Macbeth . . . " He smiled wickedly. "Looks a bit like you, don't you think?" Eyes glittering, Douglas glanced beyond MacLeod, then inclined his head before Duncan could reply. "Forgive me—I'm called away to the others. I hope you enjoyed the play." But even as he moved to leave, Jamie paused, turned back. Quietly, he said, "*Alba gu brath*, laddie. Or have you forgotten that, too?"

Dawson drifted over as the actor departed. "Challenge?"

MacLeod, frowning, also watched him go. "No." He retrieved his drink from Joe, stared into it reflectively: single malt Scotch. "Not between Immortals, at any rate." Duncan looked across the crowd toward the towering man, bright head bowed to hear a dark-haired, diamond-bedecked woman speaking animatedly to him. "I think—between Scots."

Dawson clearly was concerned. "Who is he?"

MacLeod's mouth twisted in irony. "You're the Watcher, Joe. Don't you know?"

Dawson shook his head, then grinned ruefully. "Looks

like I'd best go home and get on-line. I've got some checking ahead of me to track down James Douglas."

"So do I," MacLeod agreed. He tapped his head. "Only *my* computer is up here."

Dawson laughed. "And you have more Random Access Memory than anyone I know. Four hundred years worth!"

"So long as it doesn't crash at the wrong time."

Quite apart from the others now, James Douglas drank whisky in a febrile, avid haste.

He doesn't remember me.

His hand clenched the glass.

He doesn't remember me.

Now the hand trembled. It had taken such effort not to let the mask slip, not to do more than express affected surprise.

I remember everything about you, Duncan MacLeod.

And MacLeod, as clearly, recalled nothing at all about him.

How could he have forgotten?

Jamie Douglas remembered.

The lines were so subtle sometimes, so easily blurred. One year became ten, a decade became a day. He was two hundred and fifty years old in Immortality, and yet yesterday was today, while today was the past to another.

How many are there, like me?

How many more to come, who would know of Jamie Douglas? And how many more would die before the Gathering?

The woman approached from behind, came to stand beside him. He did not need to look. He felt her, sensed her, smelled her. *Knew* her, as he knew them all.

"Well?" she asked softly.

He smiled, watching the crowd, banishing the tension, the clenched knot in his belly. He was indeed a very good actor. "It's begun," he said lightly.

"How long?"

"It's a *campaign*," he answered. "One of my own devising, and well worth the time, the effort, and the planning, my bonnie Annie, or all will be lost as it was lost on the bloodied fields of Culloden, before the guns of Butcher Cumberland."

"Ah." Annie Devlin nodded, understanding what drove him now. They each of them were born of similar loyalties, identical dedication; that was what he counted on. "Were you there, then?"

He smiled grimly. "I was *born* there."

She knew. She was Immortal, and knew. Their true birthdays were different from those who died only once. "How long will you wait for him?"

"As long as I can," he answered. "I have time, after all."

She smiled. Lifted her glass. "*Sios e*," she said. "Down with it."

He laughed, teeth white in the blaze of his beard, as an odd joyousness welled up within his breast. Indeed, he had time, more time than most. There was no need to rush.

He set his glass against hers in a muted chime of good crystal. "*Sguab as e*," he agreed. "Take it down."

MacLeod shed his jacket as he departed the freight elevator and walked into the loft. He draped it across the back of the couch Richie had inhabited earlier, and forgot it instantly, pausing to stare deeply into distance as he summoned up the words.

Alba gu brath.

Challenge? Or recognition? Not Immortal to Immortal, as he'd told Dawson. Something different. Something more. Something ineffably *Scottish*, warrior to warrior.

Lines creased his brow as he frowned. He did not know the man, could not conjure a memory of an earlier meeting. And yet the man knew him.

There was nothing in them that made them privy to another Immortal's secrets. MacLeod knew of others what he was told, or read, and the same applied to him. Whatever fame young Colin Cameron attached to him came not through any inner awareness born of Immortality, but in the usual way, the mortal way: stories, rumor, innuendo.

It was disquieting to acknowledge that the Watchers had amassed far more knowledge of his kind than he had. He was limited to his own memories.

So many memories . . .

"Och, bonnie Duncan, what's become of you? D'ye no' recollect me?"

He did not recall James Douglas. Not even in tales and rumors.

It bothered him, that. It was wise for no Immortal to forget another, most particularly a foe, and he was not a man to forget a friend. Yet he did not recall James Douglas.

Random Access Memory, in Dawson's words. MacLeod smiled crookedly, though it faded quickly. Dismayingly random, in his case. Was it possible for the mortal computer to have a failing power supply?

But he was not mortal. He was—other. More, in so many ways. Less in other ways, and weaknesses, that made a man mortal.

He wrenched himself from reverie, walked to the liquor cabinet, took from it a glass and an old thick bottle of single malt. He uncorked, poured, replaced the bottle. Then sat himself down in the deep leather armchair and accessed the living RAM that was stored inside his head.

Despite centuries to integrate such things, he felt occasionally rootless, with neither home nor heritage. It was their curse, all of them: foundlings, fosterlings, reared by mortals to *be* mortals—save they weren't, and at some point that became all too obvious by the first death, and resurrection.

He recalled his own. Wounded in battle, his name and pride upheld, carried from the field by kin and clan to die within the nearest thatch-roofed hut.

The first death only. And then the resurrection, the "miracle" his father cursed him for, cursed and cast him out.

The taut, hard-muscled flesh over his ribs contracted involuntarily beneath the silk of his shirt. He recalled the pain of the wound, the shock of the spear thrust through his ribs, the lung, tearing up to the sheath of his heart. No pain then, only shock, and knowledge. He'd seen enough death wounds to know.

Not quite thirty years old. And killed. Though he hadn't died that moment, hadn't died on the battlefield; was brought to a stranger's pelt-bed upon the floor . . . put to bed like a babe, a bloodied, dying babe, praised for his valor by a man whose opinion counted, a man who named him his son, his heir: Duncan MacLeod.

And he had died.

Had *died*.

That death, that resurrection was long past. He was a Scot living out of Scotland, cut off from a distant past, ineluctably Immortal before he was anything else—and yet the play brought home too vividly all that he had lost when he had deserted Scotland.

The play, and Jamie Douglas.

He drank quickly, taking whisky—*usquabae*—into his mouth, held in the peaty, smoke-flavored liquor that tasted of his past, and swallowed, welcoming warmth; rested his head against the chair and tried to banish the memory, the image of his father's face, the sound of his father's voice, naming him a demon because he lived again.

And the pain. Physical, emotional. Breath, where there had been none. Lungs laboring again, where they had been stilled, one brutally cloven. The spasm of his heart that resounded throughout his body, claiming death-slackened limbs in something akin to seizure.

Viscera healing itself, bones reknitting, vessels and flesh made whole again so he did not bleed. Pain in the doing of it, that first unlooked-for healing; pain in resurrection, the acknowledgment that he lived, and there was no pain anymore, no scar, no sign he had ever been wounded. No sign he had ever died.

Miracle, and curse. It gave him endless decades and dozens of deaths, dozens of resurrections. And it robbed him of kin and clan.

Scotland forever. Scotland the brave.

What would it have cost him ... what would it have cost my father to say he'd made a mistake, had judged me dead too soon—?

Miracle, or mistake: the laird's heir not dead after all, and their clan as yet whole.

How many years of kin and clan might he have known, had his father believed it otherwise than demon-wrought?

They'd been praying, after all. Why couldn't his father have claimed it God's intercession instead of the Devil's?

There could have been respite, for a while, perhaps even years. But it would have come at some point, the casting out. He'd have been killed again in battle, probably, or in a fight over a woman—he winced as he recalled Debra Campbell, his first beloved—or perhaps even a fall no mortal man could survive any more than a spear thrust through his vitals; death in the Highlands was common. But he would have survived each time, unaccountably—or he would have lived for decades, unchanged, unaged, and been cast out later.

It would have come. One day, one way, or another.

A wholly unexpected loneliness washed up from the depths of his soul, painfully intense. *But I might have wished it to come after my father was dead, so he would not name me demon.*

MacLeod shut his eyes. It was meant to banish the memory, to relegate to a lengthy but painstakingly integrated past the knowledge of that time, those days, when he was but newly Immortal, uncognizant of what it meant never to die, or how it would shape his future. Before he knew of the Gathering, the Quickening, and the rules of the Game.

But memory remained, albeit transmuted into another. New vision, not old, bloomed against closed lids, painted in vivid colors as wet and red as blood. Another image entirely: the sight of a severed head mounted upon a pike.

"D'ye no' recollect me?"

Macbeth, King of Scotland . . . and James Douglas, as Macduff, hoisting high the head as he hailed the new king.

MacLeod's hand tightened upon the glass. *—hoisting the head—*

The dark-eyed, dark-haired head that looked uncannily like his own.

Och, bonnie Duncan, what's become of you?

Chapter Six

___

Killiecrankie, Scotland, 1689

Watchfires bloomed against the braes of Craigh Ellaich, the rain-wracked, time-warped slopes of the mountains near the Pass of Killiecrankie, where Scotsmen gathered to make war. So many Highland clans supported King James, now in exile in France in the Year of Our Lord 1689. There was no choice: James the Sixth of Scotland, also the Second of England, was a Scot, a Stuart, the rightful king—and his pedigree was preferred by every Highland chieftain who took his men into war. They were Jacobites, all of them, who supported James Stuart and his right to the throne.

King James had himself left that throne, seeking self-preservation, because a prickly Protestant England opposed his Catholicism. It had become a volatile issue, pitting faith against faith and men against men, and so devisive that James had utterly lost control of Parliament. And so he fled England altogether, and now lived in Saint-Germain upon the sufferance of the French king, Louis XIV.

James Stuart had not abdicated, but he was nonetheless

quickly replaced by joint monarchs: his sister, Mary, and her Dutch husband, William of Orange, who currently levied war against France and wanted Highlanders to aid him. When the Scots refused to fight for King William, he decreed angrily they should then fight against him. And so they prepared to, here at Killiecrankie.

This war was with William's conscripts and Lowland troops sent into the Highlands to tame the clans. But the clans would not be tamed by an enemy such as England; many of them now paid homage to King James on the braes near Killiecrankie, paid homage to his representative in the guise of James Graham, Viscount Claverhouse, styled Dundee. As Highland as any of them, born and bred of their kind, and calling them to war in the Jacobite cause.

A good cause, that, in the name of a Stuart king. The Highlanders embraced it, as did Duncan MacLeod.

Men gathered now, men wrapped in tartan plaids, weighted down with the weaponry that made them fearsome foes: deadly Scottish claymore, six feet of wicked steel; the dirk, the spike-orbed targe, the lethal Lochaber axe. Even Spanish pistols, and muskets got from England from the decks of purloined boats, from waylaid Sassenach supply trains wending their way through purple heather and the crags of ancient mountains warding the barrow-graves of the Norse.

MacLeod stood on the lower slopes, one among many. In the dying of the sun, in the rising light of watchfires, Dundee glittered in martial finery, yet was crosshatched on the diagonal across his chest by a swath of tartan cloth. Flame glinted off plaid-brooch, massive as a man's fist; off the fittings of accoutrements gracing his horse; off the seductive steel of a basket-hilted broadsword, gripped but not yet raised. He wore a dark blue Highland bonnet, black in dying light, and pinned to it by clan badge were the three eagle feathers of his chieftainship, plus a single crimson feather. Though no man save a chief could wear the triple feathers, all men wore the other to show solidarity.

Highlanders gathered around him; around them gathered mountains, the harsh and lush magnificence of Craigh El-

laich now echoing of pipes, the skirling, soaring melody of a Highland battle rant. Ceol mor, in Gaelic: the music of war.

He spoke to them, did Dundee, as if they were his fathers, his brothers, his sons, valued all, and loved. They were Gaels, he said, Highlanders born and bred of privation, honed as steel on hardship, choked near to death on the perfidy of the English. It was time, he told them, the true king regained his throne, the Stuart born as they were of Scottish blood and bones, bred up to rule them all.

Time, he said, to prove to the Sassenachs no man but a Highlander had the governing of their mountains, the ordering of their lives. In the morning the English would come marching down through the Pass, and it was their turn now, the turn of all clansmen, to prove to the Sassenachs no man but a Scot was fit to rule the Scots; that no man among them would countenance the Dutchman.

Gaels for Gaeldom, he cried, lifting his sword into the sunset, and on his shout of "Claymore!" they would fall upon the English and put them to rout forever.

It was instantaneous. Every hand snatched from a head the matching Highland bonnet with its single crimson feather and saluted Dundee. Even as the pipes skirled again into ceol mor, Duncan MacLeod and every Highlander shouted for victory. For King James, and Dundee—

—The glass fell, shattering against hardwood. MacLeod awoke with a start, hearing yet the shouts of the clans at the Pass of Killiecrankie, the wailing of the pipes, the echo of oratory. For a moment, a moment only, he remained in Scotland, and then he shed disorientation and decades as he had learned to do four hundred years before, lest he be killed for carelessness.

The loft, not Killiecrankie. And the tang of Scottish whisky spilling across the floor.

He pushed up from the chair, went into the kitchen to pick up a towel, whisk broom, and dustpan—

And stopped short before he retrieved any of those things, staring in startlement at the single crimson feather lying upon the floor not far from the back door beside the elevator.

When he could, he went to the feather and took it up from the hardwood, wondering if—and how, and who by—it had been blown in beneath the door. He studied it, thinking strange coincidence, hearing again the wailing of the pipes, the words, and the thunder of approbation from the throats of so many others as well as from himself, on the braes of Craigh Ellaich at the Pass of Killiecrankie.

A single red feather marked him Dundee's man, bound to King James and the Jacobite cause.

Dundee, who died of a musket ball after his clansmen routed the English.

Abruptly MacLeod set the feather down upon the countertop and strode purposefully across hardwood and rugs to a brass-bound leather trunk set against the brick wall in an unlighted corner. Swiftly he unlatched and flipped open the hasp, raised and tipped back the lid to rest against brick.

The contents were there amidst the mothballs as he had packed them away: tartan plaid, leather baldric, a badger-hide sporran, the glint of muted light off stag-handled dirk and smaller *sgian dhu*—and also a Highland bonnet.

He picked up the bonnet, lifting it gently from the other items put carefully away, and turned it so the clan badge showed, silver tarnished. Pinned to the wool was a lone crimson feather, its edges bruised by the passage of more than three hundred years.

He had pinned it on at Dalcomera, when the clansmen gathered, and wore it proudly all the way to Killiecrankie, where he had killed Sassenach soldiers on the cry of *"Claymore!"*, as ordered by Dundee.

Not his, then, the feather blown under his door. Not his at all.

In three strides Duncan MacLeod reached the katana and took it out of its stand. In four he felt the thrumming awareness, the uncanny sensation, and fell immediately once into a defensive stance of quiet, loose attentiveness.

Only another Scot would know of Dundee's feather. And he had only that evening met one who was also Immortal.

* * *

Smiling beatifically, Richie Ryan lifted the slatted door of the freight elevator. "Hey, Mac, I saw your light on and thought I'd stop by . . ." One stride off the elevator, he froze. He knew that posture, that infinitely *poised* preparation. "Mac—hey, it's just me—" He spread his hands placatingly, knowing better than to move; he had learned immense respect for Duncan MacLeod's reactions and reflexes over the years. As he saw the coiled readiness slacken into recognition, he relaxed in relief. "What's got *you* so on edge?"

MacLeod sighed and flipped the katana up beneath his arm in a deft motion Richie still had not mastered, safed the blade between bicep and rib cage. He tilted his head toward the kitchen, the red feather on the counter. "Was that some kind of joke?"

Richie stared. "Joke? What joke?"

"The red feather. It was on the floor."

Richie knew that tone, that cold deadliness. MacLeod had banished the physical preparedness, but not the tautness of his mood. If it *were* some kind of joke, clearly it was unsuccessful. And one was never quite certain how MacLeod might react, depending on circumstances.

Bewildered, he shook his head. "I haven't even been back here since I left earlier today . . ." He went to the counter, picked up the feather, examined it, then shrugged. "Sure you haven't decided to take up birds as a hobby, Mac?" He grinned, trying to ease the residual tension. MacLeod's eyes bespoke the impenetrable opaque darkness no one, not even Richie, had ever gotten through. Until it was permitted. *Except maybe Tessa*—But Richie dismissed that image. It hurt less that way. "Somehow bird-watching just doesn't seem quite your style."

"*Someone* put it under the door so I would find it." MacLeod set the katana down, then went to the kitchen to get towel, dustpan, and whisk broom.

"Not me." Richie got out of his way, marking MacLeod's foul mood, then spotted the bonnet on the floor beside the trunk. He picked it up, saw the feather—a twin to the one on the countertop—and looked sharply at MacLeod. "What does this mean, Mac?"

MacLeod, cleaning up, hitched a single shoulder. "It's a kind of code."

"Like taggers?" Richie grinned, twirling the bonnet on one hand.

"More like Crips and Bloods. Showing colors." MacLeod dumped the remains of ice in the sink, slid glass shards into the trash. "A man—a Scot—who wore the red feather in his bonnet was showing his support for King James."

"Which one?"

"James the Sixth of England, Second of Scotland. And a man called Dundee. A Highlander himself: James Graham."

Richie shrugged. "I never could keep all those kings straight."

MacLeod, relaxing now, smiled. "Just think of them as sequels."

Richie smiled back, relieved to hear the habitual irony in MacLeod's tone. "So, you supported this King James and Dundee?"

"Most Highlanders did. He was a Scot, a Stuart, and the rightful king."

"But he got tossed out on his butt, right?"

"Not quite. He left." MacLeod sighed. "It's complicated, Richie."

"Most history is. One of the reasons I ditched class a lot. Boring." Richie grinned. "Did you win?"

"At Killiecrankie? Yes, we won. One of the few times, fighting the English." He paused, very still. "One of the *last* times."

"So . . ." Richie turned to drop the bonnet back into the trunk, stopped when he saw the other items. Curious, he set the bonnet down and pulled out the stag-handled knife, the smaller weapon. "What is all this stuff?—oh, wait, *I* know." He laughed, turning to look at Mac. "It's the play. The 'Scottish play,' right? It's got your Highland blood up."

MacLeod grinned briefly, more at ease than he had been; Richie knew the subtle signs. "Something like that."

Richie inspected the two knives, checking weight and balance. "This one's wicked enough—it's a 'dirk,' right?—but what's the little one for?"

MacLeod crossed the room, boot heels thumping. "The 'little one' is a *sgian dhu*," he said. "You wear it strapped to your calf, here"—he slapped his leg briefly—"and you can use it for whatever purpose you like. Meat-knife, weapon." He took both knives from Richie, dropped them back into the trunk. "So endeth the lesson. If you want a drink, fix it yourself; it's late, and I'm going to bed."

Richie took the hint, but affected deep disappointment as Mac headed toward the bathroom. "Don't you want to know how my date went?"

The answer was as resounding as it was succinct: *"No."*

Richie laughed, turned to close the trunk lid—but not before he fingered the tartan fabric, its texture: stiff, obviously old. "Blood," he murmured, as humor died away. So many battles fought, so many enemies killed, so much blood spilled by the man he knew as friend and mentor. MacLeod's own blood, as well as that of others.

Richie sighed, lowered the lid. He was as Immortal, though infinitely younger, and would fight his own battles, kill assorted enemies, spill much blood. He had no choice. None of them did, who were part of the Game. Even if they didn't choose to play.

He glanced toward the closed bathroom door. Privy to confidences, to insights, to heritage and history, he more than most understood Duncan MacLeod. But equally he acknowledged there were times he knew nothing at all of what the man was, or who. Or how he endured.

How would *he* feel when he was four centuries old? And what would others think of him?

If he lived that long.

Richie shivered as a chill walked his spine. Then he turned on his heel and departed the loft, leaving Mac to his memories.

At dawn, Joe Dawson gave up. He had spent the intervening hours between the play and sunrise on his computer, digging through directories and files, accessing as much data as possible that might give him information on James Douglas, Immortal.

The Watchers had existed for countless centuries, but a constantly mutating technology altered data collection and storage tremendously, relegating certain practices to abrupt inefficiency despite the historical implications. Handwritten Chronicles, even meticulously kept, were vulnerable to the depredations of age and man, and gaps existed. Even computers and modems, the blindingly swift transferral of data from one Watcher cell to another over telephone lines, were subject to human error, to the exigencies of weather, malfunction, dirty lines, even viruses. It was not a perfect world, despite startling advances.

And things went wrong. Such unexpected things as disks falling into dangerous hands, as had happened once already.

Dawson had been a Watcher for nearly thirty years, recruited out of his hospital bed in a medical unit in Vietnam by a man known as Ian Bancroft. Until the moment Bancroft told him there were men and women who could not die, men and women who survived all but decapitation, Dawson had been powered only by an agony of helplessness and self-hatred: a mine had cost him both legs, and his world was forever changed.

Nearly thirty years later the world continued to change, but he had learned in those decades that the world was far larger, and contained more oddities, than he had ever envisioned. Men and women, Immortals, who could not die, unless one took their heads. A world apart from his own, where a Prize was promised in a very private battle between Immortal and Immortal, moving toward the day, the moment, when only one would survive, when all the Quickenings of forever would reside in a single soul.

And he, as others, Watched. And committed the lives of Immortals to an infinitely *human* kind of immortality: written, typed text. To past, and to present.

Unaccountably, James Douglas was absent from the files. Dawson could find no entry, no mention of the man, in any of the data he had on hand. And so at dawn Joe logged off and shut down the computer, listening idly as the CPU fan ceased. His eyes were gritty; he rubbed them lightly, stretching lids out of shape, massaging weary sockets. Tension bled away.

Then bled back again as he recalled the giant Scot and the look on his face, on MacLeod's face, as Duncan admitted he did not remember him.

"And it'll eat at him," Dawson mumured. "I've seen that look in his eyes before."

Not fear. Joe had never seen any hint of fear in Duncan MacLeod; if it existed, it was hidden under layers of competence, confidence, the reliance upon swift and startling reflexes honed to an instant and deadly response. But self-castigation, yes, for not recognizing a man, particularly an Immortal, he was supposed to recall. MacLeod too often took on responsibility for the entire world. He would not stint blaming himself.

It was challenge, what James Douglas extended, but not to battle, not *by* battle. By blood, by heritage, by something even MacLeod himself clearly did not understand.

Dawson rubbed at his close-trimmed beard. "Or understands all too well . . ." A thing between Scots, between Highlanders, apparently. Joe had seen it before. It promised the same kind of bond that war often forged among men, a bond never broken, never forgotten, a bond of blood and battle and a merciless clarity, an unflagging comprehension that time might dull the vividness but never the memory of commitment.

MacLeod had said it once as he coldly dismissed Joe from his life before circumstances permitted entree again: they were different. He and Joe Dawson could never be other, could never be more or less than mortal and Immortal, separated by the chasm of their different natures, by the knowledge of a mechanism that functioned independently despite physical similarities that were wholly superficial.

One man, frail and vulnerable as all mortals were, doomed to die of decay, or injury, or illness. And another doomed to live perhaps forever, if the Gathering permitted.

Once, Dawson would have gladly surrendered his mortality for MacLeod's gift of resurrection. But Immortality carried a price he was no longer prepared to pay.

"Too many deaths," he murmured. He himself had seen so many die in Vietnam during his single mine-aborted tour. But MacLeod had fought in wars too many to count, had seen far more friends and lovers murdered.

Too high a price. How many times, how often, Joe wondered wearily, would Duncan MacLeod pay it? How many times, and how often, *could* he pay it?

"Forever," Dawson murmured. "If the Fates are wise."

He sighed, gathered himself, pushed himself from his chair. Sleep was required if he were to think clearly, to link together pieces of anomalous data of an insular, secretive race. In the morning he would contact other Watchers to see if any of them had information on James Douglas.

Chapter Seven

Killiecrankie, Scotland, 1689

*Dundee had made it clear: They were to charge, all of the
Highlanders, to draw the initial volley; and it would kill hundreds of them but was worth the sacrifice, because then as
the army scrambled to reload muskets, to fix the new-style
bayonets that no longer plugged the barrel, they would have
those moments to attack in a way that would deliver the victory.*

*—down over the Pass of Killiecrankie, into the valley
warded by cliffs and crags, sliced in two by a ribbon of river.
That first terrible volley, the barrage of flame and ball, the
acrid stink of powder as black clouds enveloped the valley,
shrouding in funerary finery the massed Highlanders charg-
ing down the slopes.*

*—bodies beneath his bare feet, blood and weapons spilled
on the ground; the shouting of the enemy, the shouting of the
clans, the ranting of the bagpipes resounding against the
mountains.*

Engagement. The round targe on his forearm warded

*away the bayonet with a screech of metal on metal, and then
the first strike, catching briefly on leather baldric, then slicing through crimson uniform jacket, the shirt beneath, and
into flesh. English flesh, or the flesh of a Lowland Scot in
thrall to King William; none of it mattered now, save
MacLeod defended his life as he took the lives of others.*

*The body fell. He followed it down, pulled his dirk free,
twisted and thrust up with the targe again as a bayonet-
crowned musket barrel came down toward his spine. Block,
and block again—*

*—and the dirk employed, again, slicing into the throat. A
gout of blood arced forth, drenching MacLeod . . . he spat,
swiped his eyes clear, felt stickiness on his face, in his hair—*

*Behind him a musket roared. He felt the ball strike, felt it
score the flesh of his ribs even as he turned; and it saved
him, that turn, that agile twist of spine . . . flame bloomed in
his side but nothing penetrated, nothing was injured beyond
the affront to his flesh, bone-blunted ball turned off his ribs.
He bled, he hurt, but nothing would disabuse him of his intent: to kill in the name of King James and Dundee as many
of the enemy as he could.*

*And then the sword came down, arcing out of the sky: a
blinding slash of steel that found him, cut him, bit into his
neck; and he would die now, die forever in the way of his
kind, deprived of life, of Quickening—*

Drenched in sweat, MacLeod jerked out of sleep into brutal wakefulness, wrenched upright in his bed from dream
into reality. Heart pounded, lungs labored, naked flesh stip-
pled with gooseflesh. He could not help himself: one hand
went to his throat. To warm, whole flesh, and the beating of
his pulse, leaping beneath his touch.

Breath rasped in his throat as he expelled air, expelled the
dream. And it *was* a dream: he was whole, unbloodied, tangled in the bedclothes, and utterly alone.

He was bone-weary, dream-wracked. Dawn blossomed beyond the shutters, but he was unprepared.

MacLeod chilled as sweat dried. He let go then, shook
himself briefly, banished the coiled tension, the rigidity of

shock, the residue of recollection. Then turned down against the mattress, burying face into pillows, emitting a noise akin to growl, to groan: sheer frustration, and a protest of the night that had refreshed nothing at all, neither body nor soul.

He twisted, hearing vertebra pop, and one hip; he had not slept comfortably, oppressed by vivid dreams, and his body paid the price. So many years ago, the battle at Killiecrankie. So many wounds taken, so many wounds healed. So many men killed, including Dundee.

Including Duncan MacLeod, who died of multiple musket balls in the shadows of Craigh Ellaich, born yet again into daylight and delight as the English army retreated, defeated and disarrayed.

The day belonged to Scots, to Highlanders. As much to Duncan MacLeod as to any man who wore the crimson feather.

Backstage, James Douglas was meticulous about preparation. He placed in the florist's box a bundle of dried purple heather against a scrap of tartan cloth, a clipping from the newspaper, a tape cassette. He closed the box, tied it with twine, then handed it to the stagehand. "You still have the address?—good. Go now."

As the young man left, Jamie turned to the curtain in the wings, to the woman waiting there, shrouded in cloth and shadow. "Almost," he said. "The invitation, the feather—now this."

Her face cried out for pure light, though the shadows were kind to the arch of her brow, the oblique angle of her cheekbones. "Are you so certain of him?"

"He's a Scot. A Highlander."

She did not smile. "Are you so certain of him?"

"I was once," he answered honestly. "I believe I can be again . . . but there is you as well, bonnie Annie, Irish though you are."

Her head tilted up; faint light burnished ruddy hair lying loose around slender shoulders. "Don't try to charm *me*, Jamie Douglas. It's been tried by the best."

"By MacLeod?" he asked mildly, and saw color bloom in

her cheeks. "Och, my bonnie lass, I ask for no sacrifice beyond that which you'd make anyway—and perhaps have?" Still she said nothing. "He's a man I'd have at my side in any circumstance, and this one most of all."

"Then why not ask him outright?"

He smiled warmly. "This amuses me."

"Trickery and nonsense!"

He feigned amazement. "Och, lass, but you're too impatient!" Douglas grinned. "You're a cannon ball, Annie, crushing a body to bits . . . but I'm a *sgian dhu* snooving between the ribs just so, and all unexpected. You've forgotten how it is to savor anticipation, to set the scene—" He laughed, indicating the props and scenery stacked behind the curtain. "He's a long time out of Scotland, and not given to thievery. How do I ask a man outright to sacrifice his morals? And that, I believe, is something you know of, about him—he wouldn't stay with you in Ireland, would he, to fight against the English?"

Her face tightened. "He said it wasn't his war."

Jamie smiled. "This one is. There's no one to kill, Annie. Only something to *take*, something tangible, something real—"

"Symbols," she said sharply.

"Scotland," he retorted, "and the history of our people, Annie, yours and mine, Irish and Scottish alike—before England killed so many."

Anger kindled in her eyes, and fierce dedication. "We should kill them all instead of stealing from them!"

Jamie smiled. "This is a start, my lass. But I'll have him with us first. Only a fool would not."

Her eyes glittered in shadow. "I said that to him once. He left me anyway."

"Then fetch him back," he said calmly. "Surely a woman such as you knows how to catch a man, and keep him."

Color flared anew against the fine bones of her face. She turned from him then, turned away, walked away, left him in the shadows. He listened to her boot heels, the ratchet of the door, the thump and click of its closing.

Another piece in place.

He smiled. "Ah, the taste of it . . ." Annie would have him

gulp, but he refused to do so. Better to anticipate, to imagine the taste—and then take only a small sip one after the other, savoring the flavor one has dreamed of for so long.

James Douglas took up his sword, his massive Scottish claymore, carried it with him as he walked out onto the stage. The cavernous theater was empty now, save for Macduff. He paused, raised the blade, fixed his eyes on the costly and elaborate crystal chandeliers adorning the slanted, serried ceiling so high over his head, threw that red-maned head back and filled the auditorium with the thunder of his voice.

> *"Cut short all intermission; front to front*
> *Bring thou this fiend of Scotland and myself;*
> *Within my sword's length set him; if he scape*
> *Heaven forgive him too!"*

* * *

This time sweat was intentional, sweat and focus and fierce determination: banishment of the tension, of the residue of recollection. MacLeod, in sweatpants and a tank top, worked out on the heavy bag with great absorption, letting tautness bleed away into a steady pounding rhythm that eased the bones, the muscles, even the weary spirit; leached tightness from shoulders and neck. The sheer pleasure in physical labor, the release of endorphins, vanquished weariness and distraction. When Richie came in from the street, clutching a newspaper, MacLeod was in a far better mood than the night before.

"Check it out, Mac."

MacLeod, turning from the bag, caught the folded paper as Richie slapped it against his sweat-sheened chest. Grimacing, he unfolded the paper, glanced at it, looked curiously at Richie even as he caught his breath. "It's a supermarket rag." That did not erase the expectant expression from Richie's face. "Most people read 'em and leave 'em *behind*," he pointed out, "they don't usually bring them home." MacLeod paused for emphasis. "Not if they want to be taken seriously."

"Humor me."

"I do that all the time."

"*Look* at it, Mac."

MacLeod heaved a long-suffering sigh and obligingly looked at the front page. Dutifully he scanned the banner headline, the subheads touting inside exposés and sidebar stories, examined the grainy photo of a dark-haired fat man in slacks and shirt.

Elvis Presley, alive and well, buying beer in a convenience store. Or so the banner claimed.

None of it made sense. "Yeah, Rich? So what?"

"Elvis," Richie said crisply.

Nothing more was forthcoming. "It's *supposed* to be," Mac agreed with elaborate patience. "What's it got to do with me?"

"With *us*," Richie corrected. "That's it, isn't it? The truth?"

"Which one?" he asked dryly.

"Elvis is an Immortal."

That stopped him cold. "Elvis *Presley*—?"

"Hey, it's possible, isn't it? You don't know 'em all. And it would explain all the sightings."

It amused more than expected, alleviating the last remains of the dream. "You make him sound like a UFO." Laughing, MacLeod slapped the tabloid against Richie's chest, returning the favor. "Elvis *died*, Richie."

"Did he?" Richie asked seriously. "Really, I mean? And how can you know?—unless . . . " He leaned close, speaking quietly. "You didn't take his head, did you?"

Still grinning, MacLeod turned away, picked up a towel from a nearby weight bench, dried his face, hung the towel around his neck. "I gotta hand it to your imagination, Richie— but don't you think this is a little far-fetched? Even for you?"

Richie feigned hurt feelings. "*Think* about it, Mac. The guy dies—or does he? I mean, there are all those stories about the death certificate being falsified, that they smuggled the body out and it wasn't really Elvis they buried—"

"I think you're forgetting one thing, Rich."

"Yeah? What?"

"Lisa Marie. Elvis fathered a child." Mac folded his arms across his chest, evincing elaborately startled consideration. "Unless you're suggesting . . ."

"Oh. Yeah. I mean—no." Richie's face fell. "But it fit so well."

He grinned. "Trust me, Richie, Elvis isn't an Immortal."

"You ever meet him?"

"No, but—"

"Ever see him in concert?"

"No, but—"

"Ever get close enough to him to know?"

Duncan rubbed his forehead. "Richie—"

"Then he *might* have been. I mean, it still fits. All those sightings."

MacLeod studied him a long moment. "You," he declared finally, wagging an accusatory finger, "have been watching too much television. And this stuff"—he nodded at the tabloid—"will rot your brain." A hard knock sounded at the front door. "Why don't you get that?" Duncan deadpanned. "Maybe it's Elvis."

"Aw Mac, c'mon . . . " Richie headed toward the door. "With all the weird shit you've seen in your life—your *very long* life—can't you admit it's possible?" He disappeared a moment, came back with a florist's box in both hands. "Can it only be right if it's printed in a real newspaper, instead of in one of the supermarket rags?" He bestowed the box upon MacLeod, changing subject abruptly. "You seeing someone new?"

"No." Frowning, MacLeod slipped the twine, opened the long box, and set it down on the weight bench to peel back the tissue paper.

"Roses—?" Richie began, then frowned. "What *is* that? Dead flowers?"

"*Dried* flowers," MacLeod clarified. "Not roses—heather."

"Heather?"

MacLeod stilled. He felt the spasm of his heart, then it resumed its steady beat. From beneath the dried sprigs of purple heather, he lifted a scrap of muddied tartan cloth.

"What is it?" Richie asked, as if from a great distance.

The dream came rushing back. He heard the pipes again, smelled the tang of powder. Wind whipped the watchfires, tangled in hair and plaid. Down the braes of Craigh Ellaich, through the Pass of Killiecrankie—

"There's a cassette here," Richie said, taking it from tissue paper. He nodded at the boom box in the deep sill of a window. "Want me to play it?"

Distracted, Mac didn't answer. Beneath the tartan scrap was a folded newspaper clipping. He picked it out of tissue, sat down, read it. He was vaguely aware of Richie's movements as he loaded the boom box, then switched it on.

His head jerked up as the sound of bagpipes filled the dojo. Hastily Richie lowered the volume, muttering something about squalling tomcats. MacLeod, frozen on the bench with the clipping in his hand, heard the proud music, the skirling notes climbing to the rafters of the room.

"Not exactly what I'd call a catchy tune," Richie observed.

Oh, it caught. It caught the heart, and squeezed.

"Is this Scottish Week, or something?" Richie asked. "First *Macbeth*—excuse me: 'the Scottish play'—then a red feather you say is a secret Highland code, and now this"—he paused pointedly—"*so-called* music. What's going on, Mac?"

" 'Scotland the Brave'," he said only.

"What?"

" 'Scotland the Brave,' " MacLeod repeated. "The song."

"So, what does it mean?"

MacLeod frowned. "It means I'm a long way from home." He rose then, dropped both the scrap of tartan and the clipping about the Highland Games into the florist's box. "I've got to go out."

"Anything I can help you with?"

"No." MacLeod walked swiftly to the elevator, stepped inside, and lowered the slatted door. "It's personal."

"Scottish?" Richie called.

MacLeod did not reply. As the elevator rose the bagpipe music ended abruptly: Richie had shut it off. But the melody, and the unsung words, lived in MacLeod's head.

> *Hark when the night is falling,*
> *hear, hear the pipes a'calling,*

Loudly and proudly calling down through the glen

He raised the door, stepped off the elevator into the loft.

There where the hills are sleeping,
now feel the blood a'leaping!
High as the spirits of the old Highland men!

Walked straight to the bathroom and stripped out of sweat-crisped clothing, feeling tension seep back into tendons.

Towering in gallant fame,
Scotland the mountain hame.

Turned on the water, ran it hot, hot, stepped naked beneath the torrent and let it pour over him.

High may your proud standards gloriously wave!

Hot, steaming water, quite unlike the cold, clear water that ran in the burns, the rivers, was wind-whipped on the lochs. Streaming against his scalp, over shoulders, down ribs, belly, into the hollow at the base of his spine.

Land of the high endeavor, land of the shining river

Duncan MacLeod closed his eyes and gave himself to the memory of the man he had been. At Killiecrankie. At Culloden. In the name of a Scottish king.

Land of my heart, forever, Scotland the brave!

Chapter Eight

Joe Dawson logged onto his computer, waited for the menu to come up, went to the *Mail* feature and addressed a memo to his string of Watcher contacts.

Check: "James Douglas": Scottish, approximately 6'7", guesstimate 250 lbs; red hair, beard, light brown eyes, freckled, apparent age early to mid-30s. Now touring as an actor with the Highland Shakespeare Company. No data found in initial check. Cross-check: "Colin Cameron," Edinburgh. Dawson paused, then typed again, deleting quote marks; this name was known, and accurate. *Cross-check: Duncan MacLeod.* No more than that was necessary. The individual cells would check their own data, then E-mail him back what was found, if anything. The Watcher organization was infinitely careful, but gaps did occur. Information was lost, or never recorded; Watchers died before they could report. It was not widely known among Immortals there was such an organization; MacLeod knew, as did a handful of others he had seen fit to tell. But for the most part the Watchers were unknown to Immortals, which was precisely the way it should be. Despite several unfortunate instances where certain Watchers had misused the information to hunt and kill Immortals, the organization was what it purported to be: a group of men and women dedicated to *watching* Immortals, but never interfering.

Dawson knew MacLeod didn't like it, didn't like knowing his whereabouts were tracked, his activities catalogued, his hobbies and interests entered into a file by a network of faceless, nameless strangers. Joe supposed *he* wouldn't like it, either, but MacLeod appeared to have arrived at a fairly philosophical acceptance of it. And short of attempting to kill every Watcher worldwide and destroy the entire network, there was nothing MacLeod or any other Immortal could do about it.

Except trust to the precepts of the organization that there would be no interference in their playing of the Game, the Game Immortals claimed had no bearing whatsoever on human life, and yet no Watcher alive felt certain of that. What if the rumors at the Cabal and the Priory were true? How could men and women with the gift of Immortality *not* be tempted to use it, to plot dominion over humans who were all too mortal? It was what James Horton had feared to obsession; was what the fringe group feared also, and why they hunted. Better to kill, the Hunters believed, than to be ruled by genetic freaks; and so they had tried to eliminate known Immortals.

Dawson sighed wearily, reread the text of his letter, then sent it. Time to find out precisely what James Douglas wanted in the city, and with Duncan MacLeod.

In addition to the elegant theater, the Cultural Center boasted an interlocking complex of plush conference rooms and exhibit halls. The night before, MacLeod had gone straight to the theater to attend the play, but this time he went instead to one of the exhibit halls, absently noting the multicolored flags hanging from globe-topped light poles, the banner draped across the front of the building touting *Treasures of Scotland*. Indeed, Richie had been bang-on. It was Scottish Week in the city.

He paid his fee, accepted the brochure containing maps,

information, graphics, entered the hall—and came face to face with a life-size wax figure in full Highland regalia, except it derived from books, from portraits, not reality. The tartan cloth was far finer, richer, brighter—and cleaner— than any MacLeod had worn: heavy folds of draped plaid flung across a jacketed shoulder and pinned on with a massive Celtic pennanular brooch of ornate silver knotwork, the elaborate badger-skin sporran, saffron-dyed shirt, silver-studded leather baldric, patterned trews and stockings, *sgian dhu* tucked into the calf-garter, good leather shoes aglint with silver buckles, and the badge- and feather-bedecked bonnet atop a cascade of golden curls.

MacLeod did not recognize the figure. He did recognize the tartan: a red field cross-hatched by blocks and narrow lines of blue, green, black, yellow, and white. The royal sett, the pattern, associated with Prince Charles Edward Stuart.

He looked again at the proud and haughty face, rendered lifeless in wax. "No," he murmured. "He looked nothing like that."

Not at Culloden, retreating from the field; nor had he with Flora MacDonald, clad for escape in a serving woman's cap and apron.

How that had grated on his fine manners, his prickly royal pride. More, MacLeod had feared, who had been there, than the acknowledgment of loss, of destruction. Of the deaths of thousands of Highlanders rallying to his name.

Drummossie Moor, 1746, known as the Battle of Culloden, where England defeated Scotland and changed forever the face of the land, the lifeblood of her people, the culture of the clans.

"A sad day, that," said the quiet voice beside him. "Have you read about Culloden?"

MacLeod looked at the woman. Young, pretty, scrubbed clean, dressed in pleated tartan kilt and white blouse. But her nametag proclaimed her Heidi.

"I've read a little," he said dryly, recalling how no book had ever gotten it right, that terrible day when Butcher Cumberland killed so many Scots.

Guileless, she asked, "Can I answer any questions for you?"

"No," he answered politely. "No, I'll guide myself." And he could not help himself: *"Tapadh leibh."*

Her expression was utterly blank. "What?"

He smiled faintly. "Never mind."

"Well, enjoy yourself," she said. "The Honours of Scotland are through there." She gestured toward a distant hall. "But we close in a half hour, so I'm afraid you haven't much time to see everything."

He had started to turn. Now he stopped and looked at her more sharply. "The Honours of Scotland?"

She nodded. "Most people like to see the jewels. Since there's not very much time left, I thought I should tell you."

"They're *here?*" he asked.

The girl smiled brightly. "Oh, yes—they're the star attraction of the tour! Shall I show you?"

"No—no, thank you." This time he used the English in place of the Gaelic. "Thanks," MacLeod said again, and left behind the wax figure for the crown, the scepter, and sword of state that would have been the bonnie prince's, had he defeated the English.

But he hadn't. He had *lost,* as Scotland had lost. The prince went to France, to exile, and the proud and loyal Highlanders who died for him that day in volley after volley of brutal roundshot and grapeshot, cut to ribbons within one hour by ceaseless Hanoverian artillery, were buried in mass graves dug deep in the bloodied field, never knowing as they died that their bonnie Scotland died also, Scotland the brave.

In the hall, beside the alarm-rigged display case full of glittering Scottish jewels, James Douglas waited. With so little time before closing most of the people were gone; only stragglers and latecomers rushed through the individual exhibits. He waited patiently—and felt it at once, the sudden thrumming *presence.*

Jamie watched him come in, watched the way he moved, watched the way the dark eyes found him at once, then swiftly assessed the hall, the exits, the lighting, the guards at the doors. MacLeod knew just as *he* knew an Immortal was present; what MacLeod could not be certain of were his intentions.

Jamie waited, and let him come. Watched him walk from the door, smooth steps steady and unflagging, arms hanging loosely from wide shoulders beneath the long, loose coat. Simple clothes: jeans, faded denim shirt, boots. Two hundred and fifty years later and the very same man, if clad in different clothing; if with shorter, neater hair.

Duncan MacLeod of the Clan MacLeod.

He knew more of that man now than he had ever known or suspected then; that he ever could have *dreamed* of, in the days before James Douglas died.

He doesn't remember me.

Impossible, that. But all too plain. And it took him in the gut, punching deep into viscera. Yet he managed to smile as MacLeod approached.

Power, Jamie thought. *There's power in the man, and grace, and swift agility . . .*

It would never do to underestimate Duncan MacLeod. Fools had before, when no one, least of all Jamie, knew what he was, though none of them had died; had merely been humiliated at the field games. But now Jamie knew better: those innocent games were replaced by the grander Game, and other fools *had* died. MacLeod yet lived, testament to the legend.

The giant waited, aware of a febrile anticipation building in his belly. MacLeod stopped before him a sword's length away, flicked the merest glance at the display case of glittering jewelled ornaments—sword, crown, scepter—then slid one hand the barest fraction beneath one coat flap. And waited.

Jamie took note of it. "No," he said plainly, watching MacLeod's eyes. "I haven't come for that."

The deep, slow voice, nearly devoid of accent, though what existed was of England, lacked utterly in Scots burr. "Then what *have* you come for? What game are you playing?"

"Game?"

"Answer me," MacLeod said steadily. "No more games."

Jamie laughed. "Is it truly a game to remind a man of his roots?"

"I need no reminding of my *roots*," MacLeod said sharply.

"Oh, no? I think you do. I think you've forgotten. How can you not forget, after four hundred years?"

MacLeod cast a sweeping glance across his shoulder at the distant door, marking the guard's placement: far enough for their conversation to remain private. When he turned back the lines of his face were as stone, the clean, dark planes of bones beneath taut flesh hard as Scottish granite. "What do you want? I'll not ask it again."

Suddenly it was easy. Was true, and right. Jamie grinned, then barked a brief, disbelieving laugh; could he be so blind? "I want you to look, MacLeod!" he hissed. "Christ, man, look around you! Look at *this*!" He indicated the display case holding crown, scepter, sword. "What do you see, MacLeod? What do you *see* when you look at the Honours of Scotland? Pride? Heritage? Folly?"

Douglas smiled as he saw the faint frown that passed all too quickly. "Aye, *folly*, MacLeod. How can it be anything else? We lost. We *lost*. England defeated us. Now we're naught but a tourist attraction, we Highlanders, a dramatic, romantic notion of times gone by, when men were men and knew what honor was, what pride meant, and loyalty—" He broke it off, then shook his head. "God knows there's little of that anymore, in all the grand cities. Do you recall it? Do you recall what it was to come of a village, of kin and clan . . . to answer the burning cross summoning us to war?"

MacLeod's eyes were nearly black, swallowed by pupil. Eaten by memory. "I recall it."

"Do you? *Do* you, MacLeod?" So easy now, all of it. His passion was genuine, the words telling because of it. "Or have the two hundred and fifty years since Culloden blunted your memory, leached you of your pride, made you a Sassenach in place of a Scot?" That told in the tightening around the eyes. "Good Christ, MacLeod—you don't even *sound* like a Scotsman anymore! Has the Butcher had his revenge? Has England remade you? Tamed you? Emasculated you?"

"That's enough," MacLeod said sharply.

"Is it? I think not. Look around, MacLeod! Scotland is *on tour*." Jamie broke from him then, moved throughout the hall, indicated this display, that exhibit. "Here's a piece of it, aye? And here . . . and here . . . they've carved up chunks of Scotland to send it out into the world where people can see it, can share a bit of the life we knew as lads. I'm younger than you—oh, aye!—but not so young as to forget what I was, what *Scotland* was, in the days before the Butcher blew us to pieces on that field! We were *kings,* MacLeod, kings of England, of the world, and it all went for naught. All of it blown to bits in the thunder of his guns, the cunning royal butcher . . . and what was left was stripped from the survivors on orders from Parliament: no more Gaelic permitted, no more kilts or tartan, no more *bagpipes*—" And he was back before MacLeod, looming over him, close enough that even the small *sgian dhu* could take a man's life, were he not Immortal. "Even the pipes," he whispered, "so we could only grieve in our minds, in our hearts, and in our souls. But never in our language. Never on the pipes. Not even within our own glens."

There. It was done. He saw the bright shifting sheen in MacLeod's eyes, the bleak and deep acknowledgment of the pain in his soul, a Scotsman's soul after all.

"D'ye no' see it?" Jamie asked softly, slipping into dialect, into the soft-cadenced, singing rhythm. "D'ye no' ken what we were, we Highlanders, and how they've neutered us?"

MacLeod swung away, took a single long stride, then swung back. One stride brought him very close, clearly unintimidated by Jamie's great height. "And what are we supposed to do about it?" he asked. "We can't go back, Douglas. Times have changed—time is *gone* . . . we may live forever, but we live in the here and now, not in the past—"

"*You* do," Jamie retorted. "Indeed, I see you do. And you born of the bones of the land, Duncan MacLeod"— he let disgust into his tone —"bred up to be a warrior, honoring your land and its rightful king . . . you were a Jacobite, as I was, and you took an oath to James! You took an oath to his son! You took an oath to *his* son, to Charles Edward Stuart!"

"We lost," MacLeod said tightly. "We lost at Culloden. We can't remake history!"

"Not remake it. *Take* it."

"Take it how?" MacLeod demanded.

Jamie put out his hand, his broad-palmed, long-fingered hand. His tone was kept soft, but was no less passionate for its self-control. "With this, MacLeod—by reaching out, and grasping, and *taking*, and making it ours again!"

"What, by stealing?" MacLeod asked, indicating the case with an outflung hand. And then he stopped. Realization entered his eyes, and startlement, as he looked at the Honours of Scotland. Hastily he glanced at the guard again—the man was on his walkie-talkie—then lowered his voice. "Is that it? Your solution is to *steal* back what we had?"

"It's ours."

"Why? What good would it do?"

"Show them we're serious."

MacLeod shook his head. "We are not the IRA, Douglas. We are Scots—"

"All of us?"

"—and we've never been militant the way the Irish have."

"Maybe we should be."

"Is that your plan, then? To steal the Honours of Scotland and begin a war?"

"No war, MacLeod. You said it: We are not the IRA. But we are one in this: Celts, Gaels, Irish, Scots—and we prize our heritage." He paused. "Or have you forgotten what that was, Duncan MacLeod of the Clan MacLeod?"

The guard stepped into the room. Behind him were several others. "Time to leave," the man said, one hand resting lightly on the butt of his gun.

"Aye, so it is," James Douglas said, smiling, employing immense and tangible charm. "You'll forgive us, I hope, two actors . . . two Scots far from home practicing lines—and arguing over such things as make no matter anymore!"

That settled them. He laughed as the guards relaxed, recognizing him now; actors were forgiven many things.

And then his smile altered; was meant now for MacLeod—and there was no humor in it. "Go home, MacLeod, and think

on this, think on what we were. Remember the pipes, bonnie
Duncan . . ."

MacLeod said nothing. His expression was closed as he
turned toward the door. But James Douglas had seen the bitter acknowledgment in the eyes, the dark and expressive
eyes of a man too far from home, and freshly reminded of it.

James Douglas smiled as MacLeod walked away from
him. "And remember *too* when Scotland was brave."

With brisk economy Richie racked the hand weights,
stacked the barbell plates near the wall, took an industrial
push broom to the hardwood floor. He recalled when Mac
had first bought the dojo from Charlie DeSalvo, how the jan-
itorial duties had annoyed him. And yet now the work was
second nature, a part of a new discipline brought on by
tragedy and rebirth. Richie Ryan was no longer a kid from
the streets, half punk, half thief. He'd grown up in the years
with MacLeod in body and maturity, so that it was the man
who died in place of the boy; a man born again into unexpected Immortality. He knew it as intimately as any mortal
could, because of his friendship with Duncan MacLeod; and
yet it was still a shock, still painful and astonishing, to waken
out of mortal death into something quite apart.

"And now here I am, playing janitor again," he murmured.
"What kind of a job is this for an Immortal?"

But it wasn't a job. It was a sense of responsibility, something Richie Ryan had eventually come to understand was
within his power despite self-doubts.

His smile widened. "Not so stupid after all, are you, Mac?
You gave me enough rope to almost hang myself God knows
how many times, then reeled me in—" Richie stopped sweeping. It was there, abrupt and all-encompassing . . . "Mac?" He
gripped the broom handle more tightly and assumed a balanced stance, staring at the dojo entrance as the outer door
was opened. He had learned, had been taught, never to make
assumptions. "Mac, is that you?"

The outer door slammed shut. The dojo door was open, as
usual; the woman came through, stepping into the studio,
into light. And stopped.

"Are *you* still here, then?" She slid the hood of her raincoat back, baring her face, her obvious if startled amusement. "D'ye mean to say no one's taken that foolish head off your shoulders yet?"

Chapter Nine

Richie knew her at once despite his stunned disbelief—no Immortal could forget the first opportunity to take a head, a Quickening—and was struck anew by her delicacy, her petite beauty, the burnished glow of her hair, and the unrelentingly fierce brightness of blue eyes, fixed on his face.

"Annie Devlin," he murmured. Then, swiftly, *Sword . . . sword in a rack on the wall*—

"Ah, no," she said, smiling, reading his face, his body, "we'll not be needing that . . ." She paused, eyes narrowing. "Unless you insist upon it."

His chest tightened. The knot crept into his gut even as he stayed his response, as he gripped the broom handle and tried to relax, to give away nothing of his tension. He had thought never to see her again, this woman; had believed his generosity in leaving her her head would make her grateful. But Annie Devlin had never been that kind. Woman or no, Immortal or no, she was ruthless and obsessed, dissuaded by nothing, and no one.

Except Mac—"Him," Richie said sharply. "You've come for MacLeod."

Annie's smile altered, sweetened, and the Irish took her words. "Oh, I've come for MacLeod, indeed—but not in the way you're thinking."

Last time he had seen her was on the shore, weaponless, virulently furious, goading him to violence despite the precariousness of her position: awaiting the stroke of his sword that would truly end her life. At that moment he had seen only the angry woman, the terrorist, the killer, who had sworn to avenge the death of her husband, to kill Richie because of his interference in a planned assassination that, gone wrong, had resulted in her husband's death. Then he had been so new, so young in Immortality, but now—

"All grown up," she said softly. "No more the boy, are you?"

He reddened, body tensing. "I could have killed you."

"Oh, indeed, you could have . . . but you didn't. You're not ruthless enough, Richie Ryan, not dedicated enough to a cause—"

"The IRA?" he interrupted. "Terrorism, bombings, the deaths of innocent people? No, no, you're right—I'm not that ruthless." Derision shaped his tone. "That *dedicated*."

"Then why did you leave me my head?" she prodded. "If I'm so bad a person, so deserving of death, why did you let me live?"

He had no answer for her.

"Because I'm a woman?" She smiled, came two steps closer; he was put in mind of a predator on the stalk. "Or because you're soft?"

He thought of what MacLeod might do, might say, and mimicked it. He held his tongue, and waited.

"Ah," she said, "you're learning." She took two steps more, assessed her surroundings. Then assessed him, seeming to arrive at a conclusion. "I'm not here for your head, or his."

He drew in a silent breath, wondering what she thought of the man who might have killed her. "Then why *are* you here? We've no business with you."

"You don't, no, that's true," she conceded, "but I've business with MacLeod. Private business."

"And I'm supposed to believe you?"

Annie Devlin shrugged. "Believe as you will," she said. "Trust your gut, boyo, if not your ears. Would I announce myself?"

"Why not?" he countered. "You might expect to take us by surprise, with our guard down."

"No one could ever catch Duncan MacLeod with his guard down," she said plainly, "nor would I try. As for you? Well . . ." Unexpectedly, she laughed, if bitterly. "You beat me once. I won't try you again."

His turn to assess her. "I don't think so."

Brows arched up. "What? You don't believe me?"

"I don't *trust* you. There's a difference."

She tilted her head in consideration, then spread her arms wide, showing him her palms. "No weapon," she said. "Peace between us, Richie Ryan; I promise it."

"And what are your promises worth?" he shot back.

"Good Christ," she cried, stung, as her hands slapped back down, "it was me who nearly died, not you! It was *your* blade at *my* neck, not mine at yours! What more would you have me say?"

He shook his head, certain of his course. "Lady, don't even bother. No one in this world should trust you. I know what you are."

"You know nothing about me," she snapped, clearly angry now. "You know nothing but what you've created out of imagination, out of newspapers and magazines—"

"I saw you try to murder a man," Richie declared. "A mortal, not part of the Game—"

"Part of *life*!" she cried. "Part of Irish life, you fool—or what's left of it—"

"Politics have nothing to do with us," Richie said heatedly. "We don't die, not like they do—we shouldn't get involved—"

"No?" she hissed. "Well, maybe that's because you've never known anything worth dying for! You've been coddled all your life—"

"Coddled? Me?" He laughed sharply. "Lady, you don't know anything about me."

"I know you killed my husband," she said in a deadly tone.

"Oh no," Richie said, flatly denying the purposeful provocation. "Not me. The gun was in *your* hands—"

"And you interfered," she declared tightly. "Had you not been there that day—"

"—an ambassador would be dead," he finished. "A man trying to bring about peace—"

"There will *never* be peace in Ireland," she said viciously, "until all the fat bastards such as that man are dead!"

"And what about you?" he asked. "What do you get out of this? You're *Immortal*, Annie—you've outlived how many Irish patriots? And how many *more* will you outlive? What happens to you when the war is ended, when Ireland is at peace? Do you just pack up all your bombs and bullets and go home to a cottage on the coast?" He shook his head. "It isn't that easy."

Color stained her face. "What do *you* know about it?—still tied to MacLeod's apron strings!"

"He's a friend—"

"He's my friend, too!" Sudden tears glistened in her eyes, shocking him into silence. "Are you a blind man, then, not to see it? Not to know it?"

He had known it even then, though he wanted to deny it. It was easier to.

Annie read his face. "Why not?" she asked tautly. "We've more years than you, boy—and something more than friendship binding us."

He offered her contempt. "So much for marriage vows."

"I meant those vows," she said, strung tight as wire. "Twice. Kerry died in Dublin more than seventy-five years ago, and it was MacLeod who got me out before they could kill *me*. As for Tommy—" Her face twisted to reflect a more recent grief, and an abiding anger directed now as much at herself as at him. "Between us, boy, we killed him. You and I."

That much he never expected out of her. It was acknowledgment. Admission. Perhaps a form of confession. More quietly, he said, "Then what does MacLeod have to do with this?"

After a moment she shook her head. "You've never loved one of us, have you?"

It took him completely off-guard. He had, actually, but Annie didn't give him opportunity to answer.

"It's better if you don't," she said, "because there isn't an Immortal alive who stays with one mate." Bitterly, she said, "Monogamy is difficult when you may live for a thousand years."

Complicated, complex, the lives of Immortals, Richie thought. And now his own as well.

"Fine," he said, still gripping the broom. "Private business, you and MacLeod. But he's not here."

"Then I'll wait."

"So will I." He motioned toward the elevator with a tilt of his head. "Go on up. I've got work to do down here."

Annie Devlin smiled sadly. "He doesn't need the warning," she said quietly. "Oh, he makes me angry at times, does the bonnie Highlander, but I could never harm him. Nor he, me."

With hard strokes, Richie began to sweep again. "I'll reserve judgment on that."

Her tone was odd. "Then he's taught you well."

He swept briskly, obsessively, as she walked by him; until the elevator carried her up a floor, and away. Then he stopped, clutching the handle tightly, and recalled the moment he had slammed her sword away with his own, steel screeching on steel, rendered her helpless and vulnerable—and had known in that instant he would not do it. *Could* not do it.

Especially before MacLeod, who was present, and yet who said no word, made no move to interfere, to stop his friend from killing a woman who was also his lover.

Complicated. Complex. Immortal with Immortal, Immortal *against* Immortal.

Richie lowered his head, lightly banged his forehead against the butt of the broom handle. "Will it ever get easier?

Any of it?" He lifted his head, looked at the elevator. "Or does it just get harder?"

MacLeod parked the T-bird in the alley behind the dojo, as usual, but didn't get out at once. Instead he sat there several moments, recalling the red-haired actor, his rhetoric, his challenge; recalling also the glitter of jewels, the sheen of gold, contained in a massive display case: the Honours of Scotland.

As James Douglas said, Scotland was *on tour.*

MacLeod gripped the steering wheel, visualizing again Douglas' fierce pride, his unassailable passion for Scotland. His ridicule of a fellow Highlander for neglecting his roots.

Stung by the memory, MacLeod pulled the keys from the ignition abruptly and climbed out of his car. He considered going in through the front, to speak to Richie, but reconsidered and went up the exterior staircase instead. James Douglas had roused recollections and emotions within him that were intensely personal, requiring thought and resolution, and he did not care to share them with Richie just now, because Richie would know something was wrong, and would ask.

Had he become predictable? He thought not. But Richie knew him. Of all the Immortals MacLeod had met in four hundred years, he believed Richie Ryan knew him best of all, because he permitted it. Because he let Richie *in,* knowing he would be Immortal and required training, lest he lose his head at once. Father, uncle, brother, guardian, friend, mentor—it took dedication, that kind of relationship, and intense commitment, patience, and loyalty, yet he knew of no Immortal who had not done the same for another despite the requirements of it.

Up the exterior stairs, key inserted, door opened—

—into awareness, and shock. *Not Richie after all . . .*

Annie saw the sword in his hand before anything else. The sheen of polished, elegant steel; the flash of light off edge; the hand gripping the ornate ivory hilt ending in an exquisite dragon-headed pommel. And she saw the curve of the fingers, the fit of hilt in palm, the tension and flexion across the back of the tanned hand as tendons shifted minutely. It was a dangerous, deadly and *personal* grip, that hand on that hilt, ineffably Duncan MacLeod.

"No," she said only.

One deft flick of his other hand swung shut the door behind him. "No?"

She rose from the couch, leaving behind the coat, the sword. "When have you ever needed that with me?"

He laughed. He *laughed*, even as he tucked the blade beneath his arm. "Annie," he said, grinning, "I need it always with you. I remember a dock before the lighthouse, and a very angry woman. With a sword in her hand."

She flared; he always did that to her: got under her skin. Or set it afire. "I was drunk."

"If I remember, Annie, the challenge came first. Drinks after."

"I'm not drunk now."

He smiled. "Neither am I."

She drew breath. "Would it help?"

Cautiously he ventured, "That depends."

"I remember it," she said evenly, not retreating; she was not that sort of woman. "That dock, that lighthouse . . . that night."

"That whisky?" His smile was kind, though he promised nothing but that he would not attack her; he came into the loft, set the katana on the kitchen counter, stripped off the loose raincoat. "Annie—"

"They're all dead," she said quietly, holding her tone steady with effort.

He stilled. "Who?"

"Kerry. Tommy. Others. All of the men I have loved." She saw the flare in brown eyes, the kindling of comprehension, compassion; he took it to his soul, that statement, and absorbed it. Altered it to fit himself. Had he lost another? Another Tessa? Painfully she managed, "How many for you, MacLeod?"

He turned from her then, draped the coat across the

counter beside the sword. Set his hands along the edge and leaned there a moment, not turning back. "Annie—"

No man would name her a coward. She would hear it straight out. "Say it, MacLeod. We were drunk. Lonely. Grieving. No more than that, was it? Two empty people aching inside, two of us dealing with the knowledge that mortals always *die,* no matter how we love them, no matter how we protect them. No matter how we lie to them." It ached even now, deep within her heart. "No more than that. Was it?"

It was none of it coming out right. This was not how she had envisioned it, dreamed it, planned it. But she had never been a shy woman, nor one who beat around bushes; Annie Devlin saw what she wanted, and took it.

But MacLeod was not a man who let any woman take him, unless he permitted it.

Inside, she died a little. "Was it?"

That much accomplished; she saw it at once as he turned to look at her. He remembered, clearly, recalled it all: the words, the whisky, the responses of the anguished bodies both had believed numb, dead, stunted, so empty as to be lifeless. And yet the bodies understood what the spirits did not in that moment of awareness intensified by whisky, by the softness of the moonlight: that an Immortal, to heal and renew more than simply flesh, but soul, required another Immortal, one who knew, who understood, who comprehended the terrible heartsick pain of life and loss, the price paid when a mortal grew old and died, or a mortal was killed.

Tommy for her. Tessa for him.

Abruptly she grieved again. Was that all there was between them? Dead mortals? Lost lovers?

He moved past her, and she put out her hand. Touched him. Stayed him. Felt the warmth of flesh beneath the sleeve of his shirt, the vitality that sheathed his bones.

He didn't move away, but neither did he move *to* her. He simply stopped.

Her campaign, all of it. Her command, her offensive, her ground to gain, or give. But he had not begun to defend.

She took her hand from his arm and raised it, put out trembling fingers, touched the base of his throat where the pulse beat full and strong. "May it always be whole," she said, "this neck. Never die, Duncan MacLeod. Promise me that."

"I can't." The flesh of his throat vibrated beneath her fingers. "None of us can, Annie."

"You more than most, MacLeod. You may not be a warrior any longer, but I've known none as good as you. And that's why—" She paused, went on. "That's why I've always wanted you with us. With me." She looked away at last. "There you have it. The truth. There are Causes—and causes."

At last he touched her. He lifted his hand, closed it around hers, then carried it up to his mouth. Lips against her palm, he said, "I can promise you nothing, Annie. Ever."

And she was free. He let go her hand, moved away, and when she turned she saw how he poured liquor into a glass.

"Two," she said. "Is it whisky?"

"*Usquabae,*" he said. "And Scots." He turned, smiled. "Does that offend your Irish blood?"

"Oh, my Irish blood is up for more than Scots *whisky.*" She smiled archly; let him see what was in her eyes, her body. "But I think I have your answer."

"Do you?" He poured another glass full, lifted it. "Drink with me, Annie?"

Something bloomed within her. It was a beginning, after all.

She moved to him, took the whisky, watched the hand again as he brought his glass to hers.

And abruptly she knew what he did. For a moment it made her angry, that he would test her; and then she understood. What was between them was of the past. The present was—the present. And there would be no future if she did not concede a form of defeat, albeit not what most would expect. From him, yes. She knew him now better than ever.

Annie nodded once, acknowledging the challenge. "To happiness." She said nothing at all again of the Cause that had always come between them. Even in toasts.

His warm smile kindled, lighting dark eyes. "Is it so hard, Annie?"

"Yes," she answered honestly. "Now, I've said it. I've

made your toast, the one you always insisted on . . . and what is yours, MacLeod?" Her turn to challenge. "What do you drink to?"

He would not do it. She knew better.

The muted chime of heavy crystal against crystal. *"Alba gu brath,* Annie Devlin . . . if you'll forgive a Scot his pride."

"Anything," she declared, meaning it.

"Not you, Annie."

"Anything."

"Not for me, Annie."

"For Kerry, seventy-seven years ago. For Tommy, far fewer. The same for Duncan MacLeod, in the here and now." She drank, watching him, reading his eyes, his heart. Because she could. She always could, then as well as now, but only now realized how much she wanted to. "Was it an accident, MacLeod? That night at the lighthouse?"

"You said it was." Arched brows lifted in reflection. "As I recall—I said it seemed pretty real to me."

"So it was."

"And I also said maybe we should have had that accident a long time ago . . ."

"And I said we *would* have."

"If I had joined you."

"Never," she said, "I know that now. No more the warrior, Duncan MacLeod. You've made your choice."

He tilted his head in assent. "What about you, Annie? Have you made yours?"

She lifted a shoulder. "That depends on which choice you mean."

"People can change, Annie. It's not impossible."

"If they *choose*," she agreed. "But what you don't understand is that I'd give my life for Ireland—"

"And have, many times." He grinned, then it faded. "But Ireland would be healthier if you gave your heart and head, instead of your blood. Instead of demanding the blood of others."

She swung away, staring hard into her drink. "I didn't come to speak of the Cause, MacLeod."

"The Annie Devlin I knew has never spoken of anything else."

"Oh, but she did," she said tautly. "That night at the lighthouse."

She didn't hear him move, but felt him. Close now, so close. "I remember."

She twisted her mouth. "Was it the whisky, MacLeod?" Behind her now. She felt him. So close. She had only to turn—

And couldn't. *Christ Jesus, you're a bloody fool, Annie—*

But he did it for her. He reached around her, lifted the glass from her fingers, set it down on the table. Then warm hands closed on her shoulders, sliding beneath loose hair to the naked flesh bared by the wide-cut neckline of thin sweater. Thumbs caressed gently. "Peace, Annie." He brushed her hair aside, then his mouth came down on the nape of her neck. Found the swelling of bone at the junction of her shoulders. "Peace, Annie Devlin."

So close against her now as he teased her flesh with tongue and teeth. "Oh, *Christ,* MacLeod—" Her body came alive. At once, altogether. There was no delaying, no denying: he was male, she female, and nothing else mattered.

She shuddered even as he laughed softly, gently, meaning no contempt but acknowledgment of response, hers as well as his; and she turned, reached blindly and captured, clung, pressed herself close, as close as could be; shaped herself to fit him as they had fit before, one night on a dock by the lighthouse. There were clothes between them now, but that would not last.

"*Anything,*" she said clearly, with explicit emphasis.

He smiled into her eyes, caught her bottom lip briefly between his teeth, tugged, then released it. "I know."

Had likely always known. But just now, in his arms, feeling the beat of his heart, the heat of his mouth on hers, she did not care what that suggested.

"You shouldn't have left me," she managed between kisses.

"When?" He slid the loose-cut neckline of her sweater

down over one naked shoulder. "In Ireland? Or at the light-house?"

"Either. Both." His hands were deft as he worked the sweater to her elbow, so that one bare breast was freed. He cupped it; she quivered. "Ever." He laughed softly against her mouth as she found his belt, set fingers to the buckle. "Why d'ye wear your pants so tight, MacLeod—harder to get them off."

His breath was warm in her mouth. "They weren't tight a minute ago."

"Oh, Christ—"

"Your fault, Annie—"

"Will you be *serious*, you bloody Highlander—? Oh, Christ, MacLeod—"

"Why?" He scooped her up then, ignoring her difficulties with belt and buckle, hooked her higher on his thighs, then carried her to the leather couch. "Although I might say I've never been more serious in my life, Annie Devlin." He dropped her on the cushions, then came down upon her. He knew how to balance his weight, to take it on knees and elbows so as not to crush her. He caught and guided her hand. "Do you doubt me, Annie?"

Annie laughed exultantly. How could she, with such evidence as that?

She bent her attentions to the belt buckle with renewed efforts, tackled the zipper as well. "Kilts are easier."

He laughed softly. "I've always thought so."

"I suspect if the Scots and Irish took to wearing them again, there'd be more of us." He had the sweater off of her now, slipping it over her head quickly. Then his own shirt, stripped off and tossed aside; she slid her hands beneath the unbuckled belt, unzipped jeans, the thin briefs; to the warm, taut flesh of his flanks, freeing them and buttocks of encumbrance with a deft motion of her hands. Muscles jerked reflexively. "There," she said, "better—"

They did not bother with divesting themselves of any more clothing than was, just this moment, strictly necessary. The couch made for close quarters, but not impossibility; and it was softer than the dock had been there by the lighthouse.

In the haze of muted light, burnishing his shoulders; in the brief opening of her eyes she saw his face, his eyes, the arch of expressive brows over the sockets, and the faint smile softening the curve of his mouth as he came down to cover hers. Certainty was sudden. "I was a fool to let you go."

He took her with him then, banishing everything of the world save the one they made within the loft upon the warmth of worn leather. She lifted her legs, wrapped them tightly around him, took him deeper and deeper.

Fool, her mind said, *to accept any other when Duncan MacLeod is in the world.*

Chapter Ten

For the fifth time, Richie walked purposefully to the stairs and stopped short. *Not my business.*

And every bit his concern. MacLeod's safety, surely, always would be—and as decidedly MacLeod's business, personal and private.

But. Annie Devlin.

Mac was not dead, Richie knew. And was in fact home; a quick trip to the alley to check on the car confirmed that. But neither had Mac come down, nor asked him to come up.

Richie sat down on one of the weight benches once more, wrestling with impulse. *None of my business.*

But he could not help conjuring the moment again, the memory of her face, her rage, her fierce pride as she goaded him to take her head. It would have been his first kill as an Immortal, his first Quickening, something he had anticipated with a commingling of emotions, among them fear. What if he failed?

He had not, but it wasn't Annie's head he took. Mako's. Dead at his hands; his Quickening, his experience and power, Richie's own.

But Annie Devlin lived, and now she had come back.

Richie turned on the bench, looked over his shoulder at the elevator shaft. "I don't get it." He wondered if he would ever truly understand Duncan MacLeod, what shaped and drove the man, the complex emotions and experiences that made Mac who he was. What Annie Devlin, quite plainly, had come to find.

Maybe when I'm four hundred years old. Or maybe not.

It was late. This served no purpose. MacLeod made and lived by his decisions with no expectations of interference; it wasn't anyone's place to question him.

And yet . . . Richie sighed, thrust himself to his feet and grabbed up his motorcycle jacket, leather tails just long enough to conceal his sword. He felt young by anyone's terms, mortal or Immortal.

At the door he paused, glanced back. "Watch your head," he murmured, and took himself out of the dojo.

Joe Dawson sat up late reading all the E-mail from Watcher cells all over the world. It took hours, and yet each report was of deepening concern for its extreme brevity. There were comments, extrapolations, myriad theories—but not a single file contained any concrete information. Nothing verifiable, quantifiable. So far.

Dawson gritted his teeth. He detested gaps. They were at odds with his orderly mind, his desire for thoroughness, his need for full information, but as much for the implication. Such things were dangerous, to mortals and Immortals alike. Gaps suggested sloppiness, ineffectiveness on the part of the organization, but something even worse: a secretiveness on the part of Immortals, and that betokened cause for alarm. Such alarm had, in fact, laid the groundwork for those Watchers who went fanatical, who believed every Immortal should be killed lest they threaten the lives and lifestyles of humans.

It was possible James Douglas had changed his name. Some Immortals did across the generations, hiding their existence beyond the present. It was simply easier. Yet many of them did not. Many of them took great care so as not to need new identities, but the inevitable happened. Even Immortals were prey to accidents. Many had been "killed" as a mortal would be killed—except they all survived. And that in and of itself was complicated, because that "death" required them to go away entirely, or to go so deeply underground that no one they knew would ever see them again.

There was, however, one thing on an Immortal's side, even if he or she were "killed" as a mortal would be. Disbelief. No lucid, reasonable mortal (who was not a Watcher) believed in immortality, and thus so long as a "dead" Immortal avoided those who knew him well, brief chance sightings were relegated to imagination or, in some instances, to the theory that every person alive had an exact double, a doppelgänger, somewhere in the world.

Joe Dawson no longer believed that. He had not believed it since Ian Bancroft first explained to him, in Vietnam, that Immortals existed. Had not believed it when Ian Bancroft died, killed by a Watcher grown too close to her assignment.

So. Some Immortals took new names, new identities, started over somewhere else. If they returned to where they'd been "killed," it was in another generation. Although large cities made it far easier, more convenient, to disappear. One could remain anonymous in a sprawling city, so long as one did not gravitate to the same interests.

How difficult was it, Dawson wondered, to remake oneself any number of times? Over centuries?

He did not envy them that. He had even stopped envying them their Immortality; he had learned too much of MacLeod *from* MacLeod to wish for the gift himself.

Dawson tapped a key. The next step was to cross-check other referents for James Douglas. Name was no longer important. Physical description, habits in dress, in speech, hobbies, employment; what was known and could be learned of him now was more important than what he called himself.

Once again Dawson wrote his inquiry and E-mailed it to the cells. A more detailed physical description, and facts Dawson knew without consulting further, though he would do that as well: an actor with the Highland Shakespeare Company, touring throughout the world. A man who wielded a sword with consummate skill. A man standing head and shoulders above most men. Hair could be dyed, a beard grown or shaved, weight could be gained or lost, body reshaped through weight training and conditioning, an inch or three added via lifts in shoes and higher heels—but natural height of such magnitude could not be altered.

Time, Dawson knew. It always required time. Technology rendered data easier to find, to retrieve, to receive, but the gathering, collation, analysis, and transferral still required time.

And time could kill an Immortal. Could kill Duncan MacLeod, if Douglas wanted his head.

Dawson sighed. Irony in its purest form. A man who was Immortal had all the time in the world. And yet could also have none.

"Time," he murmured, sending E-mail. "God grant me enough of it."

God grant it to Duncan MacLeod.

James Douglas sat on the floor, long legs bent and crossed as he worked backstage, beyond the backdrop. One length of wood approximately five feet in length, big around as a man's wrist; a second length as thick, but only three feet in length. Both pieces were rough-hewn, pocked with insect holes, divots, small knobs of "eyes" where new-sprouted branches and twigs had long since been stripped away. With meticulous care he set the short one across the long one and began to lash it in place: a bit of sisal twine first, then limber strips of bark.

As he worked, he whistled. Mostly under his breath; it was tradition, superstition, that one did not whistle in a theater. But he was not a man bound much by tradition or superstition beyond that which he made himself. Acting suited his temperament, his taste for performance and presentation, but he paid only lip service to many of the superstitions. Just now, as he worked, he whistled, tongue set against the roof of his mouth immediately behind his teeth. Not *true* whistling, that, merely a snatch of sound now and again cradled in sibilant hiss.

He heard the step, glanced up. Colin Cameron, come to see what he did, to reassure himself what *they* did was right and just.

"Jamie?"

Jamie smiled briefly, tending his business: looping, wrapping, tying. "Here, Coll."

The young man came around the backdrop. "I was just over at the exhibit hall . . ."

"Reconnoitering?" Jamie nodded. "Doesn't hurt to check, and check again. There is safety in diligence."

Colin's tone was startled. "What are you doing?"

"Me? Och, I've become a Boy Scout." Jamie grinned, still not so much as glancing at Cameron. "There's much you don't know, even of your own people. You should tend your history, Coll."

"I'm learning," Cameron said diffidently. "I'm reading the books, Jamie."

"Books, aye—they'll help. But there's no substitution for having been there." More wrapping, more knots. "But then, you can't help that you're a wee sprat, can you?" Finally he looked at the young man, saw the red tint of his face. "Oh, now, don't be so embarrassed, lad. You are what you are. You'll learn."

"What is that?" Cameron asked.

"The cross of war," Jamie answered. "And every Highlander knew it, understood it. Answered its call, save he was a coward." He stood up then, uncoiling long legs, rising to his full height. In his hands the cross was a toy. "Duncan MacLeod is not a coward, and he'll answer it."

"How can you be so sure? It's robbery, Jamie. He may not wish to join us."

"He will."

"Because of a cross?"

Jamie smiled, carried the cross around the backdrop. "You'll see."

"But—I *don't* see."

"You will. He's already been baited, lad . . . now he's rising to the lure."

"What lure?"

Jamie climbed the false rocks, the tumbled pile of prop construction that, from a distance, appeared hard as granite and real. At its top he looked for and found the slot that held the pike upon which Macbeth's head was stuck for Macduff's final climactic speech. Jamie placed the heel of the staff at the lip, dropped the cross into the slot.

Then he grinned at Colin. "Annie, my lad. Annie is the lure."

And as the boy stared, he boomed out in resonant bass a verse of the song he'd been whistling:

> *"Far off in sunlit places, sad are the Scottish faces,*
> *Yearning to feel the kiss of sweet Scottish rain!*
> *Where tropic skies are beaming, love sets the heart a'-*
> *dreaming,*
> *Longing and dreaming for the homeland again!"*

He broke off, grinned down at Colin Cameron. "Don't you feel it, lad? *Scotland,* lad! Scotland the brave!"

Near dawn, MacLeod awoke. He lay quietly, listening to her breathe. The bedclothes were tangled around her legs, leaving most of her bare, and him; carefully he pulled the sheet and coverlet up and settled it over her, but not before he saw the line of her spine in dim light, the pale sheen of her flesh. He could see nothing of her face, the fine fragile bones, only the curve of one hip, the jut of a single shoulder. And the spill of burnished hair, dark against the pallor of pillow and sheets.

Carefully he slipped from the bed, walked soundlessly to the nearest window. The chill of near-dawn did not offend him as he stood there, gazing out through slatted, half-open blinds. But instead of the trees, the vistas, the crags and braes of burn-broken mountains, he saw rooftops and antennas, heard in place of an eagle's cry the sound of the city.

So far now from Scotland. So far from Glenfinnan. And a woman in his bed who was Irish, but still a Celt.

Behind him, she stirred, murmuring of desertion. Softly she asked, "What are you thinking?"

Did she miss Ireland as much as he missed Scotland?

"MacLeod?"

He turned then, went to the bed, to her, slid down onto the mattress. She said something about the chill of his flesh, and pulled the sheet up over him. He shifted and she moved close, tucking into him. The curve of her skull fit perfectly into the hollow between his chest and shoulder.

She was drowsy, her accent heavier. "D'ye ever dream, MacLeod?"

He smiled into darkness. "Yes."

"About death?"

Not what he expected, that. "Mine? Not if I can help it."

"No. Others. Mortal deaths, even. In the battles, in the wars."

Fingers found her hair and stroked it away from her brow. Her flesh was so fair, and his so dark in comparison. "What do you mean, Annie?"

When she answered at last, her tone was reflective, scoured of habitual challenge, taut defensiveness. "I see their faces, MacLeod. The children. The women. Even the men, sometimes."

He had never heard such wistfulness in her, such vulnerability. "That was your choice," he told her. "No one holds you to it. You can change anytime."

"Can I?" She was warm against him. "I wonder, sometimes, if I ever could. It's been so many years."

The flesh of her brow was soft beneath his fingertips. She was twenty-five, and ninety-five, and everything in between. "And in the daylight?" he asked. "How do you feel then?"

She was very still. "In the daylight . . . in the daylight, I see the need. In the daylight, everything is clear. There is no choice anymore."

He let her think about that even as he did. "You have the advantage of time," he told her finally. "You could do more for Ireland as a peacemaker, not as a warrior."

"It's what I *am*—"

"But you can stop, Annie."

"I can't."

"Darius did." It still hurt, that death. "He realized that kind of life wasn't for him anymore, and he stopped."

She was quiet a long moment, and then she laughed softly. "Would you have me take the habit, then, and become a nun? While I'm here in your bed?"

He smiled into false dawn. "Well, no, I wouldn't go so far as that."

"But Darius became a priest. Is that what it takes to stop?"

"I stopped, Annie. And I am not a priest."

"Jesus, I should say *not*." She turned to him then, sealing herself more closely against the length of his body, trapping an ankle between her feet. "And if I stopped—if I pledged myself to something else, something as justified, but with no bloodshed involved . . . would you believe me?"

"I might."

"Would you join me?"

That set off alarums. "Annie—"

"Stop." She turned close, put a hand over his mouth, stilled his question. "Stop."

He removed her hand. "Annie, you can't start something like that and then just leave it. Tell me what you mean."

"Later," she said, moving adroitly atop him, straddling powerful thighs. She swooped down to nip briefly at his lower lip, then traced the contours of his face with her tongue.

Nothing approaching a comprehensible language issued from his mouth.

"Hush," she said severely, easing down upon him. "You talk too much, MacLeod."

He caught his breath, held it, let her undertake the sweet, urgent labor as she captured him, held him. He arched beneath her, buttocks clenching, barely aware of anything in the world save the singular rocking of her body, the rhythm of give and take.

"Mine," she murmured.

He might have argued it for the sake of the contest. But Annie Devlin gave him no opportunity to shape or complete a single sentence.

Chapter Eleven

Dawson worked again, but this time over receipts and books, the mundane requirements and responsibilities of his life, his "real" life, quite apart from the Watcher organization. The bar was his to fail with, to succeed with; it paid the bills, provided a stage for young musicians, offered those with similar tastes in blues a place to go, to listen, to while away the hours. A place where Watchers might gather also, after hours, to play cards, talk shop. To discuss such men and women, such lives and deaths as could be discussed nowhere else as plainly, as openly, in such dramatic and evocative imagery as decapitation by sword blade.

And to quietly mourn the deaths of those who were not supposed to be friends, and yet were more than merely strangers. Watchers devoted years to specific individuals, conceived of likes and dislikes and hard-won tolerations in the name of their service. But some Immortals were more than merely assignments. Some were heroes, some villains. Some were philanthropists, while others were assassins. Some lived as Immortals merely a matter of months. And some were legendary.

Dawson sat hunched at the desk tucked into a corner of the tiny office in the recesses of the blues bar. The desktop was littered with charge receipts, creased and tattered checks, register tapes, order forms, business cards, letters of inquiry from aspiring musicians, even a sprawled stack of cassette tapes. And a handful of IOUs from people with whom he played poker.

He jumped as the phone rang. Glad of reprieve, yet annoyed also by the interruption, he snatched it up on the cusp of the second ring. "Joe's."

A woman's voice. *"Joe Dawson?"*

Dawson sat upright. "Yes."

There was a pause on the other end of the line. When the woman spoke again the tone was flattened, stripped of character. *"You've been asking questions about a red-haired actor. A Scotsman."*

Dawson drew a quick breath. "What have you got for me?"

"Not what you need, I'm afraid."

"You don't know him?"

"I've seen him. I didn't know he was an Immortal." She paused. *"Are you certain?"*

Dawson sighed. He was, thanks to MacLeod, but not in a way he could divulge; no one in the organization knew he was so personally involved with the Highlander. To do so broke his oath, and that they would not tolerate. "I've seen him around MacLeod," he said, which was not precisely a lie. "Figured I'd better check him out."

"Has everyone reported in?"

"Not yet," Dawson replied. "But so far you're the only one besides me who can confirm there is such a man."

"But not that he's an Immortal." She paused. *"If he is one, and he's come for MacLeod—"*

"I can't interfere," Joe finished, irritated. "I know that. I just don't like not knowing the names of all the pieces in the Game. It goes against my nature."

"If he's part of the Game, someone will know who he is."

Before or after he comes for MacLeod's head? Joe was tempted to ask. "Yeah, I guess." He wanted badly to let her know how vital it was for him to learn the truth of the big actor, but beyond what he'd already said there was little that would not tip his hand. All he could do was ask, and wait—and hope.

"If I learn more, I'll let you know," the woman said, and disconnected.

Dawson set the handset into its cradle and stared blankly at the piles on his desktop. Such things as bar receipts were abruptly rendered distractions, annoyances, when a man's life was at stake.

When a man's *head* was at stake.

They were not in Scotland, nor in that time, and so MacLeod showed Annie what had been his world, his time, his country, the only way he could. He took her to the exhibition hall at the Cultural Center and let her see what the tour contained: Scotland as she had been, but also as she was translated by those who knew nothing beyond books. It was illuminating to walk the halls and displays, to correct the mistakes, to comment on what was truth. With Annie there was no need for prevarication: she was Immortal, and knew what it was to live so long. He could speak of such things as if they were yesterday. To both of them, they were.

But it was when they came to the hall dedicated to Culloden that he understood at last.

So many bits and pieces of history acquired over the years and assembled now in one place. Mannequins wearing faded, stained kilts, clothing outlawed by the English; display cases of shot, small arms, dirks, *sgian dhus*; a wall arrangement of swords, Lochaber axes, the muskets, powder horns and bayonets. A handful of discolored coins. One time-twisted, age-dried shoe, a Scottish brogan. A clan badge—MacDonald—and a wallet full of oatmeal, proof of a Highlander's breakfast. Enlarged photographs of paintings and etchings, of the field itself, of grave-markers placed decades later; of battle plans, of orders, and descriptions of the battle, the aftermath, the destruction of Highland culture.

So much was known, and so little. Reports differed, as did opinion. For MacLeod, a man who had been there, the truth was part of all sides, all opinions, all convictions. And yet it hurt to see it rendered here in painstaking miniature, spread out upon a huge table beneath a protective plastic bubble in vast, serried detail: Drummossie Moor, the battle, broken down to match the diagrams drawn by Douglas Campbell, engineer.

Men, transmuted to lead figures. Tactics into ink marks. So many Scots, dead, at the Battle of Culloden.

He heard again the pipes, the crackling of musketry, the roaring of artillery, ceaseless for one hour. Was blinded by powder that blew hard across the Jacobite army; tasted its grit between his teeth, smelled the stink of heated metal, shredded flesh, fresh-spilled blood.

"Where were you?" Annie asked softly.

His vision came back to the present. He saw the armies before him, no men of flesh and blood but tiny lead figures in painted-on clothing. "Here." MacLeod pointed.

She nodded. "In the midst of carnage."

"All of it was carnage," he said tautly. "It was butchery, Annie, nothing more. The English had more men, horses, superior artillery . . . we were outnumbered, outweaponed, and outfought. He'd studied us, had Cumberland. He knew Highlanders too well. He was ready for us." He stared hard at the lead figures. "The English army lost three hundred and sixty-four men in the entire battle, out of nearly ten thousand. Only that. Within one hour—*one hour, Annie*—we lost twelve hundred. And later . . . later, when the English found survivors, they killed them. Wounded, whole—it didn't matter. They shot them there, or hanged them later. Burned them alive in barns. Or stripped them of clothing, gave them no food or water, and let them die of exposure in the jail in Inverness."

"And you?" she asked softly.

He shook his head. "I was away by then. My duty was to my liege, to Prince Charles Edward Stuart no matter what else there might be to do—" And he stopped. Broke off at once, into rigid stillness.

"MacLeod?"

In his mind MacLeod played it out again, heard Fergus

MacDonald call him away from a dying man in the name of his oath, when he had just given one to the badly wounded clansman upon the ground.

Duncan MacLeod had made his choice between prince and dying man because he was sworn first to Scotland and to her Stuart kings and living heirs. But he saw the dying man again: a mask of blood and brain matter, albeit the latter was not his own; and black powder, sweat, tears . . . hair darkened and matted by mud and wet turf, a nose so badly smashed it altered his features; the broken jaw that warped the shape of his face. A gangly young man in immense pain, all bent over to hug it into himself as he staggered nearly to knees; then down, those knees drawn up to belly.

A mother would not recognize a son in such straits.

"—Douglas . . ." he blurted.

"What, MacLeod?"

"I know him," he murmured, transfixed. "I *know* him—now—"

"Who, MacLeod?"

"James Douglas. I remember . . ."

"Ah," Annie said, with infinite satisfaction.

James Douglas stood up from the false stone upon which he perched, the cairn of a king, the podium of a prince. Headstone, gravestone, funeral cairn; as much a throne as barrow-grave. But not holy ground; this was no more than theater, than drama, than fantasy.

He stood up and smiled, looking upon the battlefield, the ranks of seats downsloped, upsloped, curving crosswise in elegant symmetry to permit each member of the audience good view, good hearing. Exquisite acoustics, superior lighting. Perfection. A director, an actor, could not desire better.

Beneath his feet stretched the polished wood, laid down with such meticulous care that no nail caught at soles, no scratch altered footing, no divot set a prop aslant. But he forsook wood for prop stone and climbed upon the cairn.

Anachronism personified. In one hand: claymore. In the other: a lighter.

He watched him come, and laughed. Boomed out the

deep, joyous laughter that carried so clearly, so cleanly throughout the theater empty of all save Duncan MacLeod, who came swiftly, so swiftly, face fixed in disbelief, in astonishment, and something akin to relief.

No more the laughter, but lyric:

> *"Let torrents pour then, let the great winds rally,*
> *Snow-silence fall, or lightning blast the pine;*
> *That light of Home shines warmly in the valley,*
> *And, exiled son of Scotland, it is thine."*

MacLeod halted abruptly, gracelessly, near the wide central aisle cross-cutting the ocean of seats. Struck into stillness, to silence.

> *"Far have you wandered over seas of longing,*
> *And now you drowse, and now you well may weep,*
> *When all the recollections come a-thronging*
> *Of this old country where your fathers sleep."*

"Stop," MacLeod said; and it too carried, that single word.

"Och, laddie, dinna fash yersel'," Jamie said in broad Scots, dropping into converse out of declamation. "I've but begun!"

"I remember you now," MacLeod said intently. "From Culloden. At the last, as you died."

"Ah." Jamie smiled. "Then you *do* remember." He paused. "All of it?"

MacLeod understood. "I couldn't tell you," he said. "You know that."

"Now." Douglas shrugged massive shoulders. "Though I've never understood it, myself, this rule of saying naught of so important a thing as Immortality to a man or woman who'll know it." An odd glint passed quickly through his eyes. "D'ye know how long it took me to find out? How many deaths?"

"Douglas—"

"How many Immortals I fought, not knowing what they

were? Took me time, it did; I nearly lost my head twice before I realized I had to take *theirs* to keep myself alive."

"Didn't you have a teacher?" MacLeod thought of Connor, with him; of himself, for Richie.

Jamie thrust a fist into the air. "None but my strong right arm!" He grinned, winking. "And my wits, laddie."

That was incomprehensible to MacLeod. What would it do to a man not to know what he was, or why his head was hunted? Why he never died? What kind of man did it shape, that lack of knowledge, that slow and painful education as others tried to kill him? He remembered so clearly his own misery and confusion before Connor found him.

"I meant to stay," MacLeod said. "To see you through it. To explain when you roused—"

Jamie's brows arched up theatrically. "But you *left* me!"

"For the prince, Douglas—"

"Of *course* for the prince; what else could you have done?" Jamie grinned, then shrugged. "Still, it might save a man some grief, aye? The knowing?" He laughed. "I suppose you might have met some measure of disbelief in me—although at that moment I'd have grasped at anything! Had you told me then, in those last minutes as I lay dying a mortal death—my *first* mortal death—"

"I couldn't." MacLeod moved again, approaching.

"But you knew," Jamie hissed.

"I knew."

Jamie stroked his beard, affecting hurt feelings. "I thought you'd know me, when you came to the play," he said mournfully. "Oh, I'll admit I've changed a wee bit since then—I'm *clean* now, and my hair's properly combed, and my face isn't smashed, or my chest so broken I can't stand up, and I've gained weight and grown me a beard . . ." He stared down from the stage, challenging. "Was I so easily forgotten, MacLeod? The Red Douglas, the giant, the Highlander who wanted so badly to wrest control of Scotland back from the Sassenachs?" He paused. "Ah, but I suppose I was no' so different, in wanting that freedom . . . was I? Didn't you desire the same. *Once?*"

MacLeod's confession: unadorned, unmitigated. "I did."

"And now?" Douglas smiled within the trimmed thicket of ruddy beard, enjoying himself. "Would you swear it again, laddie?"

"Douglas—"

And into his role again, sliding effortlessly into Shakespeare's Macduff in stance and elocution: " '*This avarice/ Sticks deeper; grows with more pernicious root/Than summer-seeming lust:*' " Douglas hoisted the claymore so that light ran off the steel—" '*and it hath been/The sword of our slain kings*"—he smiled down upon MacLeod—" '*yet do not fear; Scotland hath foisons to fill up your will/Of your mere own: all these are portable/With other graces weigh'd.*' "

"Douglas—"

" '*O Scotland, Scotland!*' " He laughed, then lamented: " '*Bleed, bleed, poor country!*' "

MacLeod halted at the stage. "What do you want, Douglas?"

Jamie stared down upon him, motion and quoting arrested. In his left hand he held the claymore; in his right, shut up within a fist, a lighter. With infinite care he opened his hand and displayed the lighter, then kindled flame.

He lifted that flame to his face, so that its modest light danced within the shrinking pupil of one amber eye. Beard and hair glinted ruddy. Then James Douglas turned, knelt, held the lighter to the foot of the cross.

It licked up, a tongue of fire that ran up wood, then shrouded the wrapped cross until every part of it blazed atop the cairn of stone.

The flame was reflected in the mirror-bright blaze of claymore blade; backlighted the huge man in an eloquent, elegant statement: *No man may ignore this. No Scot may turn his back.*

Shakespeare was banished. No more Sassenach playwright out of place in this thing of Scots, of Highlanders, of warriors sworn to princes, but a proper man in it: Robert Burns, Scotland's greatest poet, roared out of a massive throat. Transforming a modern theater into a battlefield, and the summoning of Gaels to war.

> *"Scots, wha hae wi' Wallace bled,*
> *Scots, wham Bruce has aften led,*
> *Welcome to your gory bed*
> *Or to victorie."*

MacLeod placed hands upon the edge of the stage and with one fluid movement hoisted himself up. He came to the base of the prop cairn, downslope of the burning cross. Reflected flames blazed in dark eyes, set hollows into his face, defined contours and rigidity. "Stop this, Douglas. Speak plain English to me—or Gaelic, if you will!—but no more of this quoting. If you've come for my head, say so."

But James Douglas merely stepped back from the blazing cross, hoisted the massive claymore, shook back his mane of hair and quoted Burns a final time.

> *"Lay the proud usurpers low!*
> *Tyrants fall in every foe!*
> *Liberty's in every blow!*
> *Let us do, or die!'"*

Chapter Twelve

She came in near closing, and stayed through last call. Dawson noticed her because she was a woman, and alone; it was not a response born of sexism—Joe knew better than to make any assumptions of women—but of rarity. Women for the most part still did not walk into bars alone; if one did, generally she was met in short order by a friend or a date. The club was not a singles joint, but it was not unheard of for a man and a woman to meet there for the first time in common appreciation of the blues.

But this woman did not share that appreciation. She ordered a drink indifferently, watched the musicians without interest, bided her time, bored; and he knew she was there for something more than a drink, the music, or male companionship. Joe wasn't certain why that should be so: she was an attractive woman, if lacking in the sort of blatant appeal that stopped men dead in their tracks. Late thirties, he judged; clean-featured, dark-haired, blue-eyed, clad in nondescript clothing. But it was her hands he noticed most: they were slender, long-fingered, elegant, and beautifully manicured. The hands of a pianist.

His bartender, Mike, had handled last call a half hour before, but Dawson took up his cane and made his way to the table nearest the front door. He marked the hands again as every man would: a ring—a flash of silver—but not on her wedding finger. On her right hand.

Joe smiled, preparing to offer greeting, but as she glanced up he was met with a smile of dazzling beauty—it lighted up her face—and, oddly, amused curiosity. Startled by the unexpected bounty of her smile and the juxtaposition of a curiosity quite apart from the interest displayed by a woman looking for a man, he could find no words sufficient to his intent, which was merely to welcome her; but he began again mentally and managed it after all.

"Welcome," he said. "You've just missed last call, but I think I can make an exception if you'd like another drink. The owner's a friend of mine."

"Is he, now?" she asked. "And here I'd been told he's a lawful man, Joe Dawson—are *you* telling me he bends the rules?"

He laughed quietly, if self-consciously, and reached for something inane to turn the embarrassment. "You're Irish."

"I am. Mary Margaret O'Connell." The smile came again. "And you are Joe Dawson. You're better looking in person."

He blinked in surprise. "Thanks, but—I'm afraid you have me at a disadvantage."

"Only because I knew I was coming, and looked you up." She made a fluid gesture with one lovely hand. "Can a woman invite a man to sit down in his own pub?" She paused, amended it. "Bar."

"She can, and he will." Joe pulled out a chair. "And I like the sound of the word 'pub' in place of 'bar.' Sounds warmer, friendlier." He glanced at her left wrist. "Since you know me, you must be——"

"Oh, indeed." Mary Margaret O'Connell's blue eyes lighted with unalloyed amusement. "Would you have me show you, or will you take my word for it?"

"Well, seeing as how I could go look you up in the files, I'll assume you're who you say you are. Mary Margaret O'Connell."

"You'll do it anyway, when I'm gone. But you'll see I'm

there." She slid her sleeve back to check her watch; it displayed the tattoo briefly, as perhaps she intended. "I've come for the game."

It startled him. "The Game?"

"Oh, not *that* Game—no, I mean the other one. Joe Dawson and his legendary poker game."

He rubbed thoughtfully at his short-cropped beard. "I didn't realize so many people knew about it."

Dryly she said, "There are not so many places in the world where we may congregate for a friendly game."

"That's true enough." He eyed her curiously. "But surely you didn't come only for my poker game."

She shook her head. "Because of Annie Devlin."

It shocked Dawson. "Annie Devlin's *here*?"

"She is."

"But—isn't that dangerous for her? She was arrested here three years ago for attempted assassination—"

"And died here," the Irishwoman said. "Oh, the body disappeared, but no one who saw that body broken against the ground would believe it was she, alive, if they saw her again. Would you?"

After a moment he shook his head. "No. Not if I didn't know what she was."

"But you do, and so do I." Her face was abruptly stiff, as if it hurt her to speak. "She's a murdering bitch who ought to be hanged for her crimes, except she'd only rouse to murder again."

Her expression chilled Joe. "Ms. O'Connell—"

"Mattie," she interrupted.

"Mattie," he agreed. "Do we have a problem, here? If you're unhappy with your assignment, you can be reassigned."

"And leave her to whom? I have certain credentials that make me ideal for this assignment."

"And I have certain responsibilities to the organization," Dawson declared. "If there's a problem—"

"There isn't."

"You've heard about Horton. The Watchers who hunt."

"I've heard." Her mouth twisted faintly. "And no, I'm not

one of them; it's only *this* Immortal I don't care for, Joe. And I honor my oath. I Watch, I don't interfere."

He relaxed slightly. "What credentials, Mattie?"

She drew in a breath. "Hugh O'Neill," she said.

"Annie Devlin's teacher."

"And my lover," she said plainly. "It's how I came to be a Watcher, Joe. I knew what he was—he trusted me with it—and when he was killed, the organization decided to make use of me." Her eyes were steady as she looked at him. "Because of Hugh, I know what Annie is. I know her habits. I more than any am suited to be her Watcher—but I don't have to like it."

"Fair enough," he agreed. "But if you were O'Neill's lover, why are you so opposed to Annie Devlin?"

"I'm Protestant," she said. "And I've no problem with being a part of England. Ireland has *never* ruled herself adequately; this is the only way we may survive."

Dawson nodded. "And Annie, raised Catholic among other things, wants Ireland free from English intervention."

"It's not that she *wants* Ireland separate," Mattie said. "It's how she goes about it. Annie and others like her kill the innocents."

Dawson felt a chill touch his spine. "Is she here for that again? To kill another ambassador?"

"I don't know why she's here," Mattie answered frankly. "But I will find out. It's why *I'm* here."

Dawson picked his way with care. "If you know Annie because of Hugh O'Neill—"

"I know *of* Annie because of Hugh O'Neill. We never met. By the time Hugh and I became lovers, Annie was decades gone. But he followed her career; in Ireland, among the IRA and others, she's a bloody hero." Her face twisted briefly. "I know her by what he's said of her."

"But Hugh O'Neill was himself a patriot," Dawson said. "He *trained* Annie as much in fanaticism as in the tools an Immortal needs to survive!"

"He did," Mattie said quietly, "and repented of it."

"Hugh O'Neill?"

Her smile was brief and bittersweet. "There was a precedent," she said quietly. "Darius killed for centuries in war after war, until he found God. Hugh didn't find God, perhaps—not the way Darius did—but he found something other than fanaticism. Than terrorism." She closed her left hand over her right, over the silver ring: two hands clasping a heart. "Things have changed in the last few years, Joe. Even now there is a kind of peace in Ireland; even now there are attempts to settle the troubles. In the year before he died, Hugh found reason to believe it might hold, to believe there might be sense in it. Peace, instead of war. Progress in place of habit, instead of rhetoric for the noise." She looked steadily at Joe. "Men do change. Even Immortals."

"Even Annie Devlin?"

The woman's face hardened. "I don't know."

"Because if she's come to kill another political figure—"

"Would you interfere?"

"I don't know," Dawson answered forthrightly. "Would you? With all that's at stake if we're investigated?"

She weighed that, assessed his expression. Finally she sighed. "I don't know."

Joe nodded. "And now would you care to tell me why you called last night about a certain red-haired actor?"

Delicate color suffused her face.

"Why the secrecy?" he prodded. "You could have told me who you were. And you certainly didn't need to hide your accent."

She stared hard at her hands a moment. The silver ring glinted in the muted light. "It's been a long time," she said finally.

That baffled him. "Long time?"

Mattie O'Connell drew in a deep breath, released it quickly in a brief gust of sound. "I'd heard about you, Joe. From a woman-friend of mine, one of us. She showed me your picture in the files. And I, well . . . I wanted to hear if the voice fit the image."

With effort he contained a cough of startled laughter. "And what's the verdict?"

Mattie O'Connell smiled. "Will there be a game tonight?"

"Tomorrow night," Joe said, diverted. "Same time, same place."

"Good." She rose, picked up the raincoat she'd draped over the chairback. "I'll be here."

He sought to delay her. "You haven't given me an answer."

"Tomorrow night," she said, smiling. "Same time, same place."

The cross of war blazed atop the cairn in the theater, illuminating the backdrop. Flames bled the length of steel blade raised beside it, polished near to blinding. MacLeod, on the stage, eased into a balanced stance with the faintest shifting of weight. "Is it my head you want?"

James Douglas stopped quoting poetry and laughed. "No, laddie. I want all of you, and whole. I want an oath of you, but better than the one you gave me at Culloden."

That stung. "He was my liege lord," MacLeod declared sharply. "Yours, as well as mine. You'd have done the same."

"Left you there? With your jaw smashed so you choked on your own blood—so you could not so much as pray!—and your chest cut to pieces—? Oh, aye, I suppose so . . ." Douglas lowered the claymore and set its tip by one foot. An immense man, commanding cairn and stage. "I agree, you had no choice. But now you do."

"What choice?" MacLeod asked.

"To give such service to Scotland as you gave to her then, in the carnage of Culloden." The actor paused. "If you have anything left in you that is Scottish, and honorable."

"A campaign, was it?" MacLeod asked grimly. "To remind me of something you believe I might have forgotten?"

Douglas bared teeth. "I'd have tried talking with you, laddie, but you'd not have heard. It served me to *show* you such things as what we were, we Scots: Gaelic, the play, the things I had delivered by unsuspecting mortals . . ." He shrugged.

"The feather under my door?" Anger cracked in MacLeod's voice. "You weren't even alive at Killiecrankie!"

Douglas was unperturbed. "But *you* were. And it was nearly the last victory we had of the English, that day by the river. Och, I read about it—I've read about them all, the battles we won, and lost. So, the red feather, Dundee's symbol; and the heather, and the wee scrap of tartan, and the pipe music . . . all intended to remind you of what you were."

Coldly he said, "I know very well what I was."

"But what are you *now*, MacLeod? Oh, I know—four hundred years and more can bend a man's spirit in ways he wasn't born, but his soul?" He shook his head. "Bred of her bones, MacLeod, those old, unassailable stones, and suckled on the water running free and cold in the burns." Douglas placed a hand against his chest. "She lives here, does Scotland; a day doesn't go by when I don't think of her."

"And so you will steal the Honours."

"And anything else we can that belongs to the people."

"To what purpose?"

"To remind what is now little more than an extension of England that once we were more, and separate from the Sassenachs."

"That's not good enough."

"But it *is*, laddie! The Honours belong to the people, not the government. And the government—"

"Is Scottish," Duncan reminded him. "Scotland owns the Honours, Jamie—"

"And England owns Scotland!" Douglas roared back. "Good Christ, man, have you forgotten what we fought for, that day at Culloden? How we swore to King James at Dalcomera? How we marched out so neatly before the guns of Butcher Cumberland, who blew us to shreds in the space of an hour—and most of our culture, too?" Beside him, the cross yet blazed. "In the name of all that's holy, MacLeod, *I died for my king* that day at Drummossie Moor! And if it weren't for some uncanny stroke of Fate that brought me back from mortal death, I'd *still* be dead, thrown down into a mass grave with all the other lads so that no one could mourn us at the place where our bones lie." His face was white and tense. "How can you even suggest any other reason is required than to stuff our pride up English arses?"

"Not everyone sees history as you do," MacLeod retorted, "or the repercussions. Would you care to explain to the Scots people what stealing their Honours is all about?"

"And so I will!" Jamie shouted. "But first we'll have them, laddie-boy . . . first we'll take them, and then we'll hide them, and then we'll mount our campaign. It's not so different than what the Irish do, aye?"

"The Irish kill the English, they don't steal from them—" And then MacLeod stopped. "Annie." It hurt, that comprehension. Sharply. Unexpectedly.

Douglas might have laughed, but he did not. "The Irish understand better than most what it means to lose one's soul to the Sassenachs. But Annie came of her own free will. She is a Celt, as we are, with her own stake in this."

MacLeod conjured it again into his mind, the quietude of her voice, the words that were, for her, as alien as any he had heard. *"And if I stopped—if I pledged myself to something else, something as justified, but with no bloodshed involved . . . would you believe me then?"*

And he had hoped, had believed, had abetted. Had brought himself to this point, to this place, before the cross of war.

"They're in their graves, all of them," James Douglas said quietly. "Montrose, who was hanged for his service. Wallace, drawn and quartered. Dundee: shot dead on the field of battle. And every man before them who died in the name of our homeland." The pale amber eyes were steady. "Do you not believe it's time we honored the oaths we made?"

"We are *different*," MacLeod said; as he had said it once to Joe Dawson. But this man understood. "You know that, now. We are not like other men—"

"Mortal men?" Douglas hitched a broad shoulder in casual dismissal of the obvious. "Do you mean to say the oath of a Highlander to his king, to Scotland, means nothing be he Immortal? That he owes the service of his soul only to himself, and not to his people?"

It was discomfiting logic. Duncan MacLeod had been a Scot for thirty years before he died and learned the truth of his kind; was indeed bred of her bones, her stones; had suckled on the water running fast in her burns and rivers. Whatever the truth of his Immortal begetting, MacLeod had been a Scot before anything else.

But he was something different, now. There was more at stake than oaths. And yet as he looked on the blazing cross, the unsheathed claymore, the giant Scotsman, he was not certain he could be other than he had been once: Highlander, sworn to Scotland and her kings. He had *died* for Scotland and those very kings, as he died at Killiecrankie, in the name of an oath.

With difficulty he said, "And if I walk away from you now, Douglas . . . is it my head you'll come for then?"

The man grinned. "Laddie, if I'd wanted your head I'd have come for you before now." The cadence of their homeland crept again into his words. "And I dinna think Scotland has so many men in her service she can sacrifice Duncan MacLeod." He motioned with his head toward one of the back exits. "Go, MacLeod. Go again to the exhibits, look again on Culloden, look again on the Honours of Scotland. And tell me, once you have done so, that a man who has killed in the name of his country cannot steal in it as well." He paused, smiled affably, shifted the pitch of his tone from dramatic to nonchalance. "There's a tale told of Scots patriots who once went in secret into an abbey, into the sanctity of a Sassenach church in the heart of London, and robbed a king."

MacLeod went very still.

James Douglas laughed. "I know you, Duncan MacLeod. You have killed for your king. You have stolen for your people. How dare you play the hypocrite and stand before me now, mouthing *bullshit* about my decision to liberate the Honours not being good enough? You're a bloody fool, MacLeod, if you expect me to accept that excuse. I know what you are, I know what you've done." He slammed the point of the claymore into the prop cairn. "Steal for her again, MacLeod! Steal Scotland's past in the name of Scotland's future!"

Chapter Thirteen

Westminster Abbey, London, 1950

It was undeniably daring, dangerous, and wholly intoxicating. Here they were in London, on the grounds of Westminster Abbey next to the Houses of Parliament, sneaking around like Highland laddie-boys snooving down through the heather.

Which, MacLeod thought, was entirely appropriate in view of who they were and what they did. The differences, however, were manifest: there was stone and brick beneath their feet instead of turf and heather, they wore baggy trousers and ragged sweaters in place of kilts and plaids, and they were weaponless. No man among them carried a dirk or a sgian dhu, and certainly none of them intended to kill the enemy. This time, they meant mearly to steal from him.

Killing was a demonstrably impressive insult, but too quickly forgotten by the man who no longer breathed. This insult would stick in Sassenach craws for all the many years of Duncan MacLeod's life, even long after the mortals he assisted were buried themselves.

*A proposition made over ale, among a handful of Scots pa-
triots, Glasgow University students, who studied the history
of their ancestors in addition to their contemporaries. For
Duncan, too old for student but of their company because he
was, like them, a Scot, drank in the same pub, and knew more
of the history they studied—albeit of a far more intimate acquaintanceship. It was a mad scheme he doubted they could
accomplish. But it was worth the trying. And worth far more
if they actually succeeded—which he had every intention of
insuring. They had proposed the idea; he had helped them
plot the plan and offered to see to the riskiest part of it.*

*Westminster Abbey was, after all, a church. Tourists vis-
ited it, kings and queens were crowned in it, but it also
served its true function. And worshiping was difficult when
church doors were locked. It required only that they plan
how to hide within the Abbey when it was time for tourists
to leave; but where else was so ideal as the undercroft, the
catacomb-like vaults deep beneath the stone floor?*

*Afterward it was merely a matter of creeping up the nar-
row stairs, of flitting down the side aisles of the spectacular
Gothic cathedral like wraiths chased out by God, and to find
the throne. The Coronation Chair.*

*And to liberate from it the stone beneath its seat, fastened
into place so that any monarch of England also became
monarch of Scotland according to the old ways, because the
rightful king or queen was, by Scots tradition, to be crowned
while seated upon the Stone of Scone.*

*For centuries the Stone had been in English hands,
trapped beneath English arses. It was time to take it back, to
give it into the keeping of the Scottish people, so they might
know some pride again as they had in the days of the clans,
before Culloden ended them.*

*MacLeod handed out the tools, kept some for himself, then
banished everyone to their tasks: to pretend they tended the
carved floor markers in the Abbey under which the remains
of kings and queens and certain gifted commoners were
buried, so that no one, entering, would suspect what MacLeod
did, kneeling in poor light beside the ornate wooden throne.*

Beneath the throne, beneath the Stone, he slid a piece of

wood, padded and wrapped in cloth. Then he worked quickly and carefully at the fastenings, prying out the nails, the wires, the brackets. When he felt the Stone shift he held his breath; it dropped easily and quietly onto the padded wood.

He smiled, peered beneath the throne to make certain all was well—and was struck by horror.

"Holy Mother," he blurted, "it's broken!"

Half of the Stone lay on his piece of wood. The other half remained fastened beneath the throne.

Had he—? Surely not. He had been too careful. He had used no chisel, no pry-bar; had merely eased out the fastenings to allow the stone to drop but inches onto the wood.

"You bloody fool, MacLeod," he berated himself. "Have you split the Stone into pieces the way the Sassenachs split the clans?"

It was ironic, that: that he, a Highlander who had died for his country more times than anyone else—save perhaps for Connor MacLeod—might have sundered the thing held by his people to be the most sacred of all.

No time for recriminations. MacLeod dragged the padded wood out from under the throne, transferred the chunk of stone to a gardener's wheelbarrow, and bent again to free the other half. When it too resided in the wheelbarrow, he enfolded both of them in thick cloth, piled his tools on top, then began a hasty but silent journey toward the nearest door giving out into the gardens.

He told no one it was broken. He did not know how he could. They would see it soon enough, when he handed it over to the students bound home to Glasgow; his task was to remain behind and observe what the English did in answer to the theft.

There would be much outcry and calls for punishment. But by then the Stone of Scone would be safe at home in Scotland, and Duncan MacLeod would be most content to read the newspapers and laugh up his sleeve at the red-faced Sassenachs outdone by bold Highlanders.

It wouldn't make up for Culloden, for what was lost that day, but it was a piece of Scotland won back from the enemy.

* * *

In the theater, from atop his personal stone, James Douglas flung his claymore without warning through the air. It glinted in flames, came down from the cairn without a hand to guide it beyond the one that had released it. MacLeod caught it, took its weight, settled it into his palms as if it lived in his grasp, as indeed once one very like it had, on the braes of Craigh Ellaich by the Pass of Killiecrankie.

"We *are* different," Douglas said, "we who cannot die save by the separation of head from body. But we are also men, and in this we are the *same*: born of Scotland, bred of the Highlands, reared to honor oaths. And so I ask you, one Scot to another: Do you honor the one you made to our home?"

No one had honored oaths and home quite as MacLeod had. And Douglas plainly knew it.

Annie. MacLeod had told Annie that night beside the lighthouse how he had stolen in Scotland's name.

And Annie had told Douglas, who used it now.

Time, MacLeod thought, he took control of the conversation.

With pointed deliberation, Duncan looked at the cross atop the cairn. "Do you mean to burn down the theater?" he asked lightly. "That might piss me off. My taxes paid for it."

It stopped James Douglas, who stared.

MacLeod slung the sword back to arc through the air, slicing toward the flame. "I know the weight of my soul, I know what lives in it. No man but me *can*."

Douglas was on his feet as he caught the claymore. "Damn your eyes, MacLeod—"

"You'll know," he said evenly, "when I am ready to tell you. Not before. Save your wind, Red Douglas. You'll need it for the play." He paused briefly. "Or perhaps to put out the fire. You've got enough hot air in you to float the Goodyear blimp."

Richie lounged back bonelessly in the glass-and-wood partitioned dojo office, phone set against one ear. He nodded, heavy-lidded, smiling fatuously. "*Oh* yeah," he murmured. "Oh *yeah*—no, no, I like the sound of that. Keep it coming, babe—it's hot . . . yeah, I think I can get off on that—"

But cold water intervened in the personage of Joe Dawson coming in the dojo door. The arrival *and* the expression on the older man's face prompted Richie to cut short his conversation despite its attractions; Teresa, he hoped, would understand. And if not, well, he could always make it up to her. Wherever, whenever and however she'd like it, which was how *he* liked it. Wherever, whenever, and however.

By the time he was off the phone Dawson stood in the office doorway. "Where's MacLeod? Upstairs?"

"No." Richie untangled the phone cord from a cup of pens and pencils before all could be tipped out. "Something wrong, Joe?"

"I don't know." Dawson was rarely this serious. "Maybe. I tried calling last night, but his machine was on—and it was busy when I called a while ago."

Richie's face warmed. "I, uh—that was me. I grabbed something to eat out of his refrigerator and made a call." The first of three to Teresa, but he wouldn't confess to that. "What's up?"

"Trouble, maybe. Maybe not." Dawson shrugged. "When do you expect him back?"

Richie shrugged. "No idea. You know Mac: he comes, he goes . . ." He banished levity. "If it's that important, I can give him the message."

"I know." Dawson shook his head. "It's not any of my business, and yet it is . . . I am his Watcher—"

"Joe—"

Dawson sighed. "Annie Devlin's in town."

Richie stood up all at once, kicking the chair out of the way. He moved past Joe in the doorway, went into the dojo proper, and grabbed the push broom. Something to do. "Yeah. I know."

"What about MacLeod?"

"Oh, I think he knows." Richie wielded the broom with ferocious intent, tending a spotless floor. "Matter of fact, I *know* he knows. I assume he's out somewhere with her now."

"Why?" Dawson asked, puzzled.

Bristles scraped wood. "Because she spent the night last night."

"Here? With MacLeod?"

Richie grimaced, scraping harder. "Not with *me*, I can tell you that!" He stopped sweeping, straightened, hitched one shoulder in a self-conscious shrug. "No accounting for taste, I guess. Even Mac's."

Dawson didn't respond to the halfhearted and failed attempt at sarcasm. He was in deadly earnest, clearly concerned. "It could be a setup, Richie."

He barked a brief, disbelieving laugh. "Annie Devlin could never beat Mac, Joe—and I don't think she wants to. She said as much when she came here."

"And you *believed* her?"

Richie sighed. "I don't know. It's none of my business, you know? MacLeod doesn't exactly ask my opinion on who to date."

"He's very good, and he's very lucky," Dawson declared flatly, "but he's not immune to manipulation. No man is."

"Then *you* tell him," Richie said, curbing a shout of frustration with effort. "You might have better luck."

"Maybe I will," Joe agreed. "If I knew where they were."

Richie shrugged. "Beats me. She's Irish, he's Scottish . . . what's the likeliest place?" He laughed briefly, bitterly. "Besides bed."

Dawson's eyes were distant. "I think I know. I think just *maybe* I know where they are . . . where a Scot might take an Irishwoman with history in common."

"Do you want me?" Richie asked.

Joe shook his head. "No, thanks."

Richie, leaning on the push broom, watched Joe Dawson make his deliberate way out of the dojo. He watched, considered, then set the broom against the nearest weight bench. From the wall rack he took down one of the practice katanas, ignoring the shorter wakizashi, moved to the center of the floor where there were no obstructions—and with grave, self-absorbed intensity began to perform one of MacLeod's favorite katas.

In a world of Immortals where the Game had deadly results, no such thing existed as being overtrained. And no one, *under*trained, survived an encounter to regret the lack of practice.

Furious, James Douglas watched Duncan MacLeod stride away up the center aisle and into the lobby, long coat rippling. He thought of shouting after him, but caught himself in time; they had said what there was to say between them for the moment, and more would be overkill. Instead, shaking, Jamie turned to the still-burning cross and caught it in one hand, ripping it from the pocket in the prop stone cairn. That it burned his flesh, that it blistered the outer skin and then ate through into fat and muscle and tendon, blood and serum sizzling, meant nothing more than assuagement.

He hurled the cross down onto the stage itself and stood there atop the cairn, breathing noisily, one hand burned and the other clutching claymore. "Damn your eyes," he muttered. "I *will* have you!" He drew breath to shout it, to release residual tension, but before he could fill the theater with his voice Colin Cameron was there, hastening out from the nearest wing with a fire extinguisher in his hands. Douglas, startled, watched him put out the flames, and then began to laugh. "Good lad," he said, grinning. "A pity to burn down this grand new building before our run is through!"

Cameron shut off the extinguisher. Dry chemical—monoammonium phosphate, mixed with silicates and mica—coated the cross in a white shroud and frosted his hands and forearms. He coughed, scrubbed an arm across his forehead, left a streak of chemical dust in his dark hair that aged him on the spot. "Are you daft, Jamie?"

"No," Douglas answered, "dedicated." He climbed down the cairn. "As you should be, Coll, if you are to survive." He stepped from the last tumbled pile of "stone" onto the surface of the stage.

Cameron set down the extinguisher. "Should I call a stagehand?"

"No, I'll tend it." Jamie smiled; his palm tingled already as flesh healed itself. "Since you're so good at spying, why not spy for me now? Follow MacLeod, see where he goes, whom he talks to, then come back to me."

"Jamie . . ." Colin's brow creased. "What do you really want with MacLeod?"

Douglas sighed. "He's a proud, stubborn Scot, Coll-my-lad. He is granite, is bonnie Duncan, like Signal Rock in Glencoe, unmoved by such irritants as snow and wind and rain. When he gives his heart to a thing it *stays* given, aye?—and thus he keeps it locked away until he's certain of the giving."

"But—this . . ."

"Dramatics," Douglas said briefly. "A way of chipping away at the stone. Of setting a chisel into the crease and hammering at it with unflagging effort, bit by bit, until a crack is set into the granite and the stone opens its heart."

"You can't *force* him, Jamie!"

"Oh, but I can. One need only know how and where to set the chisel." He put a broad hand on Cameron's shoulder. "You see, I've found the crease, and I've set the chisel, and I've whacked away at it. The chips have begun to fly. I've let in the daylight, Coll, and the bonnie brave heart knows it." He squeezed the shoulder briefly, then released it. "Go, lad. As Will Shakespeare might say: He'll be ours on the morrow."

"But—how can you be so sure?"

"Because he knows the truth of himself," Jamie answered. "Because he knows *I* know that nearly fifty years ago a group of rebellious Scots stole the Stone of Scone from beneath the Coronation Chair in Westminster Abbey, and he was one of them."

"MacLeod?"

The giant Scot laughed. "Och, laddie, you've a wee bit to learn of people. Especially of Duncan MacLeod." He jerked his head toward the seats. "Now, go—before you lose him."

Cameron hesitated. "Won't he know I'm there?"

Patiently, Jamie explained: "You're not one of us yet, Coll. Only incipient, like a sneeze."

"But you knew what I was right away. You said so!"

"Because you ran right into me, Coll, and bounced off so

hard you fell. I picked you up, remember? We were close enough to *kiss,* laddie." Jamie arched a brow. "So long as you keep your distance, MacLeod will never know. That I promise."

Joe Dawson, carefully navigating the low-risered polished granite steps onto the plaza before the glass facade, was relieved when he saw MacLeod come out of the theater. The relief compounded itself when he saw MacLeod was alone.

"Mac!" One last step, and he was on the same level though distance yet separated them. "MacLeod—wait!"

The Immortal tensed, then swung toward him. Nowhere was the lethal katana in evidence, and yet Dawson knew it was present. Only rarely did MacLeod go anywhere without it, and certainly not when he was with another Immortal.

Which brought Joe to the point as he closed the gap between them just before the main entrance. "Look, this is awkward for me—and maybe I shouldn't be doing this at all, but, well . . ." He paused, balancing against the cane.

"Spit it out, Joe," MacLeod said curtly; there was nothing of patience or ease in him this morning. Dawson had seen that before, that tight-wound tension, the barely suppressed anger. Not often—MacLeod was an infinitely and impressively charming man, and had had four centuries to learn to control his emotions—but no man was blind to it when Duncan MacLeod let the mask slip.

Mentally girding his loins, Dawson joined the fray. "It's none of my business who you sleep with, MacLeod—"

"You're right about that."

"—but I have to tell you that she's dangerous. Annie Devlin *lives* to kill people, mortal and Immortal—"

"She isn't here for me."

"And what about James Douglas?" Dawson shifted tack. "What do you know about him, MacLeod?"

"More than you know, Joe."

Dawson managed a brief laugh, trying to ease the moment. "And you can bet I don't like it. Gaps in the record are dangerous."

"*Frustrating* for you and the others, maybe, but not dangerous, Joe. And not exactly something I'm opposed to. It affords some privacy." MacLeod glanced briefly at the theater behind him. "What Douglas wants isn't my head. It's something personal, private, and it has nothing to do with Immortals."

"No?" Dawson shook his head. "An Immortal who knows you, but you don't know him—and Annie Devlin. In the same place. Don't you think that's odd?"

"Not particularly. We do occasionally hang out together." The tone was exquisitely dry. "We have a lot in common."

"Yeah, like the Game," Dawson retorted. "Put two or more Immortals together, and sometimes one of you ends up dead!"

"This isn't about taking heads, Joe. I've told you that. It's—" But he broke off, stilled, and Dawson knew.

He twisted, using the cane. "Where—?"

There: Slim, petite, lovely woman, auburn hair flowing over slender shoulders, hands tucked into the pockets of her raincoat.

Smaller than I thought . . . He knew her at once, as every Watcher did; as Mattie O'Connell, her current Watcher; as Tara Kelly, her former Watcher; as Hugh O'Neill, Immortal, who had taught her to fight. Had forged her into a weapon in the fires of Ireland.

The light in her old/young eyes was not of curiosity, not of courtesy, but of something akin to challenge. He was a mortal. He did not count. But he was with MacLeod in a place were Immortals plotted.

MacLeod smiled at her briefly, intimately, then glanced at Dawson. "See you later, Joe."

Dismissal. Dawson acknowledged her with a strained smile, cast a speaking glance at MacLeod, and went.

Later. If there was a later.

His world was flame, and pain. Blood painted his vision so that what he saw was red, red and black, or the fading colors of sodden tartan cloth loomed in Highland glens, now trampled into blood-soaked, shredded turf.

Everywhere, blood. The stench of ordure, of vomit, of fear so thick it was tangible. He had not lost self-control yet, not faced the final indignity of a body controlling the brain, of the will gone flaccid as flesh split apart, rent by bullets, by cannon shot, cut open by bayonets.

He tried to speak and could not, tried to call out, tried even to pray, and found his mouth could not shape the words, the curses, even the slogan of his clan: A Douglas! A Douglas!

James Douglas was dying, and he knew it.

Denied it.

Challenged it with all the immensity of his body, the integrity of his spirit.

Up . . . somehow up, gagging, spitting. He could not help but swallow the blood, and he choked on it, fighting not to vomit. Bones grated within his chest, moved as they should not. A sound issued from raw throat, unformed but furious protest that his body dared challenge his will with its weakness.

Up, somehow up . . . and then a man was there, running through a haze of powder smoke, calling out to him amidst the thunder of the artillery, stretching out blood- and dirt-stained hands; he too had done his share of killing this day, this blood-wracked travesty of a day.

Not gone yet, this day . . . nor was he; and now a man with him, a Scot, kilt-clad, plaid-brooch glinting through a smear of blood in wan sunlight. Bearing him up, helping him to rise, to steady himself. Through the unceasing roar in his head he heard the man's voice, the Gaelic, the words that would drive him on as the whip drove on a flagging horse.

Chapter Fourteen

MacLeod leaned close, kissed her. Annie met it with quick answering passion, but withdrew abruptly, turning to look after Joe Dawson as he made his way down the steps.

"Who is he?"

MacLeod shrugged. "A friend."

"More than that," she said. "He knows something—I saw the way he looked at me."

He offered his most impish smile. "Joe has very good taste in women."

Annie was not dissuaded. "I tell you, he knows something."

He shrugged, carefully casual. "What can he know, Annie? I never told him what I am, or what *you* are." Which was quite true; Joe Dawson already knew very well by the time he and Duncan MacLeod met.

"Is he a cop?"

MacLeod laughed, thrusting his hands deep into coat pockets. "No, Joe is not a cop."

"A reporter, maybe."

"He owns a saloon."

"And that's all?" Annie pressed, still suspicious. "I'm wanted, MacLeod . . . and I don't want to be sent to prison. It would be dead boring—and difficult to explain how it is I outlive everyone else!" Her stare was steady. "If you don't tell me the truth, I'll go ask the man myself."

She would. He knew it. She knew he knew it. She depended on it.

"He might not tell you."

Annie Devlin smiled coolly. "Oh, I think he would."

MacLeod stopped bantering. "Leave Joe out of it."

"Then tell me. *You* tell me, in your way, instead of him in his."

It was something. More than nothing. But not much. "All right." He glanced beyond her to the fountains. "He knows."

"How much?"

"All of it." MacLeod shrugged, giving up. "They Watch, Annie. Nothing more. They Watch, they record. They don't interfere." He sighed, looking across the plaza to the greensward; Joe Dawson was safely gone. "We are insects, mounted; datapoints, stored—"

Bitterly, "Trophy heads on the wall?"

"No."

"Sweet Jesus, MacLeod—"

He grasped her arm and escorted her to one of the fountains, where he shoved her down on the curve of marble bench carved out of the surrounding wall. The fountain's pool was already speckled on the bottom by copper pennies, as well as the silvered shine of the occasional dime and nickel.

"Sit," he commanded brusquely. She sat because he made certain she had no choice, but thrust to her feet the moment he released her arm. He caught her again. Insisted she sit again with a deft maneuver. "Stay."

Her glare was sulfurous as he loomed over her, but she stayed lest he apply markedly undignified force again. Which he *would* do—and she had the grace to know it. Also there were people, mortals, going in and out of the exhibit halls; her avocation in Ireland's behalf had trained her not to draw attention to herself.

"What do you mean?" she asked tightly. "They watch? They *record*?"

"Just what it sounds like, Annie." With the spray behind her and mist droplets settling onto her hair, it was easy to see her again as he had seen her more than seventy-five years before: in the green hills of Ireland, at dawn, on the run from English troops. "It's an organization that apparently has been around nearly as long as Immortals. They Watch. They commit us to Chronicles." He hesitated, then repeated with telling emphasis what he had said so casually before. "Joe Dawson's a friend."

"He's a mortal."

"A *friend*, Annie. He owns a bar, plays blues guitar, likes a good single malt as much as I do. He's been there for me before, just as he's here for me now." MacLeod paused. "Even if I don't have to like it this time."

"He'll die. They all die." Unappeased, she still glared. "Like Kerry. Like Tommy. Like *Tessa*."

He took the wound, let it bleed, sealed it closed again. "Yes," he answered steadily. "Which is why we ought to be more careful of them."

"They've nothing to do with us, Duncan!"

He used the weapon before she blunted it. "And is that why you married two of them?"

It took breath and color from her, leaching her spine of rigidity, her face of stony pride. Annie looked elsewhere then, away from him, hooking a lock of hair behind one ear. Tears shone briefly, dried as she blinked them away. Bitterly she said, "They served a purpose. For a while."

"And what purpose do *you* serve, Annie? What have you to do with Jamie Douglas?"

Now he had her full attention. "Do you think I've come for your head?"

"If you had, we'd have fought already." He smiled briefly. "One thing about you, Annie—you don't believe in games. A man knows where he stands with you."

"No lies," she said. "Not from me. Truths. I'm not in this for blood this time, MacLeod. My oath on it."

Deliberately he asked, "Does that oath serve a purpose? For a while?"

That wounded *her*. "It means something, my oath! It always has!"

"Your oath to Ireland, maybe."

"And yours to Scotland!" She tossed back mist-weighted hair so that her face was unobscured, painted hard and sharp by sunlight despite its loveliness. "No heads, no blood. We've come to steal, not kill."

It was preposterous. "You've never been a thief, Annie!"

"But you have."

It was fact, was truth; and he and Annie Devlin had not shared as many truths as perhaps they should have. "Yes."

"Then why not steal again?"

"The reasons were different then."

"How could they be different?" she shot back. "Sweet Jesus, but it's the same thing, MacLeod! You stole the Stone for Scotland in the *name* of Scotland, because you didn't want the bloody Sassenachs to have it!"

"It was a rock." It required effort to sound so matter-of-fact. "It doesn't bleed, it doesn't die."

Annie's retort was viciously succinct. "Enough men died for it. Enough men bled in its name. Even I know that."

He swung away from her abruptly so she wouldn't see how that simple truth told. Men *had* bled in its name, as had women. The young Countess of Buchan had been imprisoned by the English in a cage hung outside the wall of Berwick Castle for daring to crown Robert the Bruce upon the Stone, thereby sealing his claim in the old way as King of Scotland.

MacLeod stared blindly a long moment at the colonnaded, banner-bedecked breezeway connecting the theater with the exhibit halls. Where Scotland was *on tour*.

He heard her move. Heard the whisper of her coat, heard the sound of a single footstep. And then she clasped his right hand in both of hers, shut it firmly in her grasp. Small, slender hands—and as dangerous as his own.

"I know it," she said softly. "I know how it hurts. It's our curse to know what we had, and to know we've lost it, except for what lives in our hearts." She lifted his hand to her mouth, kissed the back of it. "And that is why we must guard so *very* carefully what little is left of our worlds, lest others destroy them. Even in innocence."

Blood, and pain, and a coldness in Jamie Douglas that filled first his belly, then spread outward to tantalize his limbs.

"Away," the Scot said. "We'll go away, apart—"

Jamie was considerably taller than the stranger, but privation had peeled pounds from him, and the wounded chest kept him bent. It was not so hard after all for the other to bear him up, to keep him on his feet, albeit they both of them staggered and stumbled.

A braw lad, MacLeod—and now that braw lad took him in hand again, bearing him away from the battle that had already sore taxed him.

More words, more cannon. And then MacLeod was down, wounded, fresh blood blooming against the darker stains of his plaid, and Douglas felt a great cry welling up within his violated chest, filling his lungs, his throat; they would die here together on this moor this day.

But MacLeod was up after all, regaining his feet, renewing his efforts to help a fellow Scot from the field. "I promise you," he said. "On my oath as a Scot, as a Highlander, as a MacLeod of the Clan MacLeod, I willna leave you."

Comfort, that a man need not die alone.

"We'll go apart, where no one may see . . ."

See what? Death? Surely they knew what it was, here at Culloden.

Down. Down after all, and limbs twisted awry, until MacLeod put them right again.

He summoned what little strength remained to him. "S-Stay—"

But he did not stay after all, MacLeod. He promised. He swore an oath. But he did not stay. As the blood bubbled into a smoke-burned throat, as Jamie choked upon vomit after all, felt his bowels loosen despite his best efforts at self-control, MacLeod deserted him.

"Jamie?"

Not MacLeod. MacLeod was gone.

"Jamie?"

Ah. Colin Cameron. And it was many miles and many years from the Battle of Culloden.

Douglas opened his eyes, found he sat in the audience, albeit there was none present; sat quite alone in a front-row seat in an empty theater, with a naked claymore resting across thick thighs.

No kilts, no Gaelic, no powder-smoke. No blood.

Douglas sighed, banishing the thunder of cannon. "Aye, Coll?"

Cameron's thin young face was very pale. "There's something you should know, Jamie. About—about men. Mortals. Who know about Immortals. And *watch* them."

Same time. Same place. Joe smiled as Mary Margaret O'Connell came into the bar, as promised. This time he wondered how he could have thought her anything but beautiful. It was in the lustrous black hair; the fine, fair skin; the steady blue eyes; the curve of her mouth. Hugh O'Neill, he decided, had been a very lucky man.

Until someone took his head.

Mike was tending bar, but Dawson was handling the last call overflow when she came in the door. She looked for him, smiled; the smile widened as he jerked his head in greeting, making change and a weak joke for a man halfway through his last beer. This time she didn't go to a table, but came directly to the bar.

"Mattie." He moved aside from the patron to the very end of the bar, hooked elbows over the edge. "What can I get you?"

"Irish whisky," she answered. "If you've anything decent."

"Oh, I think we can rustle you up something suitable." He turned, caught Mike's attention, put in the order.

"So," she said, "did you look me up?"

"I did." He examined for offense taken, saw none. "Tara Kelly's replacement."

Mattie slid onto a stool, slender eloquent hands unbuttoning her coat. "Well then . . . what *about* me?"

Joe turned aside to accept two glasses of whisky from Mike, handed one to her. "What about you? Well, you're thirty-nine years old, Dublin-born; went to university in London, where you read history; and for the last three years you've been Annie Devlin's Watcher." He grinned, raised his glass. *"Slàinte."*

Her smile widened. "Back at you, Joseph Dawson." They tapped glasses, sipped, looked on one another with a sudden comfortable affinity. "And does the file also say I am a widow?"

He sobered. "It does. And that Hugh O'Neill was the saving of you."

"He was that. I didn't want to live after Patrick was killed." She hitched a slender shoulder, met his eyes steadily. "Married at thirty-two, widowed at thirty-three. Six months later Hugh came into my life like a door snatched out of your hand and slammed open in a storm, and did not go out again until Chang took his head." She lifted the glass, sipped; her eyes were dark now, pupils expanding in the dim bar lighting. "I've been three years without him, Watching Annie Devlin, and not a day goes by that I don't think of him."

Dawson took a deep, slow breath, nodded. "I lost someone to an Immortal, too. His name was Durgan. Hers was Lauren, and she was mortal. Like me."

"Ah, Joe, I'm sorry." She touched his hand briefly in honest compassion. "Here I'm thinking of myself, not of you."

"Why should you?" he asked roughly, oddly affected by her empathy. "You only met me yesterday."

Her eyes were steady. "When another door opened."

His hand gripped the glass more tightly. "I don't slam them often."

"Ah, but there are storms, and there are breezes." Her smile was calmly glorious. "And just now I'm not needing a storm."

He reached down, caught up the cane, set it atop the bar with an audible thump.

She did not even look at it. "I know," she said simply. "It matters to some people."

"Then they are the handicapped. Not you." She raised her glass again. "*Sguab as e*, Joe Dawson. Take it down."

Chapter Fifteen

Left to their own devices by, respectively, Teresa and Annie, both of whom claimed, respectively and individually, to have other things to do—vitally important things best done without interference by males who believed they knew better, but very often didn't—Duncan and Richie opted for eating in. MacLeod cooked as Richie set the table; MacLeod uncorked the wine as Richie retrieved the glasses; MacLeod tested the sauce as Richie ladled it over his mountain of noodles and carried his plate away to the table. He sat, dug in, and his host joined him a moment later, having approved the taste of the sauce.

It began peaceably enough. Richie was in the act of conveying a dangling portion of spaghetti from plate to mouth when MacLeod, excavating in his own pile of pasta, made his comment. It was, as usual, phrased in a most elaborate matter-of-factness; MacLeod's habit, Richie had learned from experience, was to mention the most vital things as if they meant nothing at all—which in fact indicated they usually meant a great deal.

Richie's fork was stopped at its zenith. "He wants you to *what*?"

"Help him steal the Honours of Scotland," MacLeod repeated.

"I thought that's what you said." Richie inserted spaghetti into his mouth. He chewed thoughtfully for several moments, swallowed, chased it down with wine, then shrugged. "Sounds more like Amanda's line of work."

"Yeah, well ... I've done my share. A very *small* share, but I have." MacLeod continued to sculpt his spaghetti without eating any. "Not as much stealing as *you've* done, but—"

"Yeah, yeah." Richie waved away the comment on his misspent youth with his unloaded fork. "My checkered past, Mac ... but I guess your past, being so much *longer,* has more room for checkers than mine."

MacLeod smiled briefly, then actually ate some of his dinner instead of building with it.

Richie kept his own tone casual. When he got too intense, too personal, Mac often retreated from the subject entirely. "So ... why exactly does he want these—Honours. What *are* they, anyway?"

"The crown, the scepter, the sword of state," MacLeod answered, "stolen from the Scottish people centuries ago, mislaid, and only gotten back in the 1800s."

That explanation proved somewhat mystifying. "Then— they *are* back. They belong to Scotland." He paused, uncertain of his course. "Don't they?"

"To the government."

"Isn't that the same thing?"

"He wants them to make a point." MacLeod drank the rest of his wine, poured more. "You know about the IRA."

Richie laughed briefly, mirthlessly. "You mean Annie Devlin's sandbox?" He saw the flash of annoyance in MacLeod's eyes, put up a conciliatory hand. "All right, all right ... yes, I know about the IRA. Why? Is this guy founding a Scottish chapter?"

MacLeod set down the bottle with a definitive thump. "There's been a Nationalist movement in Scotland for years. They want to break from England, set up a separate political party. But without bloodshed, unlike the IRA." He took up his fork and began excavating again, undermining his pile like Richard the Lionheart sapping the walls of Acre. "Stealing the Honours in the name of Scotland would do as much as setting bombs in department stores or blowing up cars," he said calmly. "It would get him attention on the world stage. He'd get the media coverage without killing people to do it."

"Oh, that's *just* what you need, Mac! Media coverage."

"That's one explanation," Duncan said. "There are others."

"Yeah?"

"The obvious one: he wants the Honours for the worth of the gold and gemstones."

"Could he sell them? I mean, they'd be too hot for honest antique dealers or collectors—"

"—and Douglas wouldn't want to break them up or sell them to a private collector," MacLeod finished. "That's not his true purpose. I think it runs deeper than that."

Richie shook his head. "This guy's an Immortal, so's Annie—why would they risk so much?"

"Maybe because it's what they believe in. It's worth the risk, to them." MacLeod drank more wine. "Remember how old Douglas is, Richie. How old I am."

"Yeah? So?"

"Modern psychiatrists attempting to find explanations for dysfunctional behavior on behalf of criminals often blame it on the society around them. The violence, the lack of respect for authority . . ." MacLeod smiled ironically, staring deeply into the depths of his depleted wine. "We were warriors, Rich, bred up of Highland pride and loyalty, of oaths made to Stuart kings—we were what psychiatrists today would claim as violent and dysfunctional, with no respect for authority." He paused, met Richie's expectant eyes. "The English. The bloody Sassenachs."

Richie inhaled a deep breath, released it gustily. "Okay. That's one explanation."

"Revenge," MacLeod said simply. "That's what Douglas wants."

"But—you wouldn't do anything that foolish. Would you?"

MacLeod smiled. "Maybe I already have."

"What—stolen something like these Honours?" Richie scoffed, then was struck by the glint in dark eyes. "Okay, I'll bite . . . what did you steal?"

"You ever hear of the Stone of Scone?"

"You stole a rock?"

MacLeod quietly ate some spaghetti, postponing his confession. Richie, hooked now, waited impatiently. "The English stole it from us in the 1200s," Mac answered finally. "It's what our kings, Scottish kings, are—*were*—crowned upon. Well, the Sassenachs wanted to rob us of that tradition—emotional terrorism, you might say—and so they 'appropriated' it."

"But—you stole it back."

"Some others and I took it out of Westminster Abbey, yes."

"*Westminster Abbey?* You stole something out of *there?*"

"In 1950. I stayed in London for a while; they took it back to Scotland."

"And did what with it?"

"Kept it. Until George VI asked for it back, so Elizabeth II could be crowned queen with it beneath the Coronation Chair."

Richie poured more wine into his glass, drank appreciatively. "This is good."

"It should be." MacLeod sipped from his own glass. "It's a 1947 Chateau Cheval Blanc."

Richie nodded consideringly. "Then I suppose I should say something clever about the bouquet or the body, huh?"

MacLeod smiled, shook his head. "Made from grapes," he answered simply.

Richie took another swallow. Grapes indeed. "So, you stole this rock, and then gave it back."

"More or less."

"Then what was the point of stealing it?"

"At the time," MacLeod said, "there was one. But a couple of years later George VI was dying of cancer—the present queen's father—and felt very strongly that she should be crowned according to tradition."

"Scottish tradition."

"So we agreed to give it back, after negotiations. But we made our point nonetheless."

"How?"

"We had a message put in it."

"In the *rock*?"

MacLeod remembered the relief he'd felt when he learned the truth of his rescued but broken Stone, once the English admitted the facts. "It was split in two by a bombing raid in World War II," he explained. "Before turning it back over to the English, we, um, repaired it. Put it back together with copper tubing. And put a message inside one of the tubes."

Richie laughed. "Clever! What did this message say?"

MacLeod frowned thoughtfully. "It said: *'This Stone belongs to Scotland. It was stolen by Edward I of England in 1296. The Church of England should be ashamed to admit that they allowed this piece of stolen property to remain in Westminster Abbey from that time. It must be returned to Scotland for the re-opening of the Scottish Parliament'*"— MacLeod raised a finger warning Richie to silence— *" 'which was never closed but only adjourned in 1707.' "*

A slow grin spread over Richie's face. "Cool!" he said admiringly.

"So Elizabeth was crowned according to Scottish tradition in 1953, seated on the Coronation Chair under which was placed the Stone of Scone."

"Have you met her?"

MacLeod smiled, shook his head. "There *are* some things I haven't done and people I haven't met, Rich."

"Not many," Richie declared, stirring the depleted remains of his spaghetti. "So—do you consider yourself one of these Nationalist guys?"

When MacLeod made no answer for several long moments, Richie thought perhaps he hadn't heard. But looking at the thousand-year stare he'd come to associate with personal, private memories locked away in Mac's brain, he knew better.

"I don't hate the English like I once did," MacLeod said at last. "But I was born a Scot, a Highlander, four hundred years ago, and I died for her honor more times than I can count."

"But—now?" Richie asked. "I mean, yeah, you're still Scottish, I know—but it's not the same, is it? The world has changed. *You've* changed."

"Have I?"

"Well, yeah. Haven't you?"

Abruptly MacLeod pushed his chair away from the table, stood up. He walked away across the loft, stopped. His back was to Richie, head bowed, spine rigid, hands on hips. "That's what *he* says. James Douglas. That's what he accuses me of. Change." Abruptly he turned, eyes kindling into an intensity few Immortals saw and survived. The head was up now, and the hands, loose again at his sides, seemed naked without a sword to occupy them. "But I was born a Scot, and on the day someone takes my head, I'll *die* a Scot. I'd have it no other way."

Richie released a long, slow breath. "So," he said, "I guess if you slip up, I'll come visit you in prison."

He lies as Duncan MacLeod has left him, betrayed him, asprawl on the field of battle with his body destroyed by the English. And there he dies as the great heart at last ceases, and the blood runs free from his throat.

And there he lives again, jerked into an agony of awareness from the otherwhere he has inhabited. And he is whole, whole, with jaw slotted back into place, and lungs that labor as they should to draw breath and release it. Ribs no longer pierce flesh, but cage his beating heart as they had before the grapeshot shredded him, before the cannon did their work.

Whole again, and alive.

He struggles up, gasping, pawing at torn clothing, pulling aside the remains of plaid and shirt. Beneath lies flesh smeared with blood, but no wound at all to cause it.

He coughs, spits powder-blackened phlegm aside, mutters something vulgar of bloody Sassenachs and their bloody guns—and realizes all over again his jaw is as it should be.

All of him as it should be.

On his knees, he laughs. And cries. And shakes his fist to the skies, occluded now with lowering clouds, and the unremitting haze of smoke.

Whole again, and alive—

And then the mouth of a musket is placed against his spine between his shoulder blades, and the hand upon the trigger blows his back to bits.

Whole again, and alive. Again.

This time he makes no sound, shakes no fist at the skies. This time he crawls away from the bodies, away from the smoke, away from the sodden ground where the English have killed him. Twice.

Away. Apart. Elsewhere. As MacLeod had told him.

MacLeod, who has left him. Who swore an oath on his honor as a Scot, as a Highlander, that he would see him clear, would not leave him; would carry him away. Would keep him company as he passed from life into death.

But such promises have proved empty after all, for MacLeod has left him, has broken his word, has thrown away his promises and his honor as a fellow Scot lay dying.

Dying.

Twice.

Surely no man can survive such wounds, can be healed of such wounds in so short a time.

Time. Is it not the same day? Is it not the terrible day when English artillery has sundered Scotland's heart?

Sundered his body?

Twice.

Jamie Douglas laughs. A quiet sound, of no great noise lest he give himself away; and then he thinks it is no terrible thing to risk, laughing at an enemy that has killed him twice and failed each time in the doing of it, because he lives after all despite the bloody lobster-backed Sassenachs who have torn him to pieces with grapeshot, then shattered spine and vitals with the point-blank blast of a musket.

He lives.

With no thanks to Duncan MacLeod, oath-breaker.

He hears shouts. English. Hears horses. Hears the hissing chime of blade as a sword is drawn from scabbard. "By God," someone says, in English, "I swear 'tis the same man!"

Douglas swings and faces them. Six men, ahorse, Sassenachs every one. Is the battle so badly lost that the English dare send men out in front of the cannon?

"The same man," the voice says violently. "I swear it!"

Jamie throws wide his arms. "Ye canna kill me, aye? Ye canna kill me!"

This time a man rides up to him. Stares down upon him with incredulity shaping his features.

"Ye canna!" Jamie cries. "Ye pawkie Sassenachs!"

Another rides up. This man draws his saber and sets its tip against Jamie's teeth, cutting into his lip. "Oh, no?" the man drawls in elegant disdain—and thrusts so firmly the blade breaks through the back of Jamie's throat, exits his skull.

He dies. Again.

And again is healed, and whole.

The fourth time he is found and killed they tie him to a horse. The rider sets his spurs, puts the horse to a gallop, and drags the Scotsman back and forth across the battlefield, across the dead and dying, across blood and broken weapons, until nothing remains of his clothing.

Until nothing remains of his face.

Joe Dawson hung up the phone and looked at Mattie, still seated on the bar stool. "That does it," he said. "It's three-handed poker, I guess; Gilman's got a sick kid, Dori has the flu, and Badger's got a big project due at her real job." He glanced at Mike, lingering at the register. "Do you want to call it?"

The bartender shrugged. "Might as well. We can try again next week." He glanced past Joe to Mattie. "Yeah, I'll call it a night. See you, Joe. Good night, Mary Margaret."

She offered the same to him as he headed toward the back door, then looked at Joe in some bafflement. "Badger?"

He grinned. "Nickname. So, shall I walk you to your car?"

She considered it. Smiled. "Well, I could do with a cup of coffee first, if you don't mind. Unless it's too much trouble."

Quite unexpectedly, he felt ten years younger. Twenty. He smiled back. "No trouble at all. I'll put on a fresh pot."

"If you'll excuse me, then." She slid off the stool. "What is it you Americans say?—I must see a man about a cow?"

Dawson laughed as he turned to the coffeemaker. "In the hall by the back door," he said, "and it's horse. See a man about a *horse*." He measured grounds into a new filter; hoped she liked it strong. Perhaps with a bit of Irish whisky in it, too; for free, so he'd not break the law. Meditatively, he said, "Although maybe in Ireland you see someone about a leprechaun."

The accent was the same. The voice, and the tone, were not. "Is that what you call us, Joe?"

He stiffened, acutely aware of the sound of the coffeemaker, hissing and churning to life. He looked for Mattie, wanted desperately to see Mattie, but knew even as he turned, even as his brain filtered the words through the machine, he would see the other woman. The other Irishwoman.

It went through his mind so quickly, like an electrical shock. *MacLeod told her. He told her about us.*

Confidentiality was breeched. But Duncan MacLeod had sworn no oaths to Joe Dawson. Some Immortals knew because they found out, even as MacLeod himself had. But Annie Devlin was decidedly not one Dawson wanted aware of the organization.

"What *do* you call us, Joe?"

He swallowed slowly. There was no more sense in prevarication. "Immortals," he said only.

"Not devils? Not witches? Not—freaks?"

The low lighting burnished auburn hair, limned the fragile planes of her expressive face. She looked not a day over twenty-six, the age she had died the first time.

But Annie Devlin was in fact one hundred and forty years

old, and one hundred and fifteen of those years had been spent as an Immortal. "No," Dawson said. "None of those things."

"Then why do you Watch us?"

He drew in a careful breath and steadied himself against the bar. "We have a responsibility to history. To be sure the truth is recorded."

"The truth about who?"

"Immortals," he replied. "It's what we do. Watch and record." Surely MacLeod had told her that much. Not that it would matter to a woman such as she.

Annie smiled, but he saw no amusement. "And what *is* the truth about Immortals, Joe?"

Behind him, the coffeemaker groaned through its cycle. "I don't have the answer to that," he said quietly.

Ruddy brows arched. "Because you haven't thought of one yet? After all these years?"

"Do I need to?"

Annie grinned. He saw the woman then, not the terrorist, not the Immortal; the woman perhaps MacLeod saw, or had. Or could.

And then she lifted her right hand from her side and brought up into the light the cold polished gleam of live steel. She set the tip, soundlessly, upon the edge of the bar. "Tell me," she said. "Tell me what you know. About *me*."

He was not her Watcher. But he knew. He had taken pains to know.

"Annie Devlin," Joe said conversationally, "born in Dublin in 1855, or so we assume. The records indicate you were taken in as an infant by Mary Deane six months after her husband died. Two weeks after her baby died."

"So I was. Go on."

"Raised Ann Elizabeth Deane, a Catholic, by a loving mother who believed implicitly in Home Rule for Ireland."

"She did that. Go on."

"In 1881, at a rally by wives and mothers and daughters protesting the imprisonment of more than a thousand Irishmen—"

"—who were themselves protesting the pathetic treatment

of us all by English landlords." Her eyes were fixed on his. "Go on."

"—a riot was started when Crown troops attempted to disperse the crowd."

"And how did they do that, Joe?"

Light ran down the steel like water. Dawson swallowed again, feeling sweat gathering at his temples, beneath the line of close-cropped mustache. He wanted to scratch away the tickle, but knew better. "They fired buckshot into the crowd."

"And?"

"And charged with bayonets."

"And?"

He wet dry lips. "They killed women and children."

"Very good," she said. "You know a little something after all." She stepped closer, slid the blade closer. The tip was near his right hand, splayed flat against the bartop. "My mother died in the first volley, shot down at close range. There was nothing left of her breasts, where she'd suckled her foundling daughter. And I, that very daughter, could do nothing at all for her, just gather her up in my arms and cradle her there in the midst of the madness." Yet another step closer; the tip of the blade touched the webbing of his hand now, between index and middle finger. "Do you know what happened then, Joe?"

"You died. The first time."

"I was murdered. Stabbed to death by police bayonets. By *English* bayonets in the hands of *English*men."

"Yes," he said. "I never claimed you had no reason to hate. No one ever has."

"I died swearing vengeance," Annie Devlin said very softly, "and vengeance I shall have. For my mother. For me. For the women and children who died that day. For all the Irish patriots before and since, taken down by the Sassenach pigs."

The coffee was done. He did not move to lift the pot from the heating unit.

"Wise man," she said as softly. Then, "Are you a Sassenach pig?"

He offered the only weapon he had. "Ask Duncan Mac-Leod."

Annie smiled. And laughed in honest, unfettered amusement. The hardness fell away and she was only a woman again, a small, lovely, unthreatening woman—until he saw her eyes. "D'ye think that's your deliverance?"

"*I* am," Mattie O'Connell said plainly, suppressing her accent, "or you'll have to kill us both."

Annie moved so swiftly Joe saw only the blur of steel. The sword was off the bar, in her hand, directed at Mattie, who stood in the hallway beside the restroom door, before the back exit.

"Ah," Annie said. "Puts a different light on it, it does."

"Indeed," Mattie agreed.

"Well, then." The sword disappeared as abruptly as it had appeared, slid smoothly beneath her coat. She glanced at Joe, pinned him with the intensity of her gaze. "Respite," she said, "*for now.*"

Joe watched her go: slight, lithe woman striding silently down the hall, moving beyond Mattie and out the exit into the night. She took the tension with her.

Joe released pent breath on a long, audible sigh. He watched, speechless, as Mattie turned abruptly and deliberately set the deadbolt. Practical Mattie O'Connell.

When she came to the bar, Joe had coffee waiting. And a bottle of whisky beside the mugs.

"Ah," Mattie said. She disdained the coffee altogether and picked up the bottle. Her hand trembled only slightly as she tipped it to her mouth, drank. Then she handed it to him.

He took it, felt the sting in the webbing between index and middle finger. The sword after all had drawn a measure of blood.

"To life," Dawson said; he drank as Mattie laughed in shaky disbelief—and then answered him in Gaelic.

"Jamie?" Colin Cameron asked, when he was done explaining about the man who watched. "What shall we do?"

Douglas smiled. Laughed.

"Jamie—"

Eyes kindling with unrepentant mirth, James Douglas bared teeth in a charming, ebullient grin. "You are an actor, Coll. You shall *act*. And MacLeod shall be your audience." He closed his eyes in pleasure. "MacLeod, even by proxy, shall be your audience."

Chapter Sixteen

MacLeod sent Richie off, then tended the dinner dishes himself. He found himself in a meditative mood, not fit company for a young man who found it difficult to sit still for any length of time. Richie would learn there was power in stillness, but for now he was yet too restless, too moved by mortal concerns. He was and always would be nineteen, albeit he lived forever; habits and disposition would change in time, but there was no hurry.

So long as he survived.

Duncan finished the dishes, dried his hands, took himself to the bookshelf. From it he pulled down an old leatherbound volume, gilt beginning to wear from the stamped title. He had no need of index; he knew the contents by heart, and their placement.

MacLeod sat down on the couch and leafed through the fragile onionskin pages. He scanned the text, then settled back, cradling the book in his lap with careful attention to its welfare. And read aloud with absorption Macbeth's soliloquy at Dunsinane, on the cusp of destruction.

> *"I have almost forgot the taste of fears:*
> *The time has been, my senses would have cool'd*
> *To hear a night-shriek; and my fell of hair*
> *Would at a dismal treatise rouse and stir*
> *As life were in't: I have supt full with horrors;*
> *Direness, familiar to my slaughterous thoughts,*
> *Cannot once start me."*

But start he did as he felt the abrupt and unmistakable sensation of an Immortal near by, very near by. Even as the knock sounded on the door beside the elevator, MacLeod had closed the book and set it aside on the couch.

The katana, retrieved on the instant. Long strides to the door, a hand upon the latch. And hesitation.

'I have almost forgot the taste of fears . . .'

"Duncan?"

Annie. Tension banished immediately, he undid the latch and pulled open the door, dangling katana beside his leg. He smiled. "Come in."

She saw the blade. Looked into his face. Waited.

"Well, if you *insist . . .*" Two long steps and he set the weapon on the countertop, and even as he turned back to her she was in his arms, pulling the tucked-in tails of his sweater from the waistband of his jeans.

It was abrupt, unexpected, but not unwelcome. Nonetheless her hands were cold from the out-of-doors; the taut flesh of his belly flinched involuntarily even as he expelled a startled breath.

This time she had no trouble with belt and zipper. She slid hands up bare torso, then took them from beneath the rucked up sweater and caught his neck, pulled down his head; she was so much smaller than he. And kissed him with such reckless, obsessive passion she took his breath away.

He recovered it quickly enough, then responded in kind. He heard the quiet husky laughter in the back of her throat, felt her fingers unfasten the clasp binding his hair. She tipped the silver ornament out of her hand and let it drop. He heard it rattle against the floor.

"Miss me?" he asked with irony, when she allowed him a chance to speak.

"You'll do," she said, "in a pinch."

He answered that literally, if carefully, catching one nipple briefly.

Annie laughed. The temperature of her hands no longer mattered. "Tonight," she said against his mouth. "Here. *Now.*"

He was not a slow starter, in wit or in anything else. One sharp kick shut the door with a thud.

Dawson escorted Mattie to the front door, unbolted it, pulled it open. He smiled at her as she slipped by him, then lingered to button up her coat. Beyond her the night was soft, but hours away from dawn. "Maybe next week," he said. As she frowned, puzzled, he elaborated. "The poker game. Depending on sick kids, the flu, and projects—and if Annie Devlin's still in town."

"Oh, yes!" Mattie laughed, stroked a lock of hair away from her brow. "The poker game."

He gripped the cane more tightly. "Maybe dinner," he suggested neutrally. "Tomorrow night?"

She gifted him with the glorious smile, and neutrality vanished. "I believe I would like that."

"Good." He nodded, infinitely pleased. "Then it's settled. Say—seven o'clock?"

"I'll come here," she offered.

"Fine by me." He glanced beyond her. "There isn't a lot of light out there . . . shall I walk you to your car?"

"No, no—not necessary. It's not far." She tied the scarf more closely around her neck. "Tomorrow night, Joe Dawson."

"Tonight," he reminded her. "It's after midnight."

"Ah, so it is." She touched him briefly on the arm. "I have this much to thank Annie Devlin for, if nothing else." And then she was gone, swiftly climbing the short flight of steps to the parking lot.

As he rebolted the door, Joe grinned to himself. Indeed, he was himself grateful to Annie Devlin, despite her predeliction for violence. He had not been this attracted to a woman since Lauren died.

Even as he turned away, setting the cane—only a little paperwork left, then he'd go home—a knock sounded at the door. He turned back. "Mattie—?" Deadbolts released, the latch undone; he pulled the door open to see in the shadows a slender auburn-haired woman in a hooded navy raincoat. Joe blinked. "Speak of the devil—"

But he was given no chance to complete the sentence. He saw only the glint of steel in pale, diffused light; cold, live steel. He fell back a single step, felt the cane slide against hardwood. . . and then the steel was in his shoulder, cutting through cloth, through flesh, into muscle. And deeper.

—falling . . .

—crashing backward into the chairs, the nearest table . . .

—poor light behind her, little before: just a woman with steel in her hand . . .

'Respite,' Annie Devlin had said. *'For now.'*

His shoulder was alive with pain. And then the back of his head struck fallen chair, or overturned table, and pain was banished with consciousness.

At one point MacLeod became aware of something digging into his spine. Muttering, he heaved himself—and Annie—up from creased leather couch cushions long enough to slide a hand beneath his torso and tug free the impediment; expelled breath on a brief laugh as he identified the book and set it down upon the floor. Then, as Annie querulously questioned the delay, he made shift to move her and himself, to twist over in one adroit maneuver of powerful hips and elbows that pulled her beneath him, though he took the weight on his arms, one knee. Clothing was—elsewhere. Flesh adhered to flesh.

He smiled against her breasts, warming them with his breath. " *'Prithee, peace . . . I dare do all that may become a man;/Who dares do more is none.'* "

"Christ," she hissed, "not love sonnets! It doesn't become you, MacLeod."

"The 'Scottish play,'" he corrected, more than a little aggrieved, "and one of the bloodiest ever written!"

"Ah. Well then, that will do for us both."

Mattie O'Connell locked her car door, buckled the seat belt, put the key in the ignition—but did not turn it over. For long moments she merely sat there, hands gripping wheel and keys, staring blindly into darkness.

She had not come here for Joe Dawson, but for Annie Devlin. And she had come for Annie because such was her assignment, because she knew Annie better than most; because of Hugh O'Neill, who had loved with an astonishing degree of dedication a fragile, short-lived mortal, who had loved him in return because he gave her no choice, and because he trusted her enough to offer the truth of his kind as well as the truth of what he had been for so many centuries. Warrior, patriot, rebel. Immortal.

He was not what she expected to love, not after Patrick O'Connell; not after seeing the horrific results of terrorism in her own country. But loved him she had, unremittingly, cherishing their bond in the wake of losing Patrick. He had taught her she could commit herself to another without fear of disloyalty; one compartmentalized such things, explained Hugh, who should know after so many centuries of experience. One boxed them up and put them into safe storage, and one took them out now and again to look at them, to remember them, to cherish them—and then one put them away.

Hugh O'Neill was dead three years. But yards away, in a bar, Joe Dawson was alive.

She closed her eyes, gripped the wheel even more tightly. And then released it.

When she opened her eyes, even as she removed the keys from the ignition and unlocked the door, she saw a figure move swiftly out of the shadows of the sunken doorway and toward the corner of the building, where more shadows beckoned. Slight build, dark coat, hair briefly burnished copper-bronze in distant streetlight. And a sword, glinting silver, put beneath the coat as the figure turned the corner into darkness.

'*Respite*,' Annie had said. '*For now.*'

"Sweet Jesus," Mattie breathed, and left the car door open as she ran toward the building in frantic haste.

MacLeod was aware the moment she left the bed, sliding out from beneath sheet and comforter. They had traded couch for bed earlier; it was perhaps three hours till dawn.

He thrust a forearm beneath his head and watched her wandering course as she gathered discarded clothing. Light from the window fell in blind-born slats across the loft, tiger-striping wall, furniture, floor, even Annie.

His own clothing, taken up, she draped across the couch. Hers she put on.

"Annie." She started at the sound of his voice, turned toward the bed. He could not see her expression clearly, save he knew she frowned. "We're well beyond the age of consent," he said dryly. "No need to sneak out."

"It's not that . . ." She sighed deeply. "It's that I've done something—something I think I should not have done."

He levered himself up higher against the pillows. "Come to bed," he invited. "Come to bed and tell me."

"It isn't something you'd want to hear."

"How do you know until I hear it?"

She was silent.

"Annie . . ." He threw back the covers and slid out of bed, walked nude across the hardwood floor. When he put his hands on her shoulders he felt the rigidity, the palpable tension in her body. "I'm not a priest," he said gently, "but I can hear your confession. If you care to make one."

"I can't."

"Annie—"

"I *can't*." She shook her head, sliding away from his grasp. "You don't understand, MacLeod. You are a decent man, a *good* man, with a sense of honor . . . and I'm poisoning that."

"Only if I let you."

"You don't *understand*, MacLeod! What I did—" She broke off again, clearly troubled. "I'm not proud of it. I suppose no man should expect me to claim pride in the things I've done for Ireland, but I do, because I believe in them . . .

but this—" She shook her head again. "This was for me, not for Ireland. Because I was angry. And frightened."

"Frightened?"

"Frightened," she repeated. "More than I have been since Hugh O'Neill found me and explained what I was." She moved slightly, into a slanting shaft of light; he saw the tears in her eyes, the fear, and terrible loneliness. "That is my confession, as much as I can make one. If you will have it of me."

He bent, leaned close, kissed her brow. Led her back to bed.

This time it was without the fierceness, the predatory possession, the bonfire kindled with every touch. This time it was slow and quiet and gentle and tender, but no less binding.

"Can I trust you?" she asked in the soft silence, later. "Can I trust all of me to you?"

"Always," he answered. "My oath on it." He smiled, wrapped her in his arms. "On my honor as a Scot, as a Highlander, as Duncan MacLeod of the Clan MacLeod."

She buried her head against his chest and, at last, gave herself over to sleep.

Such pain, so much blood; the roar of cannon in his ears, the screaming of the dying, the fell silence of the dead. But he yet lives, albeit he knows he walks the edge of the blade even now.

Such pain, so much blood; and a man with him, setting his limbs to rights, easing his last moments, telling him he won't die alone.

"I promise," he says. "I'll be here wi' ye."

He can barely form the words, trying without success to make his jaw move properly. Little sense comes of it, only a hissed sibilant and choppily expelled breath.

But the other understands. "My oath on it," he says. "On my honor as a Scot, as a Highlander, as Duncan MacLeod of the Clan MacLeod."

But he is gone, is gone; MacLeod leaves him after all; and there is the pain, and the blood, and the dying.

So much pain and blood and dying. Four times killed in less than an hour.

"On my honor," *MacLeod had said.*

No honor. No honor at all in the man.

He sits upon the cairn of stone, gazing out across the serried rows of seats. In one hand rests the claymore, point set into the surface of the stage. With detached, dispassionate negligence, he twists the sword and deliberately digs a deep divot into the hardwood.

He hears the distant door from backstage, the rattle and thump of the weight swinging closed, a hand upon the pressure bar. It ratchets in the silence, then clicks home, seating itself in the jamb socket.

Footsteps. He closes his eyes, listens to the swish of cloth as a curtain is pulled aside, as the raincoat slides against it. The sound of heavy, uneven breathing. The sound of nervousness, and relief. Smells him: the drift of perfume, the underlying tang of extremity, and tension. Of dampness, sword, and the night.

He stills the claymore from idle destruction of the stage. "So?"

"It's done. As you said."

Douglas opens his eyes, watches as Colin Cameron strips the auburn wig from his head. "Did he see you?"

"Yes."

"No, Coll—that's not what I asked. Did he see you?"

Cameron's thin, made-up face is tense. "No, Jamie. He saw *her*."

"Ah." He smiles. "Good lad."

Chapter Seventeen

Mattie O'Connell sat rigid as oak upon the edge of the thread-bare chair in the hospital waiting room. She had paced the depressing halls for a while, but found herself too often in the way. She sat in the equally depressing chapel for a while, but found herself empty of prayer, only full of bitter anger and an abiding fear. And so at last she retreated to the falsely cheerful waiting room, deaf and blind to the television chirping in the corner, to the out-of-date and tattered magazines sprawled upon the tables, to the other people who came and went, worried and/or relieved. She felt the knot seize and settle into her neck with a fiendish virulence—until a woman in surgical blues and a lab coat stopped in the door and said her name.

Mattie lurched to her feet. "Is he all right, then?"

The woman smiled, though it held professional detachment. "I think he'll be fine. The wound is less severe than it might have seemed at first. It's the concussion we're a little concerned about. We'll keep an eye on him the rest of the night and throughout the day, but I don't anticipate any problems." With that news passed, the professional demeanor altered into something more human—and, oddly, much more compassionate. "Joe Dawson is a tough man, Ms. O'Connell. I don't think a puncture wound and a bump on the head is going to get in his way."

Mattie was taken aback. "You know him?"

"Joe—? Oh, forgive me." The woman stepped forward, smiling, and extended one slim hand. "I'm Anne Lindsey. *Doctor* Lindsey; I'm working the e.r. tonight. Yes, I know Joe. We're friends, although I don't see so much of him any more." Something of regret passed through her eyes, transforming her yet again. For the first time Mattie looked beyond the faceless facade of physician and saw her: dark-haired, tall, thin, attractive in a pert, animated way. "I'm sorry," Anne Lindsey said, meaning it, "I'm working and I don't have time right now, but I know there are people who would like to know what happened, that Joe's here. Would you mind?"

"N-no," Mattie answered. "I suppose I could make some calls."

"Here, let me write down the numbers . . ." Dr. Lindsey sat briefly in a padded chair beside a scarred end table, took a crumpled piece of paper from a pocket, a pen, and scribbled. In seeming idleness, she asked, "I don't suppose you know what caused the wound, do you?"

A sword, Mattie answered. *Annie Devlin's sword.* But she said nothing of that to the doctor. "No, I'm sorry. I thought—perhaps a knife. When I got there he was already down, unconscious."

"I don't think it was a knife." Dr. Lindsey stood up, handed the paper to Mattie. "The top one is his home number, the other is for the dojo, where he works. He'll want to know." She put the pen back into her pocket. "His name is Duncan MacLeod."

Mattie felt numb. "Duncan—?"

"MacLeod," the doctor said. Then, sharply, "Do you know him? Is he involved in this?"

The numbness extended to her lips. "I don't know."

"But you know him."

"I know *of* him," Mattie prevaricated. "You see, Joe has

mentioned him." She felt utterly at sea; this woman doctor had gone far beyond mere professional concern. "I've heard his name." Inwardly she winced even as she said it; it had a lame sound, a tacked-on sound, but she was tired, worried, and too tense for careful voyaging.

"Then I know exactly what caused that wound," Dr. Lindsey said tightly, strain tautening her features. "And Duncan will want to know. Duncan *needs* to know."

This woman knew. This woman *knew*. Mattie nodded, confessing nothing, making no assumptions that though the doctor knew of Immortals, she also knew of Watchers. It went against the oath. "I'll call him."

"As soon as possible," Dr. Lindsey said plainly. "Please. Now—excuse me. I'm sorry, I have to go."

Mattie stared after her as she hastened back down the hall, already calling out to an orderly. Joe Dawson was deliberately put out of the doctor's mind, now that she'd passed along her message, the telephone numbers of Duncan MacLeod, whom Dr. Lindsey unaccountably knew was Joe's friend. Whom she also knew, from all appearances, as a man who claimed an intimate acquaintanceship with swords and sword wounds.

Mattie looked at the paper clutched in one hand. The numbers had been scrawled in haste, but she could read them. A simple matter to find a phone, drop in a coin, and dial. And she would speak to Duncan MacLeod himself, who was, despite the rules, the oath, close enough to Joe Dawson that he would want to know his friend was injured.

Bent rules, broken oaths, dispensed with at need in the name of friendship. A friendship that should not exist. There was a tinge of jealousy at the thought, envy at the assignment to a man worthy of Joe Dawson's trust. Mattie Watched, though she hated; Joe Dawson, it seemed, Watched what he loved.

Mattie O'Connell walked out of the waiting room to the pay phone in the hall. With exquisite care she set down the paper, fished coins out of her coat pocket, pulled up the obscenely thick telephone book with its lurid yellow paper.

Carefully, deliberately, she paged through the listings. It

took time, but she found what she wanted. She counted the coins lined up on the shelf: not enough. Next the handbag, the coin-purse: both yielded more coins. She would use them all.

The Watcher made many calls. The Watcher methodically told the story that had formed in her mind as she looked through the phone book, leaving out the parts she knew would not be believed, leaving *in* the parts only someone with inside knowledge could address with certainty. She answered sharp questions, verified what she could based on what she knew; and she *did* know, as she should: dates, description, real name, alias, locations, names of known confederates, case numbers of unsolved bombings. In her lilting Irish accent.

It took three hours to make all the calls, to be put through to the right people, to answer endless questions. But only after she had exhausted her supply of coins save for two did Mary Margaret O'Connell look again at the crumpled paper and the numbers for Duncan MacLeod.

Bent rules, broken oaths. But Joe Dawson was worth it.

So was Annie Devlin.

But not yet. Later.

Quite unexpectedly, a Gaelic proverb came into her mind. One Hugh O'Neill had taught her. Mattie smiled and turned away from the phone, quoting aloud softly what she felt was most appropriate. Especially under the circumstances. "'If you cannot bite, do not show your teeth.'"

She folded the slip of paper and put it into her pocket.

In addition to the theater, conference rooms, and exhibit halls, the downtown Cultural Center also featured a wide grassy quadrangle, a greensward, in front of the plaza and its myriad fountains. Ordinarily it would be freshly mowed, meticulously landscaped, posted with tasteful signs directing visitors to remain on the sidewalks.

Today it boasted displays of handcrafts, foodstalls, bookstalls; individual booths flying flags and tartan banners of particular clans; griddles full of oatmeal cakes; a fair sampling of ales and whiskies; husbands, sons, and boyfriends in kilts; wives, daughters, and girlfriends in kerches and aprons; a young man and woman setting out swords on the grass for the dance; and a group of paunchy men taking turns at heaving the "stone" over a bamboo crossbar set atop two poles, similar to a pole-vault competition, raised or lowered according to the results. Farther out on the field other men, snug Lycra/Spandex bike shorts worn beneath knife-pleated kilts—horrendous anachronism!—attempted to toss lengths of wood masquerading as cabers.

Duncan MacLeod of the Clan MacLeod, born in the Highlands of Scotland in 1592, strolled bemusedly up the walkway toward the plaza beneath the flagpoles flying the Colors of Scotland, Canada, and the United States. His pace slowed, stopped as he turned to look across the greensward, at the crowds beginning to form to enjoy a day in Scotland—or an approximation of what was *rumored* to be a day in Scotland.

He felt—odd. He could not help but be struck by the strange juxtaposition, the jumbled fragments of his ancestry assembled incompletely and yet with careful attention, with honorable intent. But he was aware of an urgent and uneasy sense of displacement. These people, most of Scottish ancestry, yearned to reclaim the days as descendants of a people long dead, resurrecting customs they knew only from books, movies, television, or tall tales. And here *he* was, all unaccountably and unbelievably: a living, breathing Highlander, born and bred of the burns and braes; the fall-carved, time-wracked cliffs; the moors and bogs and lochs of a land that no longer existed as these folk would have it exist despite their best intentions.

But it was better than nothing.

It birthed a smile, that thought: a crooked, bemused smile at his own expense. He more than any other was appropriate to the moment, but he was not so certain even *he* could manage some of the field games any more. It had been centuries since he had thrown a stone, or tossed a caber.

He could *try*, he supposed . . . but how would he feel if he failed?

Duncan MacLeod of the Clan MacLeod, son of a MacLeod chieftain, defeated by big-bellied, middle-aged accountants, teachers, and salesmen who likely had never been to the Highlands?

Aloud, he quoted: " 'Better be quiet than sing a bad song.' "

Thus relieved of temptation, he gave himself over to observation again. He smelled the whisky, the wool, the oatcakes; heard the singing chime of blades being crossed and set into the grass; heard the grunts of effort from men proving their mettle in the games that he himself had played three centuries before.

Almost, he could close his eyes and wish himself home again.

He did so. Let the wind of the morning caress his face. Shut out the sounds of the city, the stench of the city, the sights of the city—and took himself home again to the heart-stopping beauty of Glenfinnan.

The scent of rain, of damp earth . . . of gorse and heather and granite . . . the prickle of thistle against bare legs, the cry of an eagle in the air, the tang of pine and fir and cattle, the economy of the Highlands; shaggy, black-coated cattle with wicked horns upon their heads, and a wide rolling eye. Someone in the distance called out in Gaelic . . .

His eyes snapped open as the pipes began. Of course. How could they not? It was, next to *Amazing Grace* at funerals, the song most commonly heard when his homeland was invoked.

Scotland the Brave.

He felt it then and turned swiftly, balanced, at ease with his body. Saw Jamie Douglas and Colin Cameron, come out before a temporary backdrop to enact a part of the play.

But it was not as expected. He had seen them before: Cameron as Banquo, murdered friend of Macbeth; James Douglas as Macduff, who himself slays Macbeth. This time they did not play their usual roles, but changed them altogether.

MacLeod could not help but smile as he looked at Colin Cameron. This was indeed the way Shakespeare had written the play: with men cast and clad as women. He knew that very well. There was a time in his past when *he* had played one of Shakespeare's female roles: Kate in *Taming of the Shrew*. A decidedly robust Kate.

But this time Douglas portrayed Macbeth instead of Macduff, and Colin Cameron, in wig and careful makeup, as well as shrouding costume, made a lovely Lady Macbeth.

Onlookers gathered as the scene commenced. It was but a snippet of the play, a series of brief teasers meant to provoke interest, not give an accurate rendering of what theatergoers would witness when they purchased tickets. It was done as for a fair, the actors in the Company taking on different roles so as to keep the play fresh.

First, Macbeth: towering James Douglas in leather and theatrical ringmail, red mane flowing back against broad shoulders. In clear and precise diction he lent a living vitality to words long dead.

MacLeod moved aside, near the fountain; relaxed and crossed his arms as line after line echoed across the quad. He remained relaxed until Jamie, as Macbeth, looked straight at him, and declaimed several lines that of a sudden took on new meaning.

> " 'Besides, this Duncan hath borne his faculties so meek,
> hath been so clear in his great office,
> that his virtues will plead like angels, trumpet-tongued,
> against the deep damnation of his taking-off . . .' "

MacLeod stared at Douglas, who continued with effortless brilliance in his role as Shakespeare's murderous king.

> " ' . . . and pity, like a new-born babe,
> Striding the blast, or heaven's cherubim, horsed
> Upon the sightless couriers of the air,
> Shall blow the horrid deed in every eye,
> That tears shall drown the wind—
> I have no spur to prick the sides of my intent,
> but only vaulting ambition, which o'erleaps itself,
> and falls on th'other.' "

A smattering of applause started up, was hushed as Cameron, in his role as Lady Macbeth, took center "stage" before the backdrop and began his lines. There was some tittering and murmuring in the crowd as those closest realized he was a man dressed up as a woman, but the vulgar and curious comments stilled as Cameron continued and "Macbeth" answered.

Behind MacLeod, uncognizant of the play and the competition they offered, bagpipes wailed counterpoint to Shakespeare as Lady Macbeth, answering her husband, raised her voice over their music:

> " ' *When Duncan is asleep—*
> *Whereto the rather shall his day's hard journey soundly*
> *invite him . . . ' "*

A shout went up from the field games on the greensward: someone had tossed the caber farther then anyone else.

" '*What cannot you and I perform upon th'unguarded Duncan?' "*

He swung, one hand slipping beneath the coat. But it was Richie . . . Richie—

"Mac—*Mac* . . . thank God I found you!" Richie, pushing his way through the crowd, carried his motorcycle helmet in one hand. "I just got a call—Joe's been hurt. He's in the hospital."

"What?"

"Some woman called, said she found him in the bar . . . she says he'll be okay, but Anne wanted you to know."

"Anne did."

"Yeah." Richie's expression was carefully neutral, save for honest concern. "The woman said Anne gave her your number, asked her to call."

"All right." MacLeod, in his mind, was gone. "All right, Richie . . . thanks." He paused. "You coming?"

"I've got to stop and get some gas—almost ran out on the way here." Richie motioned with his head. "You go on. I'll catch up."

MacLeod turned and strode away. Behind him, as he left, Lady Macbeth continued her lines.

> " '*As we shall make our griefs and clamour roar*
> *upon his death?' "*

Chapter Eighteen

———

Mattie O'Connell stood aside and waited quietly as the man wheeled into the hospital the stack of afternoon-edition newspapers. He loaded the racks, whistling something sprightly and intensely annoying, then wheeled the handcart off to finish his rounds. Still whistling.

She remained in place for several long moments, considering what she'd done, the repercussions of it—the *hoped for* repercussions—and what had led her to it. She had now broken the rules, the oath. The wheels were in motion. She could not stop them if she tried, if she desired it. And she did not.

Mattie walked to the rack, slotted in two coins, unlatched the front door, and retrieved from the shelf the newspaper that represented revenge and repudiation.

She smiled. "The pen truly *is* mightier than the sword."

Or perhaps now it was the printing press, computers, the phosphors of television in color and black-and-white, telephone lines, even on-line systems.

It was front-page news, even if not deemed worthy of above-the-fold placement. But there was the most recent file photo with identification in the cutline beneath, plus an accompanying story. The headline was succinctly explicit: *IRA BOMB SUSPECT FEARED IN CITY.* The article itself spelled out far more of Annie Devlin's questionable credentials: implicated in bombings, shootings, and, most tellingly, the foiled attempt on the life of an ambassador three years prior that had resulted in the death of Annie's husband.

In this, the police had aided her. The media had never been given the truth of how Annie's body had disappeared, because they could not themselves explain how a woman might survive a fall from so high, or how her body could walk out of a morgue after violently subduing the pathologist. They had swept it all under the rug, hidden it away in private files—which made it all the more intriguing to a scoop-hungry media.

And now it had come to this: Joe Dawson, nearly killed the night before; and Annie Devlin the instigator of it.

This time, please God, the authorities would find her, arrest her, and *keep* her.

And Mattie O'Connell, despite her oath, was the instigator of *that.*

She saw him then in the entrance, even as she folded the paper and thrust it beneath her arm. And she realized, with a sense of shock, that file photographs and computer GIFs did not do him justice; did not and could not capture the effortless grace of his movements, the unspoken power and presence, the sheer and startling charisma that dulled the rest of humanity to a thin, sun-faded photo.

Duncan MacLeod, in the flesh.

Was it bred in their bones, she wondered, something wilder and greater than mortals? A burning of the spirit that transcended human vitality?

Unfair, she decided sourly. Everyone else was so—*ordinary.* So dreadfully mundane.

And understood, abruptly, with an inner flinching of her spirit, why Hunters grew out of Watchers, fearful of the purposes of every Immortal. Because surely those such as Hugh O'Neill, Annie Devlin, and Duncan MacLeod could have whatever thay wanted, if they decided to claim it. Even on a whim.

He was by her now, walking to the nurse's station halfway down the hall. He questioned a woman there, then turned away as Dr. Lindsey came out of a room.

It was an odd meeting constructed of subtle and strange dynamics, Mattie reflected, looking on from a distance. She could hear nothing but did not require it, needing only to interpret their movements. Lovers, once. But no longer. And yet their bodies remembered, even in ignorance of what the present prescribed for them.

He was gone, then, so quickly, turning away from Ann Lindsey to enter Joe's room.

Mattie O'Connell stared after MacLeod, thinking deeply of honor and oaths. Then she sat down in a chair at the end of the hall and waited for him to come out.

With MacLeod's hasty exit from the Cultural Center, Richie was left to awareness, the prickling sense of *presence* betokening an Immortal. He turned quickly.

The huge man clad in ringmailed leather strode over from the backdrop, his part in the performance finished. Richie saw the claymore worn slantwise across his back, the glint in smoky eyes, the massiveness of the frame. This Immortal dwarfed him, dwarfed even MacLeod.

"Shit," Richie muttered

The actor paused before him, bent his head slightly as if unconsciously acknowledging the difference in heights. Sunlight glistened off the brilliance of red hair, brushed away from strong, freckled features. "Would you be a Scotsman, then?"

"No," Richie said warily. "Local, actually. From 38th Street. My name is Ryan. Richard Ryan." He paused. "Irish, way back there."

A year before he might have cursed himself for being manipulated into declaring his identity as possible prelude to encounter; but he had learned a lot in that past year, and stood his ground unflinchingly. If the big man wanted him, Richie wouldn't walk away.

But here? In front of all the rest?

Nonetheless, he put his hand at the unzipped flap of his leather jacket. It would not take so much to meet the actor's sword with his own.

"Och, no, lad! No need for that!" A hand came down upon Richie's shoulder and engulfed it. Threatened it. "You're a wee pissant of a lad yet . . . though I suppose you always will be, now that you're 'dead' "—the wide grin was wicked—"but you're green no matter the age, aye?"

Richie detested that assessment. "I've had a good teacher."

"MacLeod?—aye, he is that, I would imagine." Amber eyes kindled with amusement. "I don't want your head, Richard Ryan. I want your assistance."

"Assistance?" This was suspicious. "What *kind* of assistance?"

"I'm an actor . . . if you hadn't already deduced that for yourself." Despite the subtle danger Richie sensed in the man, there were also high good spirits, almost as if he were drunk. "A good one, I might add, if I were inclined to immodesty"—a brief flash of strong white teeth—"and it's a theory of mine that *any* man may be an actor, albeit merely competent, given the opportunity, the practice, and the proper lines." He paused. "Would you care to give it a try?"

The guy was nuts. No question. Richie cast a quick, incredulous glance over the crowds wandering the greensward. "Look, I've got a friend—"

"Only a *moment* of your time, I promise. And simple lines, too. But tarry a moment, there's a good lad, and permit me to recite them for you."

"Why me?"

"Because I've taken a fancy to you, lad. Because there aren't so many of us who understand what risk—and challenge—are all about." There was no more amusement in the eyes. "Humor me, there's a good lad. MacLeod surely has taught you manners."

He could walk away. Turn his back and walk away—

"Stay," the actor said simply. "I asked it of MacLeod once. Now I ask it of you."

If *Mac* could put up with this guy . . . Impatiently, Richie listened as the lines were quoted for him. He absorbed little of them, wanting nothing but to get away from the man.

"Recite them," the giant invited, hugging his broad chest. "*Recite* them, Richard Ryan, for Duncan MacLeod." He leaned in, loomed. "There's a purpose to it, I promise. If you've the wit to see it, this little exercise tells you everything you need to know." He straightened, smiling benignly. "Kind of a riddle, aye? Or maybe a wager." The grin was blinding. "A wager, you see, between MacLeod and me. If you figure out what I mean, I'll stand you and all your friends to a round of drinks. If not, well"—he shrugged elaborately—"then MacLeod buys for me and the company."

Mac bought often enough that Richie felt he should do his part, and if it would hasten his chance to leave . . . "All right," Richie said tightly. "But you'll have to give them to me again."

"Say them one at a time, Richard. I'll respond, and then *you* respond."

"Fine."

"You are Young Siward."

"I'm Young Siward. Great."

"Now say your first line."

That much Richie recalled. " '*What is thy name?*' "

"Good lad." The Scot nodded. " '*Thou'lt be afraid to hear it.*' "

Richie hesitated. The actor fed him his line, and he re peated it. " '*No; though thou call'st thyself a hotter name / Than any is in hell.*' "

"Better. Now, mine: '*My name's Macbeth.*' "

Richie waited for prompting, then recited his next line. " '*The devil himself could not pronounce a title / More hateful to mine ear.*' "

" '*No, nor more fearful.*' "

Mechanically: " '*Thou liest, abhorred tyrant; with my sword / I'll prove the lie thou speak'st.*' "

And then abruptly the huge hand was on his shoulder again, shoving him down to his knees; and the claymore, deftly drawn, lingered at his throat.

" '*Thou wast born of woman—*

But swords I smile at, weapons laugh to scorn,
Brandisht by man that's of a woman born.' "

The actor grinned. "You're dead, Young Siward."

Richie's knees hurt from unexpected contact with the granite plaza, and he was decidedly displeased to have the blade in such close proximity to his neck. Was it all just a setup? A challenge? Or just an example of eccentric artistic temperament?

Or maybe the guy and Mac really did have a bet.

Richie swallowed tightly, then wished he hadn't. Even so subtle a movement put the blade closer yet to the only place on his body that was vulnerable. "Fine. Can I go now?"

"But you're dead," the other said gently.

"Then you'd better make it for real, because otherwise I'm getting up and walking out of here right now."

"No appreciation of the Bard, have you?" The blade was moved; one hand shut around Richie's arm, dragged him to his feet. "On your way, pissant. I've an afternoon performance within the half hour, and then I'll be free for such things as practice and theory."

Richie shook off the hand. "You're nuts. You know that?"

"No. I'm *flamboyant.*" The big man grinned. "Some of us have to be."

Gripping his helmet tightly—and sorely tempted to smash it into the grinning, bearded face, except the face was too high and the leverage would be wrong—Richie swung away and marched himself down the plaza toward the parking lot.

And a bike that needed gas.

A wan and uncomfortable Joe Dawson greeted MacLeod's eyes as he walked into the hospital room, but Joe was also awake and aware and seemingly not in danger of dying anytime soon. Certainly not at this moment.

"Hey. MacLeod . . ."

He smiled, approached the bed. "Guess they're not letting you sleep much, with a concussion."

Dawson was propped against pillows, clad unappealingly in a green-patterned hospital gown. "Between blinks, maybe." He managed a lopsided smile.

MacLeod stood tensely, unable to relax. He wanted to move, *needed* to move, to bleed off the restlessness. "Anne says you'll be fine." He felt intensely uncomfortable in the hospital; it was a place he didn't like to be and yet found himself too often, though not for himself. It reminded him of the fragility of mortals, the easy random occurences—or pre-meditations—that broke their bones, tore their flesh, rendered them vegetative. "How's your shoulder?"

"Sore."

"Yeah." MacLeod grinned briefly. "Been there. Done that."

"No sympathy from here—you heal too fast." Dawson winced faintly. "Let me tell you, I've got a hell of a head-ache . . ."

Courtesies offered no answers. MacLeod turned, walked a few steps, swung back, and dispensed with idle platitudes. "Who did this to you, Joe?"

Dawson shut his eyes, seemed to drift.

He provoked purposely. "Anne says she thinks it was a sword."

"And if it was?" Dawson opened his eyes. "What would you do?"

He felt his face tighten into a cold, comfortable mask, the one he put on to keep others out. "What do you think?"

Joe shifted uneasily against piled pillows, grimaced. "Listen, Mac—"

MacLeod cut him off curtly. "My business, Joe."

"Oh, yeah? And here I thought it was *my* shoulder . . ."

And again: "Who was it, Joe?"

Dawson sighed, surrendering. "I don't know. It was dark—didn't get a good look at"—he paused—"him." He swallowed, visibly fading. "Look—it could have been any-body . . . probably just wanted to rob the bar—some guy with a big knife . . ."

"You know too many Immortals," MacLeod reminded him with deliberate irony.

"*Of* them, Mac . . . I only know three." He paused. "Four. I was forgetting Amanda."

MacLeod laughed softly. "How *anyone* could forget Amanda . . ."

"Yeah. And she'd let me hear about it, too." Pain cut across Dawson's face. "Let it go, Mac. I've had worse done to me than a blade in the shoulder and a bump on the head."

Indeed he had. But that admission didn't make MacLeod feel any more sanguine about this attack. It wasn't part of the Game. Mortals were not permitted to play, and though some of them, like Horton, had forcibly and physically inserted themselves into the Game, MacLeod had no patience for those of his kind who stooped to attacking a mortal. It was like deliberately squashing a perfectly harmless bug making its laborious and inoffensive way across a busy street.

Gratuitous violence.

Joe Dawson was not a bug, and MacLeod would see to it personally that the Immortal who'd tried to squash him paid for it.

When—and if—he found out who it was.

"MacLeod," Dawson murmured, "let it go."

"Can't do that," he said crisply, and exited the room.

Mattie watched him walk through the hallway toward the exit. There was purpose in his stride, swift and effortless motion coupled with determination; but though there was anger in his eyes, rage was absent. She had expected rage. Had *planned* on rage.

Or was it that mortals didn't matter? That Joe didn't matter? That MacLeod found it *annoying* a man he knew had been injured by one of his own kind, by a woman he slept with, but did not consider it worthy of anything more?

Joe Dawson was worth more. So were innocent Irish.

She watched him as a Watcher, though he was Joe's assignment: near-black hair pulled back into a ponytail fastened with silver clasp; the ripple of dark gray raincoat away from his legs, hiding the lethal katana that was his particular weapon; thin sweater, a fine-knit silvery-fawn, concealing nothing at all of the contours and hard musculature of his chest; the powerful thighs of gymnast, wrestler, athlete.

He was himself a weapon, with blade or without.

Mattie rose from the chair as he drew even with her, took a single step into the hallway, but stopped herself from speaking to him. She was nothing to him, *could* be nothing to him: mortal, unmet, unimportant.

He glanced at her briefly, indifferently: brown eyes were hard and cold despite the warmth of their color; he looked inwardly to himself, not outwardly at her or on the world mortals inhabited—and then he looked away. Strode quickly to the end of the hall and out the sliding glass doors.

Mattie turned away, slipping the folded newspaper under her arm. She paced, considered, conjured up again the vision she had imagined. Police. FBI. Perhaps even MacLeod, negating the need for arrest.

She would not tell Joe. He would disapprove. He would suggest she remove herself from her present assignment, and then she would have to leave.

Until Annie Devlin was gone, she didn't have to leave.

Worth it, she reflected. For Joe's sake. For the lives of the Irish people.

Mattie turned sharply and walked with MacLeod's purposefulness to Joe Dawson's room.

The crowd drifted away as Jamie Douglas and Colin Cameron completed their teaser selections in front of the Cultural Center. Afterward, as they turned to fold up and carry off the portable backdrop, a small girl came up to tug on Cameron's costume; she asked if he were really a man, as someone had said.

Douglas smiled to himself as Cameron handled the answer deftly, satisfying the girl's curiosity. Then Colin turned back, expression bemused. "Why?" he asked.

"Because you *look* like a woman, Coll. You're convincing. I imagine a lot of children would be confused."

Cameron gestured sharply. "No, not that. I mean, why feed the lines to that friend of MacLeod's?"

"Maybe I wanted to see if he had the talent in him, as you do."

A brief, ironic smile hooked one corner of Cameron's mouth. "I don't think so."

"No, he's got no flair," Jamie agreed judiciously.

"Not *that*—" Colin said impatiently. "I meant, I don't think that's what you were really after."

"That's for me to know and MacLeod to find out." Douglas hoisted his end of the backdrop. "And one of the ways of making certain MacLeod comes to me—to us—is to use his friends. One way or another. Now, pick up your end, laddie."

As Cameron hastened to obey, Jamie reflected that it was *always* easiest to get the results one desired by using the target's friends.

He also reflected that it was unfortunate Shakespeare had never written a play about Machiavelli. Such lines, those would be!

Dawson drifted, longing to sleep through the night, but no one would permit it. Concussion, Anne Lindsey had explained with maddening matter-of-factness, could alter into coma if care were not taken; and so he was awakened frequently because they insisted, his torturers. He was sore and bruised, growing progressively out of sorts. MacLeod had gone and the adrenaline Joe'd accessed for the verbal fencing spilled away. He needed decent sleep, *God* but he needed sleep—

He sighed heavily as he heard the step in the open doorway. Anne, or one of the nurses. "Yeah, yeah," he mumbled, "I'm awake."

"Such pleasure in my company," Mattie O'Connell declared archly.

Startled, he opened his eyes. She saw it, smiled, nodded. "I've been told twice already that you're not likely to die from so puny a thing as this."

"Yeah, well . . ." He wished he were more alert, felt less like a horse who'd been ridden hard and put away wet. "We Dawsons are tough as old shoe-leather, Mary Margaret."

"Not old," she disagreed comfortably. "Broken in, perhaps."

He managed a muffled laugh. "I *am* flattered."

"You should be." The skin beside her eyes crinkled. What

was it about Irishwomen? Maybe the moisture in the air—or, Heaven forbid, maybe even the soap.

Another figure came into the doorway, paused, lingered. "Hey, Joe. How you doing?"

Dawson blinked. "Richie?"

"Yeah." Richie glanced at Mattie. "Some woman called earlier, said you were here."

"Me," Mattie confirmed.

"So I wanted to stop by, see how you were doing." He looked worried. "You gonna make it?"

Dawson grinned. "We were just discussing the merits of a hide tough as old shoe leather. It has its advantages."

Richie nodded, leaned against the doorjamb as if to come in further admitted him as well. "I found Mac."

"He's been here already." Joe did not at that moment wish necessarily to converse with Richie when Mattie provided company, but he could hardly be rude. "Twitchy as ever in a hospital. But I think I managed to talk him out of launching a vendetta."

Richie's brows lifted sharply. "How did you manage that?"

Joe smiled, sleepily fatuous. "By withholding information. Just as well, I think. The last thing he needs is a fight because of me."

Mattie's face was very still. "You didn't tell him?"

God, but he was so tired . . . "No point in it. You don't know MacLeod . . . once he makes up his mind you can't call him off." He looked at Richie. "And *you'd* better not tell him."

Richie raised both hands in a placatory gesture. "Not me! This is between you and Mac, if that's the way you want it."

"Good." Dawson looked at the Irishwoman again, saw the fixity of her gaze as she stared at his shoulder. "Mattie—?"

She stirred, smiled brilliantly. "I'm sorry . . . gathering wool, I guess." She repositioned the newspaper tucked under one arm. "I'll leave you to Richie awhile, if you don't mind. I've got to make some calls. I'll be back later."

"Thanks, Mattie," he said. "If you hadn't been there—"

"Oh, Mike would have found you in the morning," she said lightly.

"Yeah, but it would have been a hell of a long night!"

She waved briefly, glanced sidelong at Richie, then slipped out the door.

"Not bad," Richie commented. "That is, for an older woman."

Joe cocked a startled eyebrow. "Yeah, well—what will you say about women Mattie's age when you're two hundred years old?"

Richie considered that. "True," he conceded, and looked so deeply concerned that Dawson began to laugh.

And promptly wished he hadn't.

Chapter Nineteen

The dojo and loft were uninhabited by Immortals. MacLeod shoved open the door, stepped off the elevator, and went directly to the wall-mounted phone by the window, a conventional phone neither cordless nor cellular. He punched in the long series of numbers quickly, then checked his watch. Six o'clock in the evening his time was three in the morning Paris time. Too bad.

Transatlantic connections were far faster and clearer than they used to be, before the days of fiber optics. But for a man who for most of his life had access to nothing beyond a good horse, a carriage, or a pair of legs, such swiftness of communication still seemed miraculous.

Just now, however, anything was too slow.

After three blurry rings, the other end picked up. He opened his mouth to rudely appropriate the conversation, then realized in angry frustration it was a recorded message. Methos, despite the hour, was not at home.

He waited impatiently for the cheery, ironic greeting to end, followed by the tone; when at last it sounded, he stated his message with meticulous succinctness and nothing at all of emotion. It was everywhere in his body *except* his voice.

"This is MacLeod. I want anything Adam Pierson has on any of us who might be here in the city—and who might have a grudge against Joe Dawson."

Nothing else. Nothing more was needed. He disconnected immediately and set the handset back onto its hook.

Methos would know if anyone did. Methos, in his guise as Watcher Adam Pierson, had access to the files, the Chronicles. Methos as Immortal had access to five thousand years of memory.

MacLeod was one step away from the phone when the knock sounded at the door beside the elevator. Mortal; there was no sense of presence beyond the noise of knocking. MacLeod moved swiftly to it, undid the bolt, pulled the heavy door open.

A series of images, quickly catalogued: a woman. Black-haired, blue-eyed, of average height, weight, nearing middle-age; not exceptionally attractive but neither was she plain. Her hair and the shoulders of her coat were dappled silver in diffused light; it was raining again outside.

"Duncan MacLeod," she said with exquisite clarity in a soft Irish accent, "you know very well who it was put a sword into Joe Dawson's shoulder. You just don't want to admit it."

It was a blade in the belly, albeit her hands were empty of knife or sword. "You're her Watcher."

From beneath her arm she pulled a newspaper and dropped it so it landed flat against the floor very near his feet, the way a carrier slapped it down with the banner headline foremost. Everything above the fold was clearly visible, including the photograph. Answer in and of itself, though she chose to elaborate.

"What is it the Yanks say—'read it and weep'? Well, if you can't believe everything you read—or *choose not to*— then I'll swear on your katana I was there—*there*, MacLeod! —and saw what she did, how she threatened him. It was I who saw her leave the bar, and I who found him after she was through." Her eyes were steady, cold as those he'd seen in any Immortal's skull prior to engagement. "Don't justify it, MacLeod. You can't. You know as well as I what Annie Devlin is. Only this time it's one of *your* friends hurt for it."

"I'm not proud of it," Annie had said the night before. *"This was for me, not for Ireland."*

"She's wanted all over the world," the woman said calmly. "And if you don't find her, the authorities will—now that they know she's here."

No more than that. Her message to him, as his to Methos, was delivered without a word wasted. And she as much as he expected action upon it. Immediate and unequivocal action.

Everything in him and of him demanded the same.

She backed away, smiling faintly, as he jerked shut the door behind him. He left her there, making her quiet way down the stairs in a leisurely fashion, as he took them two at a time.

"This was for me, not for Ireland."

Even as he reached the T-bird, the proper key was in his hand.

"Because I was angry. And frightened."

He yanked open the door, sat down, rescued the tails of his coat as he pulled the door shut again. This time the key was in the ignition.

"That is my confession, as much as I can make one. If you will have it of me."

He would have more than that of her.

Richie was wet and chilled as he made his way up the exterior stairs to the back door of MacLeod's loft. He unlocked and went in, thinking of warmth, a beer; stepped square onto something that tore, and stopped long enough to discover it was a newspaper left haphazardly on the floor just inside the door. He retrieved it, grimaced as he saw the wet, gritty, waffle-soled bootprint he'd left across the now-mangled front page, then flopped the paper onto the countertop in case Mac wanted it despite its current condition. You could never tell *what* MacLeod valued; some of his antiques looked like junk to Richie. Antique junk.

He peeled off his wet jacket, got a beer out of the refrigerator, and retreated to the couch, where he promptly stumbled over something on the floor.

"Oh, great—first I destroy his paper, now I kill his book." Richie bent, caught it up, idly turned the spine so he could read the title. "*Selected Plays of William Shakespeare?*" It did not sound particularly compelling—but as he leaned to drop the book onto the coffee table he recalled the "Scottish play." And also the annoying actor who had made him spout some of the lines.

Richie sat down promptly and began to page through the book, hunting up the play. He found it, scanned it for the part of Young Siward, read the appropriate lines. He was left more baffled than before. So he went back to the beginning, to Act I, Scene I, and began to read as rapidly as could be managed, scowling in perplexed disgust. "You know, it would really help if this guy wrote in *English* . . ."

The theater was emptied of audience and, eventually, of staff and crew and actors as well. Only one was left: James Douglas, seated on a stool before a mirror in the dressing room, removing makeup. He wore still the snug breeches of his costume, the leather doublet sheathed in ringmail, wide belt, boots. None of the costume was historically accurate— as he should know better than any—but this was, after all, the *theater*.

"As bad as the games," he muttered, wiping off a smudge of greasepaint from beneath one tawny eye. "Highland Games, my *arse*. My *own* I had rather play." More makeup, the last of it, then he slathered on moisturizer and grinned toothily at his glistening reflection.

> "*Tyrant, show thy face!*
> *If thou be'st slain and with no stroke of mine,*
> *My wife and children's ghosts will haunt me still . . .*
> *. . . either thou, MacLeod,*
> *Or else my sword, with unbatter'd edge,*
> *I sheathe again undeeded.*"

He paused, then turned on his stool. *Immortal* . . . He waited mutely, feeling joyous anticipation bubble up beneath his ribs, and was not displeased when the woman opened the door.

"Annie my love!" He thrust himself up from the stool, reaching out to grasp a slim, cool, hilt-callused hand. "Did you see the performance?"

"I did." She resisted slightly as he led her to a chair, avoiding his sticky face, then sat down at his behest. "But I have seen it before, so it's lost much of its charm."

"But not like this performance. It may be my last—at least, in this country." He made a very good leg with a deft flourish of his right hand—wrong period, again, alas—and gathered up a stack of newspapers. "Have you seen these, lass? I thought you might wish to—everyone enjoys reading notices!"

She grimaced as he dumped the stack into her lap. "What are these, Jamie—" And then she stopped short, frozen into abject immobility.

"Ah," he said lightly, smoothing lotion residue into his skin, "I see you appreciate it."

The blood drained from her face, leaving her stark and pale, like bleached doeskin stretched over a drumhead. He noted with idle amusement it was the first time he had ever seen Annie Devlin look her true age, insofar as she could.

"In every one of them," he pointed out helpfully. "And on the news, too, I rather expect." He bent down, down, caught and cradled her jaw in his huge, hard palms. "Annie, my love," he whispered, "the worm has turned. See what MacLeod has done?"

Violently she shoved the papers from her lap. "Not *MacLeod*—"

He stepped back, arched a single brow. "Not I, Annie. I'll swear it on the Stone of Scone, on the Honours of Scotland, on a piece of turf cut from Drummossie Moor itself, in the name of Culloden." All said with the utmost sincerity, because it was true.

"He *swore* to me—"

"—that you could trust him? Did he make you an oath, Annie?"

Oh, but how fortunate that someone had done his work for him; had already given Annie cause to hate MacLeod, instead of leaving Jamie to plant the seeds of argument as he had planned, the seeds of division, of ending; inflammatory words of such power as he could muster, boomed out from the heart and soul of a betrayed warrior who was also brilliant actor.

It would come to a fight, of course. Highlander against Highlander. Immortal against Immortal. A simple challenge might have been enough—it served in other instances—but this appealed to the actor's sense of the dramatic. The one known as *the* Highlander, by definition a Scot before anything else, brought to comprehend the nature of his transgression, to confess his betrayal, to understand how Duncan MacLeod of the Clan MacLeod, reputed to be the most honorable of all living Immortals, was nothing after all but an oath-breaker, not fit to live among the clans who revered oaths and honor. Cast out once; now cast out again from the shabby house he had built of the remains of his birthright, denied by his father on the day Duncan MacLeod survived his first death.

And it was so sweet, this, to witness Annie Devlin of all people, hear, understand, and comprehend the immensity of what he told her now, the magnitude of repercussions. It would have come to this within forty-eight hours, as he goaded them to argument, as he lured and used Richard Ryan. He had improvised with Colin Cameron's information on the mortal Watcher to set Annie up for a fall even without the arguments, but he had planned to lure MacLeod onto his stage eventually anyway, after he had played him long enough. It all began right now because someone had aided him.

As Lady Macbeth had aided her husband.

Color began to creep back into Annie's face, bit by bit, like pinpricks of blood welling up tentatively from a bad scrape. But her lips remained white. "He gave me his *oath*."

Inwardly he exulted. Outwardly, he sympathized—and goaded her further. "Ah, and by any chance was it his Trinity? On his honor as a Scot, a Highlander, as Duncan MacLeod of the Clan MacLeod?"

A shudder wracked her. He had seen dead mortals look better.

Almost, Jamie felt pity. But this was so sweet! "You see, that's what he swore to me, bonnie Annie . . . on the field of Culloden as I lay dying that first time. That he would stay, that he would be *with* me so I need not be alone on the cusp of reawakening. But he broke those oaths, Annie. He broke his personal Trinity." He leaned down close, though he did not touch her again. "Duncan MacLeod of the Clan MacLeod is a stone liar."

Even as she turned her face up to stare at him out of eyes going black with fury, they felt it—and heard the shout from the front of the theater. *"Annie! Annie Devlin!"*

Jamie backed away from her, displaying empty hands. "Your fight, bonnie Annie."

She was here. MacLeod, entering through an unlocked front door, could sense her, *feel* her; or else it was James Douglas.

Inwardly he cursed, pausing on the threshhold between lobby and theater. Too dark; the lighting was keyed down very low, so that impenetrable bars of shadows lurked between rows of seats, shrouded the folds in heavy curtains. But the air was alive with it, setting his bones to thrumming.

"Annie!" He walked down the inclined center aisle toward the stage, striding smoothly, automatically balancing himself even in motion.

A sound issued from the stage, from behind a shielding scrim. He stopped short two thirds of the way down the aisle, just beyond the break between orchestra and loge. He saw a figure, a silhouette, behind the gauzy scrim.

Duncan MacLeod prided himself on self-control, honed over the years from the impetuosities of youth and inexperience into a habitual cool, analytical assessment of circumstances. He was not above anger, not above inseparable complexities of emotions when he engaged another Immortal—there were those who made self-control difficult at best—but he was not given to excess displays of anything save consummate skill when he fought.

And though he did not intend to engage Annie—he most decidedly did not want her head—he *did* intend to express his opinion. This time, for this reason, he let the anger loose. "Why Joe Dawson?" His shout filled the theater. "Why Joe, Annie? Because you're afraid to be Watched?"

A flicker of movement, the barest motion from behind him. He spun, coat swinging wide—

—and it was Annie, Annie *there*, not up on the stage—

"Bastard!" she cried. "I *trusted* you, MacLeod!"

He had hoped to talk eventually, perhaps first to confront and shout and argue—he and Annie had done no less at other times—but clearly it was too late.

—*Now*— And he was moving, shifting balance instantly, effortlessly, every muscle and sinew tuned to preserve his head.

Time slowed, as it did for him. Always. Time became predictable, though not always the people in it. Most of the time, many times, but not *every* time—

Still. It was— "Annie!—"

—and one hand grasping the hilt of the katana, withdrawing it in the same swift move . . . brief rotation, unweighting off one foot onto the other because of the incline . . . snapping blade up on the diagonal to block the overhand blow that would surely come, that had to come, as she went for his head . . . because he knew better than to give Annie Devlin the benefit of doubt . . .

"Annie—I don't *want* this—"

But she did. And shifted, dropped low, so low, *too* low—

"Don't, Annie! I came to talk—I don't want this and neither do you—" He heard the voice of her blade, attempted a block, realized too late she was not engaging as a man would, or even as she had engaged Richie in a signature move MacLeod had trained him to defeat.

—didn't go for his head at all, or even for his belly—

—*hamstring*—

She string-halted him like a wolf on an elk—

—*so fast*—

—only her teeth were a swordblade, a slice of shining steel slashing low, too low; that cut through pantleg, through boot top, into flesh and vessels and tendon—

"Annie!"

—that took leg and balance from him, brought him down in a tumble of pain, a garbled blurt of shock expelled along with breath, a clattering of katana as outflung arms, smashing down, crashed hard against seats.

"Annie, *stop—*"

He was larger than she, older, more experienced, much stronger, faster, and far more powerful. They both had known that on a level playing field she simply could not defeat him. But she had found the way to cut him down to size.

To Annie Devlin's size.

Chapter Twenty

Richie closed the book, held it, stared bemusedly into the distance. Slowly he set the volume on the table, picked up his beer bottle, discovered it was empty. Set it back down again without even blinking.

He began sorting them out. "There's Duncan—and Macbeth murders him. Check." He stuck his left thumb into the air. "And then Macduff kills Macbeth, because he thinks Macbeth has killed his wife and kids—or *had* them killed—and because Macbeth killed Duncan, who was King of Scotland . . . only now *Macbeth* is. Or was. Check." The index finger went up. "And then there's Malcolm—because he's Duncan's son, who's dead; and Macduff, who killed Macbeth, doesn't want to be King of Scotland, but wants *Malcolm* on the throne—"

The ringing of the phone interrupted his recitation. Still working out convoluted Scottish and Shakespearean connections, Richie answered distractedly.

For a long moment there was silence, though the line remained open. And then, in careful inquiry, *"Richie?"*

It was. He said so.

Another pause. *"Adam Pierson. Is MacLeod there?"*

"Adam *Pier*—oh." He leaned against the wall, shifting gears with effort. "No, Mac isn't here right now. I don't know when he'll be back. Can I take a message?"

Sharply: *"Where is he?"*

"I don't know where he is," Richie answered in irritation. "It's not like he leaves a Dayrunner for me to check—"

"Find him, Richie."

He'd never heard that tone in that man. A chill ran down his back. He stood up instantly, tense. "Why?"

"Look, I only just got back into town and learned Joe Dawson has been asking questions about an Immortal. I've been sorting out an emerging pattern in reports for the past few months, matching unexplained decapitations and various unconfirmed sightings, unattributed events. It's all been very random, but Joe gave me the key: the common denominator is the Highland Shakespeare Company—"

"Yes," Richie blurted sharply.

A pause. *"Do you know this company?"*

"They're here in the city. Now."

Pierson spoke rapidly. *"You've got to find MacLeod before whoever is doing this finds him. I've been trying to reach Joe—"*

"He's been hurt," Richie interrupted. "He's in the hospital. Listen, what's—"

"Then that explains MacLeod's call." He broke it off. *"Find MacLeod, Richie. This isn't part of the Game. This is revenge. This is madness. The man is insane."*

Richie stilled. "What do you mean, insane? Who?"

"He kills them twice, Richie. It's always smashed faces, pointblank gunshot wounds to the spine, sword blows through chest or skull—apparently he even drags them to death behind a car. Then takes their heads while they're dead, before they can heal."

"Oh my God," Richie murmured. *"That's* what he meant . . . it's all in the play! He was Macbeth *and* Macduff—"

"Richie—"

"Macbeth kills Duncan, then Macduff kills Macbeth! And the big guy played *both parts*—" He stopped as the implications extended endlessly before him: infinity's manifest destiny. "I think I know where Mac is."

"Richie, wait—"

But Richie hung up and ran for the elevator.

Annie knew MacLeod would heal quickly, so she had to take him before bone and muscle knitted. He was down in a most awkward position, even for her as attacker, sprawled mostly on his back on the floor between rows of seats. He was jammed there, but also shielded by seats, by chair arms and backs, hidden mostly in shadow, though she heard the hissing of indrawn breath, a bitten-off grunt of extremity. Something slid, chimed—

—katana—

"Annie—"

"Damn you!" She brought her blade down into shadow, hoping to catch flesh, knock down the katana. She needed to do it now, *now*, while fury fueled her. *"Damn* you, MacLeod—"

He shifted against the floor, the seats, seeking purchase; to come up, to defend. To attack? "Annie, wait—"

Her downward stroke caught something, but not flesh. Sheared seat cushion, or chair-back—

Movement, then . . . a huddled darker patch thrusting up from the shadows near the floor. *MacLeod*— She had lost the element of surprise. He was injured, but not made helpless. And infinitely dangerous.

She saw the glint of silver, the sheen of polished steel—

Annie sidestepped, caught the blade on her own, trapped it and threw it back, knowing he was off-balance, defending from instinct, not position or skill.

—quickly— His sword was raised as he struggled to get legs under him, a knee. He might snag a shoulder with a downstroke, but he was too low, his center of gravity altered by a crouched position. He was too disadvantaged to do more than wound her, and that she could bear.

Annie ducked in swiftly, adjusted grip so she held the hilt of her blade as if it were a butter churn, stabbed sharply downward—and heard a chopped-off grunt of pain.

—got you—

Something snatched at the seam of her coat, where the sleeve met the shoulder. Fabric tore aside, stripped away from her arm. Annie felt the sting of edged steel kiss the flesh of her arm. She jerked it away, twisting, then shifted back instantly, adjusting her grip on the hilt once again.

If he stayed down, shielded by seats and chair-backs, she would not have a good opportunity for a clean stroke. But if he got up—

If she got too close—

Do it— She brought her blade down from high overhead, hoping to cleave chest, to stop him before he could rise— "Damn you—" she sobbed. "I *trusted* you—"

Annie Devlin had trusted no one but her own for one hundred and fifteen years, since the English killed the "mother" and hacked the "daughter" to death.

Except for Duncan MacLeod, who had never been hers, ever; was only and always himself.

He learned before his first death never to trust any word or movement of the foe in battle, to make no assumptions under any circumstances; to kill as quickly as possible and to be certain of the death lest he risk his own life. He had died anyway, though not through foolishness, merely odds too great to withstand, but had awakened to another chance. And countless times beyond.

He was not a fool; he knew how to die. Knew also how to live. And Connor MacLeod had taught him the balance of knowledge, the comprehension that for all he was Immortal in nearly every instance, he should never grow complacent. Further studies with May-Ling Shen in Mongolia had taught him more, even how to fight a woman.

But not then, not ever, had he learned how to fight one like Annie. Annie, who had been in his bed, in his heart, and now came for his head. He knew himself well enough to know his own weakness—he could not kill a woman he had loved. Methos had taken it for chivalry, but it was not her sex that had protected Kristin from his blade, or not only. She had been friend and lover, once. What kind of man would kill a lover when he was finished with her? Not him. Not Duncan MacLeod.

He had been driven to it before, and life had chosen life—he had chosen to live, and live with the pain and shame of it. Not this time, please. Not Annie. He would have to find a way to win without killing her.

If Annie permitted it.

"I'll do it—" she began, but MacLeod kicked out then, thrusting sharply with one booted foot. Annie gasped as he caught her low but flush on the shin, knocking her backward as pain burst at the point of impact. She jerked away, taking weight off the leg hastily. "Bastard—"

He came up then, hampered yet up, uncoiling, moving; had shed the coat so he was less encumbered. He flipped the katana neatly as a baseball bat, slicing side-armed but tucked, elbow leading, so that the hilt was foremost rather than the blade—

—and jammed the ivory dragon's head square into her solar plexus.

Gone, all the breath gone on a keening wail—

Annie fell back, fell down, diaphragm briefly paralyzed. Sheer instinct flopped her over onto her belly; she felt cold steel beneath her body, hilt digging into one hip.

—too easy a target—

She snatched at hilt, pulled the sword to her even as she sucked knees under her body. Breath was there, if just out of reach—

But so was MacLeod. His left hand was blood-slicked; she saw the cut in the pale sweater, the stain around it. That too would repair itself as well as the severed hamstring, but for now he wasn't quite whole. Wasn't *quite* Duncan MacLeod.

He tested his foot. It gave slightly, healing but not yet healed, even as he expelled a sharp exhalation. He took the weight onto his other leg, grasped at a chair-back. The katana was gripped in his right hand, but he didn't raise it. Two awkward choppy steps took him down the aisle a stride, then three, close to the stage. Retreating, not attacking. She saw his expression, the welter of emotions: unmitigated pain, shock, denial; an odd, desperate despair.

She had hurt him. Had damaged him. There still was time.

She caught up the sword, thrust upward onto her feet. Two-handed, higher, uphill, she had better leverage—

"Annie!—" One-legged, wounded, he still caught her blade on his. Steel screeched, dragged, scraped, then sliced apart as he trapped, twisted, and knocked the weapon down, though not free to fall against the floor.

Annie jerked loose, caught her balance, then used it. She rotated into her left hip and took weight onto that leg, employed his example and kicked out with her right foot. She caught him hard on his good leg, hyperextending the knee, and smashed it from under him. "Down, you bastard!" she cried. "*Down*, damn your eyes—"

But he came up, unaccountably *up*; and was there, suddenly there— "Annie—" he gasped, winded even as she was, "*don't do this*— Don't make me kill—"

"Me?" she hissed. "So you won't, you bloody bastard— *I'll* do the killing here! It's what I do to men who betray the Cause!"

She saw his face. Saw the eyes. Saw in every aspect of his body recognition and regret. Abject resolution. And also grief.

Grief? By God, she'd make him save it for himself!

One final glorious slash with all of her strength and skill, committing everything unto him, keening as the Gaels of old going into battle.

He blocked it. Broke it.

Took her.

MacLeod tasted blood: his own. He had bitten his lip, bitten the side of his cheek. The wound in his abdomen was nearly healed, as was his ankle. But none of it mattered. Not the pain, the blood, the healing.

Despair engulfed utterly. He dropped the katana, fell to his knees in the aisle.

On hands and knees he reached out, touched one limp, outstretched hand, gripped slack fingers. The cry came unexpectedly into his chest, demanding release, though he shut it up in his mouth. *Ochone*, in Gaelic; the keening wail of the living for those they mourned who were not.

Ochone.

Never. Never Annie.

Ochone.

It was not enough, to lock it inside his head. Winded, weeping, he sucked in breath to shout aloud the grief and pain according to ritual, to loose the great ache from his soul—but the Quickening came for him then, or she did. Exited her body, the cage of useless flesh, and left her behind, empty. It betrayed and departed her, sought him out, found him—

—*became* him; and he it; and he her; and she him; and all of the other Immortals Annie Devlin had killed, and those he had killed; and he was too many people, too *many*: heads and hearts and brains and bodies and too many angry souls, too many lost and angry souls—toomanytoomanytoomany—all clamoring for comprehension.

Duncan MacLeod. Duncan *MacLeod*. DUNCAN MAC-LEOD.

Only and always himself.

It warped his body, wracked him, sheathed his bones with living fire and knotted all his muscles. He was an engine, seizing; everything stopped, *stopped*, save for what used his limbs, his mind, his self-control. Took every bit of him, every thought, and twisted, tested it.

He managed one shout for her, for Annie's sake: her name roared out to the heavens so they might hear him, hear her name, and know her, accept her.

And then he could do nothing more than let it use him, let it dictate what and who he was. It hurled him back, smashed him down onto his back, left him there struggling to get up, to make sense of the moment.

Annie Devlin.

He cried out again, denying it. Integrating the knowledge was too difficult, too painful.

He lurched to his knees, crawled to Annie. Felt the power run through him again, winding itself around his bones. It took him again, shook him again, snapped him back, arched him back onto knees with arms outstretched—

—and released him.

James Douglas saw it, though his eyes were closed. He sat behind the scrim, squatted down upon his haunches, and rocked back and forth.

How many? He had lost count. Not enough. They had come for his head, each of them, testing him, trying to outdo him in the Game he now played because at last he had learned it, after years of incomprehension, decades and centuries in which he survived because he was bigger, stronger— and impossible to kill. He was not meant to die. Therefore, he would not.

He rocked upon his haunches, knees doubled up. In his eye he saw them, all those men whom he had killed. And killed them as he himself had been killed that very first time. Easy enough for a giant to overpower a smaller Immortal, to let the man *realize* he was defeated—and then to kill him by mortal means. To extend the death, play it out, employing exquisite theatrical timing—until the perfect moment arrived. Because although each man's body attempted to heal itself as swiftly as ever, Jamie took care to injure that body again and again before the healings could be completed.

One Frenchman, because the fool insisted. An elegant Spaniard, a silent Italian. But all the rest English. All the rest Sassenachs, to pay them back for what they had done to him on the bloodied fields of Culloden, where all around him his people died in the name of the Stuart king and his son, the prince, who led them.

Into defeat.

Sassenachs had smashed his nose and jaw, cut open his chest, blown apart his spine, put a saber through his skull, and dragged him to death behind a galloping horse. Fitting punishment, then, to render unto them the same kind of treatment before he beheaded them. Although it was more difficult now to find a horse for the purpose; in the end he had switched to cars.

Jamie was content for decades to kill Sassenachs, be they

locals or visitors, wherever the company traveled—until he met Annie Devlin by chance in Ireland, who told him the man he believed long dead was not dead at all. Not *mortal* at all. Was in fact like Jamie, had been like him at Culloden, had known very well what the dying Douglas was and what he would become.

James Douglas understood then this was his task: to find and kill Duncan MacLeod, who had broken the oaths a Scotsman held most sacred. To find him, trick him, kill him, the way James Douglas had been tricked and killed by what MacLeod chose intentionally to leave unsaid.

Jamie lifted his head. Pupils expanded. Arousal was upon him. "Now," he whispered, and clapped both hands across his mouth to keep the wild laughter from escaping.

Later could come the laughter. Timing was everything.

The puppet's strings were cut. MacLeod fell, fell hard, belly-down; kept from smashing his face against the carpeted floor only by just managing to thrust an arm and hand in between. Belly heaved against the floor, trying to find air, a rhythm, to reinflate his lungs.

God. *Annie*—

He felt it then, cutting through grief in the aftermath of the Quickening. And knew—

Hands caught him up, huge hands, powerful hands; hooked beneath his arms and lifted him up as a child; clasped him, grasped him, raised him; turned him, weightless and helpless; carried him two long strides and hurled him up onto the stage.

"Look!" the voice shouted. "Look upon yourself, oath-breaker!"

He landed, slid, rolled; saw it then, as he was meant to. The pole, standing upright from a slot atop the cairn of false stones.

Duncan MacLeod's head, severed, jammed onto the pike.

James Douglas leaped nimbly up onto the stage, caught him by the hair, dragged him up. Then smashed one massive fist into his nose, the hinge of his jaw, shattering both.

"A beginning," Douglas suggested happily, slipping into dialect. "We'll see how *you* do, aye?—before I put the flesh-and-blood head there upon yon pike."

Chapter Twenty-one

Too soon . . . *too soon* after the Quickening . . .

And James Douglas knew it.

MacLeod threw himself away from the booted foot, distantly aware of blood, the unpleasant slackness in his jaw even as he slid across slick wood. The white blaze of pain was matched only by the shock, but was overwhelmed a moment later by sheer desperation and the attempt to get out of reach.

He scrambled, slid, rolled away, slipped again; felt the tip of a boot hook under his ribs and flip him. Again he rolled away, avoiding the next kick. He wanted his katana badly, but it was back on the floor in the aisle, near Annie's body.

MacLeod sobbed for air, swallowed blood, gagged and coughed, spat out spray. The hamstring was whole again, as was the wound in his abdomen, but no part of him was recovered from the Quickening.

—too soon—

It was abrogation of honor, of everything he knew as a Scot, a Highlander, a man. As an Immortal he had never once, no matter the circumstances, engaged another caught up in the Quickening, or immediately thereafter. Otherwise he could have taken Kalas on the boat in Paris, after Fitzcairn had been beheaded. All he had to do then was jump from the walkway to the flatboat, wield the katana: one slice, no more, and Kalas was gone.

But he hadn't. He had let Kalas go, then, albeit Kalas died later atop the Eiffel Tower. Because it wasn't fair or honorable, Duncan felt, to take advantage of an Immortal so physically, mentally, and spiritually weakened, so unable to defend himself on anything akin to common ground. A man of honor could not.

The boy, Kenny, had tried. And now James Douglas.

"Oath-breaker!" the giant roared. "We'll play awhile, aye? I've told the security men we're rehearsing, and the lights are automated, and the effects are powerful if as yet untried . . . no one will come, oath-breaker, no matter what we do here. I can delay as long as I like before I take your head."

MacLeod gained his feet at last, backing away carefully, wary of slick footing; cast hasty, breathless glances at stage, curtains, cairn, stairs, marking what he might need. It was essential that he retrieve his katana—

Douglas bent briefly to the cairn, took up something and tucked it into his wide leather belt, then grasped his claymore. Smiling. Declaiming. Tawny eyes blazed with exaltation.

> *"Turn, hell-hound, turn!*
> *. . . I have no words—*
> *My voice is in my sword, thou bloodier villain*
> *Than terms can give thee out!' "*

MacLeod could barely speak for the pain and blood. "Douglas—"

"Four times," the giant said conversationally. "Did you know that? Four times I died there upon the field. Right in a row, bonnie Duncan. Within *one* hour."

Four times. Four deaths, one upon another, with no knowledge of what he was, what it meant, what it made of him.

"—mad," MacLeod said. As Garrick had been, burned to death, then remade.

"Am I?" Douglas asked. "But you knew me, MacLeod. At Culloden. Remember?"

"I never knew you."

Jamie was astounded. "At Culloden, MacLeod!"

"I *never* knew you." MacLeod sucked in a breath, aware of knitting flesh, but also pain. "You were a dying man at Culloden, no more."

"But you did. Everyone did. James Douglas. The *Red* Douglas. I remember that you knew!"

"You were no more to me than a piece of meat."

That infuriated Douglas, as it was meant to. It did not fit his vision of the truth.

MacLeod, cursing, turned and ran for the edge of the stage. He slipped in his own blood, caught himself, but the delay was costly. The blade whistled down through the air; he spun, threw himself wide, aside, snapped arms out of the way.

—feint . . .

Douglas was strong enough to stop the blade in its arc, to jerk it back, then plunge it deeply through breastbone. The big Scot grinned even as he twisted, then sheared downward through ribs.

"First the jaw," he said, "the nose as we go, then the chest." He jerked the blade free even as MacLeod collapsed to his knees. "Then the spine, then the skull . . . I've no horse or car here, so I'll skip ahead." He shouted with laughter. "But I won't skip *your* head!"

Duncan MacLeod had died any number of times. He healed every time, but every time there was pain. The death was a normal death, no different save for regeneration, rebirth. Even as his jaw healed itself, his chest was peeled apart as if he were a tin can and Jamie the opener.

—no strength . . .

The Quickening had drained him, and Douglas had come too soon.

This time . . . this time?

No honor. Not in this.

MacLeod rolled to the edge, tipped, took himself off the stage. The awkward landing jarred him, robbed him of breath. He scrambled up, one hand and forearm pressed hard against the wounded chest as his heart labored to pump more blood and oxygen.

"Run, oath-breaker!" Douglas roared. "D'ye think that puny twig of Japanese steel can stop my good Scots claymore?"

It could. It could—*if* he could reach it.

"But you're forgetting," Jamie said. "The next one was a *gun*—"

And gun it was, of a sudden and unanticipated; but why should he expect James Douglas to limit himself to sword?

Up the aisle, into shadows—

—*now*—

—hurling himself down to retrieve the katana.

And the shot, the shattering, the spine ripped apart. And darkness, sudden and swift; was it to be now?

Now, after four hundred years?

Highland blood on the hands of a fellow Highlander . . .

MacLeod roused with a start, a shudder, a sucked-in hiss of pain. His entire body jerked.

"Up," Douglas suggested, prodding with a boot toe. "There's more yet, laddie."

—*not dead, not the true death*—

Not dead *yet*.

Duncan scrambled up, flung himself to the katana. Came down upon it, rolled over, ripped it free, lunged up from the ground: winded, gasping, with blade thrust out to guard, to ward away. Defense, not *off*ense; he had nothing left to offer. Too much, too fast, on the heels of the Quickening.

James Douglas, singing softly, leaned nonchalantly against the stage, claymore tip set into the carpeting beneath booted feet. *Scotland the Brave*.

Then he broke it off. "A wee bit left to accomplish," he explained, "or you'd be missing a head already."

"—not the Honours," MacLeod managed.

"Never was," Jamie agreed. "Excuse, bonnie Duncan. Part of the play. The means to an end."

"—Annie—"

"Annie was convenient. Annie knew where you were. Annie *wanted* you . . . well, so did I." He arched a single ruddy brow. "If for different reasons."

"—you set her up . . ."

"I did not. *You* did. You must have known how she'd react."

"—didn't—"

"The papers, MacLeod. The news reports."

"—not me . . ." It was easier to breathe now. The jaw was whole; his chest nearly so. He considered backing away—and then Douglas lunged.

Fast, *fast* for a man so large. MacLeod lurched backward, avoided a cut, then fouled his footing on cloth, on flesh.

—Annie—

He fell, inwardly wincing, writhed and twisted aside as the claymore came down. The blade shattered the chair arm, sliced through to clang and grate against the ground.

"D'ye remember the field games?" Douglas asked, wrenching the sword free even as MacLeod pulled himself up and ran for the lobby. There was room there, stairways, ramps, a chance to buy time, to breathe. "D'ye remember how I always threw the stone farther than any? Farther than you?"

Jamie made of it a javelin. Hurled the claymore.

MacLeod spun, twisted, blocked with the katana, knocked the point aside. The sword fell, thumped onto carpeting. He bent hastily to catch it up, but Douglas was there. One booted foot slammed down upon the claymore and the blade bit in, stripping flesh from Duncan's hand even as he jerked it back.

"Och, no," Jamie said mildly. "Bide a wee, laddie."

Too big—too strong—

He saw the blade come at him. Felt it enter his mouth, drive through—

Again, rebirth. Again, into pain and shock.

"Up," Douglas commanded. "We're not done *yet*, laddie."

Desperately Duncan heaved himself to his knees, to his feet, and lunged. The katana bit in, slid through flesh, sheared bone, cut sideways on the diagonal, carving down toward Douglas' hip. MacLeod heard the man grunt, hiss, swear furiously.

But it wasn't enough. Despite the blood, despite the pain, Jamie clamped both hands around the hilt of the katana, over MacLeod's grasp. He took the steel deeper, let the blade slide in up to the round, filigreed swordguard, jerked Duncan close.

With a wicked, bloodied grin, James Douglas smashed his skull into MacLeod's face. "I *said* we'd a wee bit left, not-so-bonnie Duncan. Och, lad—what's become of ye? All your fine looks ruined?"

MacLeod was barely conscious. He felt the man reach down and catch him up yet again, jerking him from the floor. He was flung over a shoulder, carried effortlessly. Blood from broken nose, shattered eye orbits, a split and bitten lip, poured down.

"Wait, Duncan, there's a good lad . . . nearly done, aye? Och, no, lad! Be still, lest I drop you!"

The claymore. Douglas had the claymore.

"We'll take you up here, lad—" Up the stairs, onto the stage itself. "—almost there, not-so-bonnie Duncan . . . no, no—dinna leave just yet, there's more to come . . . up here, now."

More steps. MacLeod, blinded by blood and pain, realized then where they were. Atop the cairn.

"Here, lad . . ." Douglas pulled him down from his shoulder. MacLeod resisted, but there was so little left, so very little, after so much done. "Sit or lie down, aye?—I'll get it done no matter. I think it's fitting we do it up here. Macduff kills Macbeth upon a proper cairn, and then the head chopped off, put up there on yon pike . . ."

He felt it then, felt the blade against his throat. The flat of it, not the edge, with pressure to choke the wind from him, had he any left.

"You left me," Jamie said. "You promised to stay, and you left me."

"—the prince—"

"The prince? Who, Charlie? Och, lad, you'll do better than that, aye? A poor lie, that one."

"It was—the prince . . . I'd sworn an oath—"

"As to me?"

God, but it hurt to talk. To breathe. "—an oath, first, to him . . . a command—I had to go—"

"With me dying?"

"—only—first time . . ."

"Och, aye, only the first time—but *I* didn't know that, did I? All I knew was my face was smashed, my chest cut apart, and I was dying. In most hideous pain and disfigurement. And Duncan MacLeod of the Clan MacLeod swore an oath to stay with me."

"—the *prince*—"

"Oh, lad, look—you're healing already . . . will we have to start again? They killed me four times, you see. Within a single hour."

Duncan spasmed, writhed. Felt the flat of the blade turned. Now the edge, pressed so hard beneath his jaw.

"Or should I just *do* it?"

MacLeod's boot heel found purchase against the false cairn. He didn't pull away forward, didn't thrust himself backward, but sideways, *sideways*, overbalancing Douglas as well as himself.

Both of them fell then, tumbling awkwardly into space, crashing through the wooden staff with the severed head atop it. The pole split; they tore it down with them even as they fell. Perhaps ten feet to the stage from the cairn, no farther, nothing to break or kill either of them, probably not even seriously injure a mortal.

And the claymore falling as well, crashing down onto the stage. MacLeod wrenched himself away from Douglas, felt the collar of his sweater cut briefly against his throat, taut as any blade—

And then he was free, briefly free, even as the big man came up with the claymore in his hand.

MacLeod stretched, grasped, grabbed the broken staff. For the first time he was outside the reach of Douglas' longer blade. The pole had broken off low, shedding its weight of prop head, *his* head. MacLeod found and set his weight even as Jamie lunged at him—

—and speared his Scottish boar.

—no time—

Not even as Jamie cried out and fell to his knees. The claymore tumbled free of his hands as he clutched the staff at his belly.

MacLeod let go the "spear," caught up the claymore. He straightened, reared back, strained as the great weight took him, then brought the weapon down in a swift, powerful, slashing arc that swept off the red-maned head.

"I had my duty!" he cried. "To Scotland, and to my prince. That was my honor, there upon that field. I am Duncan MacLeod of the Clan MacLeod, and I *served my prince!*"

This time when the Quickening took him, he feared it might kill him.

Mary Margaret O'Connell smiled at Mike, Joe Dawson's bartender, even as she put the money on the bartop. "Irish whisky," she suggested. "Straight up. What you gave me the last time, with Joe."

It took him little time. He set the glass down in front of her. She looked at it, nodded, then took it up. *"Slàinte,"* she said softly, and knocked it back.

Rich, peat-flavored spirits, warm, powerful, and comforting. Mattie nodded again, set the glass down. Then she slid off the stool. "I'm to see Joseph. Would there be anything you'd have me tell him for you?"

Mike weighed her expression a moment, frowned faintly, then shook his head. "No, ma'am. Other than I expect to see him back here real soon now."

"Ah." She smiled more broadly. "I'll take it to him, that."

And more.

She wrapped the scarf more tightly around her throat, buttoned up the coat with deft, elegant fingers, and went out into the darkness.

*   *   *

They had at last, at *long* last, and overdue, permitted him to sleep for more than an hour or so. Which is why Joe Dawson roused with more than a little annoyance, irritably asking who it was creeping into his room in the dark.

"Shall I turn the light on, then?"

His eyes popped open. "Mattie?"

She switched on the wall-light over his bed. "Hello, Joe."

He wished for a mirror, clean clothes, deodorant. In that order. "Mattie . . . "

"Hush now, Joe Dawson. I'll not be long." Fine fingers touched his shoulder softly, disturbing neither dressing nor the peace of his flesh. There was no pain in it, so light was her hand. "I came to tell you good-bye——and to say I am resigning."

"Resigning!"

"I must." She touched his brow then, brushing back the silvering forelock. "It's time."

"But—Mattie—"

"I'm sorry," she said. "I am that, Joe Dawson. But I've broken my oath, and we cannot tolerate such."

She was cryptic, and he not up to it. "I don't understand."

"You will." A wing of black hair slid down across one delicate cheekbone as she bent to kiss his forehead. "But I'll be gone, and you'll need not reproach me or yourself. And I'll tell no one the truth of it, what you and MacLeod share."

"*Mattie—*"

"Good-bye, Joe Dawson." She touched his lips gently with elegant fingers. "It was worth it, this oath-breaking. Some things must be."

She switched off the light, and was gone.

Richie left the bike in the handicapped zone at the Cultural Center because it was closest and quickest. He ran with single-minded abandon up the walkway beside the grassy quadrangle, through the fountains, toward the theater, not sure how he'd get in if the place were locked.

And stopped dead, ducking, as every pane of plate glass in the vast facade shattered.

He staggered back, shocked; was glad he was no closer. Slivers and shards and sheets broke out from the framework and collapsed, crashing down upon the ground. Richie spun, ducked, put his back to the theater, shut his eyes tightly. He felt the rushing whoosh of sound, the faint damp-like spray that wasn't moisture at all, but powdered glass.

Inane humor bubbled up and took him: reaction against the unthinkable. "Well, at least this answers the question of how I'll get *in* . . ."

And lightning split the sky.

"*Mac*—" He swung, took in the empty fretwork of glass-less facade. "Oh—man . . ." Richie ran, feeling the sour taste of bile in the back of his throat. He knew Mac was good, was the best, but what if . . .. what *if*—

Unthinkable.

Sound and fury. He thought that came from Shakespeare, from *Macbeth*.

"Mac—"

Mac*Leod*, not Macbeth.

Through glistening puddles of icelike broken glass, over metal frames and cement flooring, sliced carpeting; through the cacophony of alarms, piercing the air . . . and he was running again, feeling the prickling thrum betokening an Immortal's presence in the theater. Someone was alive.

Let it be Mac—

In. Low lighting, poor lighting, next to no lighting . . . he looked up onto the stage and saw one weak spotlight illuminating a prop that looked like a heap of stones, tall enough and substantial enough for a man to stand upon.

"Mac!"

He fell then, as he ran down the center aisle. He did not know at first what it was, simply cursed it, got free of it; his sword was in his hand.

Body. Headless body.

God. It looked like *Annie*—

"MacLeod!" Richie spun, stared at the stage. Saw a body there, and another: a man, all bent over as if broken. "Oh, *shit*—"

MacLeod. MacLeod. Oh, God, let it be Duncan MacLeod—

And it was, all bent upon himself as if someone had gutted him.

"*Mac*—" He tripped on something else, something that glinted. The katana.

MacLeod didn't have his katana.

Richie ran, clutching two swords now. Up the stairs, up onto the stage. "Oh, man—oh, *man*—"

And MacLeod came up, uncoiled all at once, of a sudden, sharply, disjointedly, eyes wide and blank, and blind; and there was blood on his face, a mask of blood. His sweater was torn, stretched, rent, bloodied. But he came up, spun, unwound; came up onto his knees, grasping a massive sword that appeared, to Richie, twelve feet long.

"Mac!"

And MacLeod saw him, knew him, dropped the sword. It crashed to the stage. Richie released his own as well, and the katana; knelt; dropped down onto his knees.

"Mac—oh man . . . " He had never seen such pain and anguish in any man's face, let alone Duncan MacLeod's. "It's okay . . . it's okay—it's me. It's *me*."

Small consolation. But something, something that might *ground* MacLeod, who was not . . . quite . . . whole. In body, yes, but not in spirit. Not of the mind.

Richie touched a shoulder, was shocked at the degree of tension in it. "Mac—it's okay. It's okay."

It wasn't.

"Look—we gotta go. They'll be coming any minute."

And then he saw the other coming out of the shadows. So did MacLeod, who grabbed for the claymore again even as Richie dived for his own sword.

A woman, an auburn-haired woman, in navy raincoat. She came out onto the stage in poor light, and her face shone with tears.

" 'Were such things here as we do speak about? Or have we eaten upon the insane root/That takes the reason prisoner?' "

"Annie?" MacLeod asked: a throttled cry of disbelief.

She dropped her own sword. Stripped off the wig, and let

it drop as well. Beneath it lay compressed dark hair, cropped short. " *'Worthy Macbeth, we stay upon your leisure.'* "

Man, not woman. Slight, thin man, made up as a woman, but man all the same. And very young.

"No!" MacLeod shouted, horrified, comprehending at last. "Not *YOU*—"

Richie caught him, muscled him back. "Mac." Richie gripped his shoulders. "Mac—he's not one of us."

"Annie—"

"Mac, he's *mortal*." He clutched again, felt the body shudder. "I know. I know. But you can't kill a mortal."

Colin Cameron stared. "Mortal?"

"Yeah," Richie said curtly. "You think we wouldn't know?"

"But—he said—Jamie *said*—" Stricken eyes found the body. "He told me I was like him! That I would be Immortal, once I died. That I was special, like him. He told me he *needed* me—"

Richie wasn't blind to the pain in the young man so near his own age, but he had no time. And MacLeod was—not quite MacLeod. "Yeah, well, I guess he did. He set *you* up, Annie, MacLeod . . ." He shook his head. "Everyone dies someday, but it won't be you today if you get the hell out of here before the cops find you holding a sword in the vicinity of two headless bodies." He physically pushed the stunned MacLeod toward the nearest wing. "Let him be. Come *on*, Mac—before they blame you for this!"

And reflected, as he steadied the staggering Highlander, that Duncan MacLeod undoubtedly would blame and punish himself for this far more effectively than the authorities ever could.

Behind them, Colin Cameron stood in the weak light, bereft, with a sword and red-haired wig lying at his feet.

His supremely mortal feet.

Epilogue

Last call had been called and served. All the patrons save one were gone, even Mike, the bartender. Joe Dawson, on his feet, in his bar, felt complete again, and yet oddly attenuated, stretched to breaking between the bar, where he brewed coffee, and the lone man seated at a table near the door.

Dawson wore a sling to support his left arm, for the blade wound was still sore, though it healed—albeit on mortal terms. The concussion had faded to the faintest of aches, recalled only when he thought about it. Diffidently he set about the evening chores, pulling money, coin, and checks from the register. Mike had offered because it was still difficult for Joe, one-handed, but Dawson wanted the bar emptied of all save himself and MacLeod. Who sat in silence at the table, staring fixedly into a candle. On the table was a collection of things Joe considered odd, and yet said nothing of; there were things a man, a mortal, did not ask Duncan MacLeod.

A candle. A Bible. A saucer of oatcakes, a bottle of whisky. But also a round wooden platter, bearing two small heaps. One was earth, the other salt.

Dawson, who had done his homework when preparing to

become the Highlander's Watcher, worked out what it represented. *Earth*: symbolic of the corruptible body; and *salt*: symbolic of the immortal spirit.

MacLeod was, according to Celtic ritual, seeing the dead through the night. Seeing Annie Devlin to the other side.

A noise snagged Dawson's attention: from the back door, as yet unlocked; and then Richie came into the light, eyes at once going to MacLeod. He looked back at Joe, raised his brows; Dawson shook his head.

Richie hesitated, then moved to the bar instead of the table. He looked at the sling. "You okay?"

Joe smiled. "I'll do."

Richie lowered his voice. "What about him?"

Dawson drew in a breath, held it, released it. "I don't know."

Richie glanced over his shoulder, then away. His young brow furrowed as he indicated the sling with a motion of his head. "That wasn't Annie's doing after all."

"No," Joe agreed. "But Mac thought it was. So did I. The kid was good."

Richie nodded. "And now you've got two more entries for your files, and the cops have two more unexplained headless bodies." He glanced over his shoulder again. Debated, then decided. "What the hell—all he can do is tell me to get lost."

"Richie—"

"It's okay, Joe. I know what I'm doing."

The flame was brilliant, so brilliant as to blind him, to fill his head with fire and put darkness into its place. He could not look elsewhere, though he tried; was transfixed, trapped, lost within the light.

And then someone came to it and sat down, breaking into his reverie. "I've got it figured out."

MacLeod blinked at last. His eyes were full of flame.

"Not so hard, once you think about it."

Richie. It was Richie.

"It was an impersonator."

At last MacLeod saw him.

"Lisa Marie," Richie explained seriously. "An Elvis impersonator impregnated Priscilla."

MacLeod frowned, baffled.

"See—Elvis was an Immortal, but he'd gained too much notoriety. So a bunch of other Immortals took him aside and said he'd better get lost. So he hired an impersonator." Richie shrugged. "The guy died, and Elvis went underground. But he comes up for air sometimes, which explains all the sightings."

It took a few minutes under the circumstances, but MacLeod integrated that. Then, as he saw the hope in Richie's eyes, he put his head down upon the table and began to laugh. Helplessly.

Respite. Release.

Absolution.

SCOTLAND THE BRAVE

Hark when the night is falling, hear, hear the pipes a'calling
Loudly and proudly calling down through the glen.
There where the hills are sleeping, now feel the blood a'leaping
High as the spirits of the old highland men.
Towering in gallant fame,
Scotland the mountain hame!
High may your proud standards gloriously wave!
Land of the high endeavor, land of the shining river,
Land of my heart, forever, Scotland the brave!

High in the misty highlands, out by the purple islands
Brave are the hearts that beat beneath Scottish skies.
Wild are the winds to meet you, staunch are the friends that
greet you
Kind as the light that shines from fair maidens eyes.
Towering in gallant fame,
Scotland the mountain hame!
High may your proud standards gloriously wave!
Land of the high endeavor, land of the shining river,
Land of my heart, forever, Scotland the brave!

Far off in sunlit places, sad are the Scottish faces,
Yearning to feel the kiss of sweet Scottish rain.
Where tropic skies are beaming, love sets the heart a'dreaming,
Longing and dreaming for the homeland again.
Towering in gallant fame,
Scotland the mountain hame!
High may your proud standards gloriously wave!
Land of the high endeavor, land of the shining river,
Land of my heart, forever, Scotland the brave!

(traditional)

FREE UNIQUE CARD OFFER!

Now you can play an Immortal in the fast paced card game that lets you pit your sword against others in the quest for The Prize.

In celebration of the new series of original novels from Warner Aspect, Thunder Castle Games is making available, for a limited time only, one Highlander™ Card not for sale in any edition.

Send a stamped self-addressed envelope and proof of purchase (cash register receipt attached to this coupon) to Thunder Castle Games, Dept. 118, P.O. Box 11529, Kansas City, MO 64138. Please allow 4-6 weeks for delivery.

Name: _____

Address: _____

City: _____ State:_____ Zip: _____

Age:_____ Phone: _____